Secrets
and Other Stories
of Suspense

Secrets and Other Stories of Suspense

Carolyn Hart

Five Star • Waterville, Maine

Five Star First Edition Mystery Series.

Published in 2002 in conjunction with Tekno-Books and Ed Gorman.

Set in 11 pt. Plantin.

Printed in the United States on permanent paper.

Library of Congress Cataloging-in-Publication Data

Hart, Carolyn G.
　　Secrets and other stories of suspense / Carolyn Hart.
　　　　p. cm. — (Five Star first edition mystery series)
　　　　Contents: Spooked—Turnaround—Secrets—A settling of accounts
　　　ISBN 0-7862-4328-7 (hc : alk. paper)
　　　1. Detective and mystery stories, American.　I. Title.
　　II. Series.
　　PS3558.A676 S43 2002
　　　813'.54—dc21　　　　　　　　　　　　　2002023184

Secrets
and Other Stories
of Suspense

Table of Contents

Spooked

The dust from the convoy rose in plumes. Gretchen stood on tiptoe waving, waving.

A soldier leaned over the tailgate of the olive drab troop carrier. The blazing July sun touched his crew cut with gold. He grinned as he tossed her a bubble gum. "Chew it for me, kid."

Gretchen wished she could run alongside, give him some of Grandmother Lotte's biscuits and honey. But his truck was twenty feet away and another one rumbled in front of her. She ran a few steps, called out, "Good luck. Good luck!" The knobby piece of gum was a precious lump in her hand.

She stood on the edge of the highway until the last truck passed. Grandmother said Highway 66 went all the way to California and the soldiers were on their way to big ships to sail across the ocean to fight the Japs. Gretchen wished she could do something for the war. Her brother Jimmy was a Marine, somewhere in the South Pacific. He'd survived Iwo Jima. Every month they sent him cookies, peanut butter and oatmeal raisin and spice, packed in popcorn. When they had enough precious sugar, they made Aunt Bill's candy but Mom had to find the sugar in Tulsa. Mr. Hudson's general store here in town almost never had sacks of sugar. Every morning she and Grandmother sat in a front pew of the little frame church in the willows and prayed for Jimmy and for all the boys overseas and for Gretchen's mom working so hard at the defense plant in Tulsa. Her mom only came home about one weekend a month. Grandmother tried to save a piece of meat when she could. Grandmother said her mom was thin as a rail and working too hard, but Gretchen knew it was important for her mom to work. They needed everybody to help and Mom was proud that she put radio parts in the big B-24 Liberators.

Gretchen took a deep breath of the hot heavy air, still laced with dust, and walked across the street to the café. Ever since the war started, they'd been busy from early morning until they ran out of food, sometimes around five o'clock, never later than seven. Of course, they had special ration books for the café, but Grandmother said they couldn't use those points to get sugar for Jimmy. That wouldn't be right.

Gretchen shaded her eyes and looked at the plate glass window. She still felt a kind of thrill when she saw the name painted in bright blue: Victory Café. A thrill but also a tightness in her chest, the kind of feeling she once had when she climbed the big sycamore to get the calico kitten and a branch snapped beneath her feet. For an instant that seemed to last forever, she was falling. She whopped against a thick limb and held on tight. She remembered the sense of strangeness as she fell. And disbelief, the thought that this couldn't be happening to her. There was a strangeness in the café's new name. It had been Pfizer's Café for almost twenty years, but now it didn't do to be proud of being German. Now Grandmother didn't say much in the café because her accent was thick. She was careful not to say *ja* and she let Gretchen do most of the talking. Grandmother prayed for Jimmy and for her sister's family in Hamburg.

Gretchen tucked the bubblegum in the pocket of her pedal pushers. Grandmother wouldn't let her wear shorts even though it was so hot the cotton stuck to her legs. She glanced at the big thermometer hanging by the door. Ninety-eight degrees and just past one o'clock. They'd sure hit over a hundred today, just like every day for the past few weeks. They kept the front door propped, hoping for a little breeze through the screen.

The café was almost as much her home as the boxy three-bedroom frame house a half mile away down a dirt road. Her earliest memories were playing with paper dolls in a corner of the kitchen as her mother and grandmother worked hard and fast, fixing country breakfasts for truck drivers in a hurry to get to Tulsa and on to Oklahoma City and Amarillo with their big rigs. Every morning grizzled old men from around the county gathered at Pfizer's for their newspapers and gossip as well as rashers of bacon, a short stack and scrambled eggs. But everything changed with the war. Camp Crowder just over the line in Missouri brought in thousands of soldiers. Of course, they were busy training, but khaki uniforms were no stranger to the Victory Café even though the menu wasn't what it had been before the war. Now they had meatless Tuesdays and Grandmother fixed huge batches of macaroni and cheese. Sometimes there wasn't any bacon but they had scrambled eggs and grits and fried potatoes. Instead of roast beef, they had hash, the potatoes and meat bubbly in a vinegary sauce. But Grandmother never fixed red cabbage or sauerkraut anymore.

It was up to Gretchen to help her grandmother when her mom moved to Tulsa. She might only be twelve, but she was wiry and strong and she promised herself she'd never complain, not once, not ever, not for the duration. That's what everybody talked about, the duration until someday the war was over. On summer evenings she was too tired to play kick the can and it seemed a long-ago memory when she used to climb up into the maple tree, carrying a stack of movie magazines, and nestle with her back to the trunk and legs dangling.

She gave a swift professional glance around the square room. The counter with red leatherette stools was to the left. The mirror behind the counter sparkled. She'd stood on a stool to polish it after lunch. Now it reflected her: black pigtails, a skinny face with blue eyes that often looked tired and worried, and a pink Ship 'n Shore blouse and green pedal pushers. Her blouse had started the day crisp and starched, but now it was limp and spattered with bacon grease.

Four tables sat in the center. Three wooden booths ran along the back wall and two booths to the right. The jukebox was tucked between the back booths and the swinging door to the kitchen. It was almost always playing. She loved "Stardust" and "Chattanooga Choo Choo" but the most often played song was "Praise the Lord and Pass the Ammunition." A poster on the wall beside the jukebox pictured a sinking ship and a somber Uncle Sam with a finger to his lips and the slogan: LOOSE LIPS SINK SHIPS. Grandmother told her it meant no one should talk about the troop convoys that went through on Highway 66 or where they were going or talk about soldiers' letters that sometimes carried information that got past the censors. Grandmother said that's why they had to be so careful about the food to make sure there was enough for Jimmy and all the other boys. And that's why they couldn't drive to Tulsa to see Mom. There wasn't enough gas. Grandmother said even a cupful of gas might make a difference one day whether some boy—like Jimmy—lived or died.

Two of the front tables needed clearing. But she made a circuit of the occupied places first.

Deputy Sheriff Carter flicked his cigar and ash dribbled onto his paunch which started just under his chin and pouched against the edge of the table. He frowned at black and white squares on the newspaper page. He looked at Mr.

Hudson across the table. "You know a word for mountain ridge? Five letters." He chewed on his pencil. "Oh, yeah," he murmured. He marked the letters, closed the paper, leaned back in the booth. "Heard they been grading a road out near the McLemore place."

Mr. Hudson clanked his spoon against the thick white coffee mug. "Got some more java, Gretchen?"

She nodded.

Mr. Hudson pursed his thin mouth. "Bud McLemore's son-in-law's a county commissioner, Euel. What do you expect?"

Gretchen hurried to the hot plates behind the counter, brought the steaming coffee pot, refilled both men's mugs.

The deputy sheriff's face looked like an old ham, crusted and pink. "Never no flies on Bud. Maybe my youngest girl'll get herself a county commissioner. 'Course, she spends most of her time at the USO in Tulsa. But she's makin' good money at the Douglas plant. Forty dollars a week." Then he frowned. "But it's sure givin' her big ideas."

Gretchen moved on to the next booth, refilled the cups for some Army officers who had a map spread out on the table.

The younger officer looked just like Alan Ladd. "I've got it marked in a grid, Sir. Here's the last five places they spotted the Spooklight."

The bigger man fingered his little black moustache. "Lieutenant, I want men out in the field every night. We're damn all going to get to the bottom of this business."

Gretchen took her time moving away. The Spooklight. Everybody in town knew the army had set up a special camp about six miles out of town just to look for the Spooklight, those balls of orange or white that rose from nowhere and flowed up and down hills, hung like fiery globes in the scrawny bois d'arc trees, sometimes ran right up on porches or over barns. Some people said the bouncing globes of light were a reflection from the headlights on Highway 66. Other folks scoffed because the lights had been talked about for a hundred years, long before cars moved on the twisting road.

Gretchen put the coffee on the hotplate, picked up a damp cloth and a tray. She set to work on the table closest to the Army officers.

". . . Sergeant Ferris swore this light was big as a locomotive and it came rolling and bouncing down the road, went right over the truck like seltzer water bouncing in a soda glass. Now, you can't tell me," the black mustache bristled, "that burning gas acts like that."

"No, Sir." The lieutenant sounded just like Cornel Wilde saluting a general in that movie about the fall of Corregidor.

The kitchen door squeaked open. Her grandmother's red face, naturally ruddy skin flushed with heat from the stove, brightened and she smiled. But she didn't say a word. When Gretchen was little, she would have caroled, *"Komm her, mein Schatz."* Now she waved her floury hands.

Gretchen carried the dirty dishes into the kitchen. The last words she heard were like an Abbott and Costello radio show, a nonsensical mixture, ". . . soon as the war's over . . . set up search parties . . . I'm gonna see if I can patch those tires . . . good training for night . . ."

Four pies sat on the corner table, steam still rising from the latticed crust. The smell of apples and cinnamon and a hint of nutmeg overlay the onions and liver and fried okra cooked for lunch.

"Oh, Grandmother." Gretchen's eyes shone. Apple pie was her most favorite food in all the world. Then, without warning, she felt the hot prick of tears. Jimmy loved apple pie, too.

Grandmother's big blue eyes were suddenly soft. She was

heavy and moved slowly, but her arms soon enveloped
Gretchen. "No tears. Tomorrow ve send Jimmy a stollen rich
with our own pecans. Now, let's take our pies to the counter.
But first," she used a sharp knife, cut a generous wedge,
scooped it out and placed it on a plate, "I haf saved one
piece—*ein*—for you."

The pie plates were still warm. Gretchen held the door for
her grandmother. It was almost like a festive procession as
they carried the pies to the counter.

The officers watched. Mr. Hudson's nose wrinkled in
pleasure. Deputy Carter pointed at the pie plate. "Hey,
Lotte, I'll sure take one of those." There was a chorus of calls.

Grandmother dished up the pieces, handing the plates to
Gretchen, then stood at the end of the counter, sprigs of sil-
ver-streaked blond hair loose from her coronet braids, her
blue eyes happy, her plump hands folded on her floury apron.
Gretchen refilled all the coffee cups.

Grandmother was behind the cash register when Mr.
Hudson paid his check. "Lotte, the deputy may have to put
you in jail you make any more pies like that."

Grandmother's face was suddenly still. She looked at him
in bewilderment.

Mr. Hudson cackled. "You sure don't have enough sugar
to make that many pies. You been dealing in the black
market?"

Grandmother's hands shook as she held them up, as if to
stop a careening horse. "Oh, *nein, ne*—no, no. Not black
market. Never. I use honey, honey my cousin Ernst makes
himself."

The officers were waiting with their checks. The younger
blond man, the one who looked like Alan Ladd, smiled
warmly. *"Sprechen Sie deutsch? Dies ist der beste Apfelkuchen
den ich je gegessen habe."*

The deputy tossed down a quarter, a dime and a nickel for macaroni and cheese, cole slaw, pie, and coffee. He glowered at Grandmother. "No Heine talk needed around here. That right, Lotte?" He glared at the soldier. "How come you speak it so good?"

The blond officer was a much smaller man, but Gretchen loved the way he looked at the deputy like he was a piece of banana peel. "Too bad you don't have a German *Grossmutter* like she and I do." He nodded toward Gretchen. "We're lucky, you know," and he gave Grandmother a gentle smile. *"Danke schon."*

But Grandmother's shoulders were drawn tight. She made the change without another word, not looking at any of the men, and when they turned toward the front door, she scuttled to the kitchen.

Gretchen waited a moment, then darted after her.

Grandmother stood against the back wall, her apron to her face, her shoulders shaking.

"Don't cry, Grandmother." Now it was Gretchen who stood on tiptoe to hug the big woman.

Her grandmother wiped her face and said, her accent even more pronounced than usual, "Ve haf vork to do. Enough now."

As her grandmother stacked the dirty dishes in the sink, Gretchen took a clean recipe card. She searched through the file, then printed in large block letters:

LOTTE'S APPLE HONEY VICTORY PIE

6 tart apples
1 cup honey
2 T. flour
1 tsp. cinnamon

dash nutmeg
dash salt
pastry

She took the card and propped it by the cash register.

Back in the kitchen, Grandmother scrubbed the dishes in hot soapy water then hefted a teakettle to pour boiling water over them as they drained. Gretchen mopped the floor. Every so often, the bell jangled from the front and Gretchen hurried out to take an order.

The pie and all the food were gone before five. Grandmother turned the sign in the front window to CLOSED. Then she walked wearily to the counter and picked up the recipe Gretchen had scrawled.

"Let's leave it there, Grandmother." Gretchen was surprised at how stern she sounded.

Her grandmother almost put it down, then shook her head. "Ve don't vant to make the deputy mad, Gretchen."

Gretchen hated hearing the fear in Grandmother's voice. She wanted to insist that the recipe remain. She wanted to say that they hadn't done anything wrong and they shouldn't have to be afraid. But she didn't say anything else as her grandmother held the card tight to her chest and turned away.

"You go on home, Grandmother. I'll close up." Gretchen held up her hands as her grandmother started to protest. "You know I like to close up." She'd made a game of it months ago because she knew Grandmother was so tired by closing time that she almost couldn't walk the half mile to the house and there was still the garbage to haul down to the incinerator and the menus to stack and silverware to roll up in the clean gingham napkins and potatoes to scrub for tomorrow and the jam and jelly jars

17

to be wiped with a hot rag.

Gretchen made three trips to the incinerator, hauling the trash in a wheelbarrow. She liked the creak of the wheel and the caw of the crows and even though it was so hot she felt like an egg on a sizzling griddle, it was fun to use a big kitchen match and set the garbage on fire. She had to stay until she could stir the ashes, be sure the fire was out. She tipped the wheelbarrow over and stood on it to reach up and catch a limb and climb the big cottonwood. She climbed high enough to look out over the town, at the café and at McGrory's gas station and at the flag hanging limp on the pole outside the post office.

If it hadn't been for the ugly way the deputy had acted toward Grandmother, Gretchen probably would never have paid any attention to him. But he'd been mean and she glowered at him through the shifting leaves of the cottonwood.

He didn't see her, of course. He was walking along the highway. A big truck zoomed over the hill. When the driver spotted the deputy's high crowned black hat and khaki uniform, he abruptly slowed. But the deputy wasn't paying any attention, he was just strolling along, his hands in his pockets, almost underneath Gretchen's tree.

A hot day for a walk. Too hot a day for a walk. Gretchen wiped her sticky face against the collar of her blouse. She craned for a better look. Oh, the deputy was turning into the graveyard nestled on the side of the hill near the church. The graveyard was screened from most of the town by a stand of enormous evergreens so only Gretchen and the crows could see past the mossy stone pillars and the metal arch.

Gretchen frowned and remembered the time when Mrs. Whittle caught Sammy Cooper out in the hall without a pass. She'd never forgotten the chagrin on Sammy's face when Mrs. Whittle said, "Samuel, the next time you plan to cut class, don't walk like you have the Hope diamond in your pocket and there's a policeman on every corner." Gretchen wasn't sure what the Hope diamond was, but every time any of the kids saw Sammy for the next year, they'd whistle and shout, "Got the Hope diamond, Sammy?"

The deputy stopped in a huge swath of shade from an evergreen. He peered around the graveyard. What did he expect to see? Nobody there could look at him.

Gretchen forgot how hot she was. She even forgot to be mad. She leaned forward, and grabbed the closest limb, moved it so she could see better.

The deputy made a full circle of the graveyard which was maybe half as big as a football field, no more than forty or fifty headstones. He passed by the stone angel at Grandpa Pfizer's grave and her dad's stone that had a weeping willow on it. That was the old part of the cemetery. A mossy stone, half fallen on one side, marked the grave of a Confederate soldier. Mrs. Peters took Gretchen's social studies class there last year and showed them how to do a rubbing of a stone even though the inscription was scarcely legible. Gretchen shivered when she saw the wobbly indistinct gray letters: Hiram Kelly, Age 19, wounded July 17, 1863, in the Battle of Honey Springs, died July 29, 1863. Beloved Son of Robert and Effie Kelly, Cherished Brother of Corinne Kelly. Some of the graves still had little American flags, placed there for the Fourth. A half dozen big sprays marked the most recent grave.

Back by the pillars, the deputy made one more careful study of the church and the graveyard, then he pulled a folded sheet of paper from his pocket and knelt by the west pillar. He tugged at a stone about three inches from the ground.

Gretchen couldn't believe her eyes. She leaned so far forward her branch creaked.

The kneeling man's head jerked up.

Gretchen froze quieter than a tick on a dog.

The sun glistened on his face, giving it an unhealthy coppery glow. The eyes that skittered over the headstones and probed the lengthening shadows were dark and dangerous.

A crow cawed. A heavy truck rumbled over the hill, down main street. The faraway wail of Cal Burke's saxophone sounded sad and lonely.

Gradually the tension eased out of the deputy's shoulders. He turned and jammed the paper into the small dark square and poked the stone over the opening, like capping a jar of preserves. He lunged to his feet and strode out of the cemetery, relaxing to a casual saunter once past the church.

Gretchen waited until he climbed into his old black Ford and drove down the dusty road.

She swung down from the tree, thumped onto the wheelbarrow, and jumped to the ground. The bells in the steeple rang six times. She had to hurry. Grandmother would have a light supper ready, pork and beans and a salad with her homemade Thousand Island dressing and a big slice of watermelon.

Gretchen tried not to look like she had the Hope diamond in her pocket. Instead, she whistled as though calling a dog and clapped her hands. A truck roared past on its way north to Joplin. Still whistling, she ran to the stone posts. Once hidden from the road, she worked fast. The oblong slab of stone came right off in her hand. She pulled out the sheet of paper, unfolded it.

She'd had geography last spring with Mrs. Jacobs. She'd made an A. She liked maps, liked the way you could take anything, a mountain, a road, an ocean, and make it come alive on a piece of paper.

She figured this one at a glance, the straight line—though

really the road curved and climbed and fell—was Highway 66. The little squiggle slanting off to the northeast from McGrory's station was the dusty road that led to an abandoned zinc mine, the Sister Sue. The X was a little off the road, just short of the mine entrance. There was a round clock face at the top of the sheet. The hands were set at midnight.

She stuffed the folded sheet in its dark space, replaced the stone. X marks the spot. Not a treasure map. That was kid stuff in stories by Robert Louis Stevenson. But nobody hid a note in a stone post unless they were up to something bad, something they didn't want anybody to know about. Tonight. Something secret was going to happen tonight. . . .

Gretchen pulled the sheet up to her chin even though the night oozed heat like the stoves at the café. She was dressed, a tee shirt and shorts, and her sneakers were on the floor. She waited until eleven, watching the slow crawl of the hands on her alarm clock and listening to the summer dance of the June bugs against her window screen. She unhooked the screen, sat on the sill, and dropped to the ground. She wished she could ride her bike, but somebody might be out on the road and see her and they'd sure tell Grandmother. Instead, she figured out the shortest route, cutting across the McClelland farm, careful to avoid the pasture where Old Amos glared out at the world with reddish eyes, and slipping in the shadows down Purdy Road.

The full moon hung low in the sky, its milky radiance creating a black and cream world, making it easy to see. She stayed in the shadows. The buzz of the cicadas was so loud she couldn't hear the cars, so she kept a close eye out for headlights coming over the hill or around the curve.

Once near the abandoned mine, she moved from shadow

to shadow, smelling the sharp scent of the evergreens, feeling the slippy dried needles underfoot. A tremulous, wavering, plaintive shriek hurt her ears. Slowly, it subsided into a moan. Gretchen's heart raced. A sudden flap and an owl launched into the air.

Gretchen looked uneasily around the clearing. The boarded-over mine shaft was a dark mound straight ahead. There was a cave-in years ago, and they weren't able to get to the miners in time. In the dark, the curved mound looked like a huge gravestone.

The road, rutted and overgrown, curved past the mine entrance and ended in front of a ramshackle storage building, perhaps half as large as a barn. A huge padlock hung from a rusty chain wound around the big splintery board that barred the double doors.

Nothing moved though the night was alive with sound, frogs croaking, cicadas rasping.

Gretchen found a big sycamore on the hillside. She climbed high enough to see over the cleared area. She sat on a fat limb, her back to the trunk, her knees to her chin.

The cicada chorus was so loud she didn't hear the car. It appeared without warning, headlights off, lurching in the deep ruts, crushing an overgrowth of weeds as it stopped off the road to one side of the storage shed. The car door slammed. In the moonlight, the deputy's face was a pale mask. As she watched, that pale mask turned ever so slowly, all the way around the clearing.

Gretchen hunkered into a tight crouch. She felt prickles of cold though it was so hot sweat beaded her face, slipped down her arms and legs.

A cigarette lighter flared. The end of the deputy's cigar was a red spot. He leaned inside the car, dragging out something. Metal clanked as he placed the thing on the front car fender. Suddenly he turned toward the rutted lane.

Gretchen heard the dull rumble, too, loud enough to drown out the cicadas.

Dust swirled in a thick cloud as the wheels of the army truck churned the soft ruts.

The sheriff was already moving. He propped a big flashlight on the car fender. By the time the driver turned and backed the truck with its rear end facing the shed, the sheriff was snipping the chain.

The driver of the truck wore a uniform. He jumped down and ran to help and the two men lifted up the big splintery board, tossed it aside. Each man grabbed a door. They grunted and strained and pulled and finally both doors were wide open. The soldier hurried to the back of the truck, let down the metal back.

Gretchen strained to catch glimpses of the soldier as he moved back and forth past the flashlight. Tall and skinny, he had a bright bald spot on the top of his head, short dark hair on the sides. His face was bony with a beaked nose and a chin that sank into his neck. He had sergeant stripes on his sleeves. He was a lot smaller and skinnier than the deputy but he was twice as fast. They both moved back and forth between the truck and the shed, carrying olive green gasoline tins in each hand.

Once the sergeant barked, "Get a move on. I've got to get that truck back damn quick."

Even in the moonlight, the deputy's face looked dangerously red and he huffed for breath. He stopped occasionally to mop his face with an oversize handkerchief. The sergeant never paused, and he shot a sour look at the bigger man.

Gretchen tried to count the tins. She got confused, but was sure there were at least forty, maybe a few more.

When the last tin was inside the shed, the doors shoved

shut, the chains wrapped around the board, the deputy rested against his car, his breathing as labored as a bulldogger struggling with a calf.

The sergeant planted himself square in front of the gasping deputy and held out his hand.

"Goddam, man"—the deputy's wind whistled in his throat —"you gotta wait 'til I sell the stuff. I worked out a deal with a guy in Tulsa. Top price. A lot more than we could get around here. Besides, black market gas out here might get traced right back to us."

"I want my money." The sergeant's reedy voice sounded edgy and mean.

"Look, fella." The deputy pushed away from the car, glowered down at the smaller man. "You'll get your goddam money when I get mine."

The soldier didn't move an inch. "Okay. That's good. When do you get yours?"

The deputy didn't answer.

"When's the man coming? We'll meet him together." A hard laugh. "We can split the money right then and there."

The deputy wiped his face and neck with his handkerchief. "Sure. You can help us load. Thursday night. Same time."

"I'll be here." The sergeant moved fast to the truck, climbed into the front seat. After he revved the motor, he leaned out of the window. "I'll be here. And you damn sure better be."

Grandmother settled the big blue bowl in her lap, began to snap green beans.

Gretchen was so tired her eyes burned and her feet felt like lead. She swiped the paring knife around the potato. "Grandmother, what does it mean when people talk about selling gas on the black market?"

Grandmother's hand moved so fast, snap, snap, snap. "We don't have much of that around here. Everyone tries hard to do right. The gas has to be used by people like the farmers and Dr. Sherman so he can go to sick people and the Army. The black market is very wrong, Gretchen. Why, what if there wasn't enough gas for the jeeps and tanks where Jimmy is?"

There wasn't much sound then but the snap of beans and the soft squish as the potato peelings fell into the sink.

Gretchen tossed the last potato into the big pan of cold water. "Grandmother," she scooped up the potato peels, "who catches these people in the black market?"

Grandmother carried her bowl to the sink. "I don't know," she said uncertainly. "I guess in the cities the police. And here it would be the deputy. Or maybe the Army."

Gretchen put the dirty dishes on the tray, swiped the cloth across the table.

Deputy Carter grunted, "Bring me some more coffee," but he didn't look up from his copy of the newspaper. He frowned as he printed words in the crossword puzzle.

Across the room, the officer who looked like Alan Ladd was by himself. He smiled at Gretchen. "Tell your grandmother this is the best food I've had since I was home."

Gretchen smiled shyly at him, then she blurted, "Are you still looking for the Spooklight?"

His eyebrows scooted up like snapped window shades. "How'd you know that?"

She polished the table, slid him an uncertain look. "I heard you yesterday," she said softly.

"Oh, sure. Well," he leaned forward conspiratorially, "my colonel thinks it's a great training tool to have the troops search for mystery lights. The first platoon to find them's going to get a free weekend pass."

Gretchen wasn't sure what a training tool was or a free pass, but she focused on what mattered to her. "You mean the soldiers are still looking for the lights? They'll come where the lights are?"

"Fast as they can. Of course," he shrugged, "nobody knows when or where they're going to appear so it's mostly a lot of hiking around in the dark and nothing happens."

Gretchen looked toward the deputy. He was frowning as he scratched out a word, wrote another one. She turned until her back was toward the sheriff. "They say that in July the lights dance around the old Sister Sue mine. That's what I heard the other day." Behind her, she heard the creak as the sheriff slid out of the booth, clumped toward the cash register. "Excuse me," she said quickly and she turned away.

The sheriff paid forty-five cents total, thirty for the Meatless Tuesday vegetable plate, ten for raisin pie, a nickel for coffee.

When the front door closed behind him, Gretchen hurried to the table. As she cleared it, she carefully tucked the discarded newspaper under her arm.

"A cherry fausfade, please." She slid onto the hard metal stool. The soda fountain at Thompson's Drugs didn't offer comfortable stools like those at the Victory Café.

"Cherry phosphate," Millard Thompson corrected. He gave her his sweet smile that made his round face look like a cheerful pumpkin topped by tight coils of red hair. Millard was two years older than she and had lived across the alley all her life. He played the tuba in the junior high band, had collected more tin cans than anybody in town, and knew which shrubs the butterflies liked. Once he led her on a long walk, scrambling through the rugged bois d'arc to a little valley covered with thousands of Monarchs. And in the Thompson wash room, he had two shelves full of chemicals and sometimes he let her watch his experiments. He even had a Bunsen burner. And Millard's big brother Mike was in the 45th, now part of General Patton's Seventh Army. They hadn't heard from him since the landings in Sicily and there was a haunted look in Mrs. Thompson's eyes. Mr. Thompson had a big map at the back of the store and he moved red pins along the invasion route. Mike's unit was reported fighting for the Comiso airport.

Gretchen looked around the store, but it was quiet in mid-afternoon. Millard's mother was arranging perfumes and powders on a shelf behind the cash register. His dad was in the back of the store behind the pharmacy counter. "Millard," she kept her voice low, "do you know about the black market?"

He leaned his elbow on the counter. "See if I got enough cherry in. Yeah, sure, Gretchen. Dad says it's as bad as being a spy. He's says people who sell on the black market make blood money. He says they don't deserve to have guys like Mike ready to die for them."

Gretchen loved cherry fausfades, okay, she knew it was phosphate but it had always sounded like fausfade to her, but she just held tight to the tall beaded sundae glass. "Okay, then listen, Millard . . ."

Gretchen struggled to stay awake. She waited a half hour after Grandmother turned off her light, then slipped from her window. Millard was waiting by Big Angus's pasture.

As they hurried along Purdy Road, Millard asked, "You sure it was Deputy Carter? And he said it was for the black market?"

"Yes."

Millard didn't answer but she knew he was struggling with the truth that they couldn't go to the man who was supposed to catch bad guys. When they pulled the shed doors wide and he shone his flashlight over the dozens and dozens of five-gallon gasoline tins, he gave a low whistle. Being Millard, he picked up a tin, unscrewed the cap, smelled.

"Gas, all right." There was a definite change in Millard's voice when he spoke. He sounded more grownup and very serious. "We got to do something, Gretchen."

She knew that. That's why she'd come to him. "I know." She, too, sounded somber. "Listen, Millard, I got an idea . . ."

He listened intently while she spoke, then he looked around the clearing, his round face was intent, measuring. Then he grinned. "Sure. Sure we can. Dad's got a bunch of powdered magnesium out in the storeroom. They used to use it with the old-fashioned photography." He looked at her blank face. "For the flash, Gretchen. Here's what we'll do . . ."

Gretchen could scarcely bear the relief that flooded through her when the young lieutenant stopped in for coffee and pie Wednesday afternoon. When she refilled his cup, she said quickly, "Will you look for the Spooklight tonight?"

The lieutenant sighed. "Every night. Don't know why the darned thing's disappeared just when we started looking for it."

"A friend of mine saw it last night. Near the Sister Sue mine." She gripped her cleaning cloth tightly. "If you'll look there tonight, I'm sure you'll find it."

It was cloudy Wednesday night, the last night before the man from Tulsa would come to get that gas. Gretchen and Millard moved quickly around the clearing, Gretchen clambering up in the trees, Millard handing her the pie tins Gretchen brought from the café's kitchen. She scrambled to high branches, fastened the tins with duct tape.

"You think they'll come," Millard asked as they unwrapped the chain, lifted the board and tugged the doors to the storage shed wide open. Gretchen carefully tucked the newspaper discarded by the sheriff between two tins.

"Yes." There had been a sudden sharpness in the young officer's eyes. She'd had the feeling he really listened to her. Maybe she felt that way because she wanted it so badly, but there was a calmness in her heart. He would come. He would come.

Millard took his place high in the branches of an oak that grew close to the boarded-over mine shaft. Gretchen clutched the oversize flashlight and checked over in her mind which trees had the pie tins and how she could move in the shadows to reach them.

Suddenly Millard began to scramble down the tree. "Gretchen, Gretchen, where are you?"

"Over here, Millard." She moved out into the clearing. "What's wrong?"

He was panting. "It's the army, but they're going down the wrong road. They're on the road to Hell Hollow. They won't come close enough to see us."

Gretchen could hear the noise now from the road on the other side of the hill.

"I'll go through the woods. I've got my stuff." And Millard disappeared in the night.

Gretchen almost followed. But if Millard decoyed them this way, she had to be ready to do her part.

Suddenly a light burst in the sky and it would be easily seen from Hell Hollow road. Nobody who knew beans would have thought it was the Spooklight but, by golly, it was an odd, unexplained flash in the night sky. Then came another flash and another.

Shouts erupted. "Look, look, there it is."

"Quick. This way."

"Over the hill."

If Millard had been there, she would have hugged him. He'd taken lumps of the powdered magnesium, wrapped them in net (Gretchen had found an old dress of her mom's and cut off the net petticoat), and added a string wick they'd dipped in one of the gas tins. He lighted the wick and used his slingshot to toss the soon-to-explode packet high in the air.

Gretchen heard Millard crashing back through the woods. He just had enough time to climb the oak when the soldiers swarmed into the clearing. Gretchen slithered from shadow to shadow, briefly shining the flash high on the tins. The reflected light quivered oddly high in the branches. She made her circuit, then slipped beneath a thick pine and lay on her stomach to watch.

Two more flares shone in the sky and then three in succession blazed right in front of the open shed doors.

The local *Gazette* used headlines as big as the Invasion of Sicily in the Friday morning edition.

ARMY UNIT FINDS
BLACK MARKET GAS
AT SISTER SUE MINE

Army authorities revealed today that unexplained light flashing in the sky led a patrol to a cache of stolen gasoline . . .

It was the talk of the town. Five days later, when Deputy Sheriff Euel Carter was arrested, the local breakfast crowd was fascinated to hear from Mr. Hudson who heard it from someone who heard it on the post, "You know how Euel always did them damfool crossword puzzles. Well," Mr. Hudson leaned across the table, "seems he left a newspaper right there in the storage shed and the puzzle was all filled out in his handwriting. Joe Bob Terrell from the *Gazette* recognized his handwriting, said he'd seen it a million times in arrest records. The newspaper had Euel's fingerprints all over it and they found his prints on the gas tins. They traced the tins to Camp Crowder and they checked the prints of everybody in the motor pool and found some from this sergeant and his were on half the tins and on the boards that sealed up that shack by the Sister Sue. They got 'em dead to rights."

Gretchen poured more coffee and smiled. At lunch the nice officer—she'd known he would come that night—had left her a big tip. He'd looked at her, almost asked a question, then shook his head. She could go to Thompson's for a cherry fausfade in a little while and tell Millard everything she'd heard. It was too bad they couldn't tell everyone how clever Millard had been with the magnesium. But that was okay. What really mattered was the gas. Now maybe there'd be enough for Jimmy and Mike.

Turnaround

Damn. She'd forgotten the tickets! Leigh Graham Porter swerved her silver Jag into the alley that ran behind the houses. She parked by the stone wall next to the gate. She'd slip quietly up to the house and get them without Brian knowing. It would be so much more fun tonight to hand the tickets to Brian. He would open the folder, lift them out, two tickets to Tahiti, and then his lips would curve into that lazy, crooked, sensuous smile. That moment would cap a romantic evening at The Ivy, the wonderful restaurant where he'd proposed to her four years ago today.

Leigh was smiling as she walked through the gate of the bougainvillea-draped wall. All right, she was proud to have Brian Winslow—tall, blond, athletic, thirtyish Brian—as her third husband. Whenever she saw her first husband at parties, he with his much younger trophy wife, dark-eyed seductive Courtney, Leigh and Hal exchanged cordial smiles of mutual understanding.

Youth was all that mattered in Hollywood, but she and Hal were still surviving. Leigh's body was Jane Fonda hard. No one would ever guess that she was past fifty, her black hair lustrous, her face smooth, her wide-set green eyes glowing with health and success. She continued to sell screenplays for enough money to afford Brian and a turreted house in Beverly Hills and a sprawling Palm Springs hacienda. To remember the long ago lean years, she'd kept her first little house in Topanga Canyon, and it was still a favorite retreat, especially to spend moonlit nights there with Brian. She walked a little faster, tendrils of vine brushing against her designer jeans. Perhaps she'd call in sick, skip the script meeting, stay home with Brian this morning. She was almost to the terrace when she heard his voice. She smiled indulgently. He always carried the portable phone outside with him and stretched out in the hammock to make calls. Yes, he was a creature who loved all comforts. But so was she.

". . . you shouldn't call here. I know. Yes, she's gone, but what if she ran late? Let's not take any chances now, Holly. We're so close . . ."

Leigh stopped behind the hibiscus. Brian was on the other side. He could not be more than a few feet away, his deep voice achingly familiar, and that softness when he said, "I love you, too. Of course I do. Trust me, it's going to work out . . . No, there's no chance of failure. It's all set. Then I'll be free."

Leigh crossed her arms against her body, struggled to breathe.

"Don't worry. Thursday night at the Topanga Canyon house. She thinks I'm meeting her there." He spoke briskly. He might have been describing a train connection.

Leigh felt the warm track of tears down her cheeks.

"You don't need to know about that, Holly. I've got a deal with a friend. One shot and it's over. I've got it all figured out. I'll have an alibi that can't be broken. A car wreck. She's going to get to the house about seven-thirty. When she arrives, the door will be open. She'll think I'm already there and walk in and that will be that. Then we'll be together forever. God, I love you . . ."

Leigh edged softly away from the terrace, her goal the kitchen door. Brian never came into the kitchen. Rosa wouldn't be there yet; she didn't come to work until ten.

Leigh reached the door, stepped inside. She took off her shoes, held them in her hand, ran up the back stairs in her stocking feet. When she reached her office, she hurried to her desk, looked down at the blinking Caller ID: Holly Fraser and a Valley number. She reached for a pen, repeating the number over and over in her mind. The light blinked off and the name and number disappeared as Brian deleted the listing.

In only a moment Brian's Porsche—the Porsche she'd bought him for his birthday—roared down the drive to the street. Leigh's face was hard. She knew Brian loved that car. He must really be willing to make a sacrifice to wreck his Porsche.

Her eyes traveled to her desk calendar. Today was Tuesday. According to Brian, she had two days to live.

She began to pace, the way she always worked, waiting for fragments of thoughts to swift into a pattern. They always did for her. Critics lauded the brilliance of her plots. Thursday night . . . the canyon house . . . a hired killer . . . but what if . . .

Leigh was aware of admiring glances from men at nearby tables and the icy jealousy of their women. She knew she looked especially lovely, her dark hair in a soft French roll, the kind that teased a man to loosen it and let it fall, her hard body alluring beneath the silver sheath dress. She sparkled like a many faceted diamond. Brian, of course, puffed with satisfaction, smugly certain that her uncommon iridescence grew out of passion for him.

He flipped open the ticket folder. "Tahiti! Leigh, you are unbelievable."

Was there a tinge of regret in his deep voice? Why hadn't he asked for a divorce? But Leigh knew the answer to that. She'd never been a fool, and the prenuptial agreement accorded him nothing if there was a divorce. Brian would be a very rich widower.

Leigh's lips curved in a merry smile. She picked up her champagne glass. "Brian, I have something even more special for you." Her exhilaration came not from champagne, but from the intoxication of danger.

He quirked a blond brow, leaned forward, his eyes full of warmth.

Her smile never wavered. "I've written a script that will be perfect for you—"

His eyes widened and his mouth parted. She'd let him read lines in her scripts, but she'd never made an effort to help him audition. Why should she? Why expose him to the temptations of hungry young actresses willing to barter body and soul for any perceived advantage. And a recommendation to be in a Leigh Graham Porter film was to die for.

"—and tomorrow morning I'll make a video and take it to Cameron Bachman with the script."

Cameron Bachman was currently the most successful movie director in the business.

Leigh held out the fluted glass. "To us. Forever."

Brian hesitated for only an instant, then his glass clicked against hers. He didn't repeat the toast.

The videocam was set up beside the desk. Leigh leaned against the desk. "Here's the story. You're in love with this girl. You've loved her forever. But you quarreled. She ran away and married a bandleader. He's abusive. You hear about her problems, how she's shown up at her sister's house with a bruised face, even been to the E.R. Anyway," Leigh waved her hand, "you've gotten in touch with her, she knows you care. You'd planned to meet her at your sister's house just before dark. Your sister gets called out of town. The girl's scared to be alone with you in case her husband finds out. So," Leigh pulled loose a sheet of script, "here's your sides. Let's see what you can do." Her voice was crisp now, businesslike, professional. "I'll do the voiceover." She slipped on her tortoiseshell-rimmed glasses and picked up the script. Not, of course, a script that she'd written on her computer. It was an easy matter to drive to Pasadena, find a Kinko's that rented use of computers. She'd worn a red wig, baggy gray sweats, and paid cash. She reached out, adjusted the angle of the camera, turned it on, then casually leaned back against the desk, one hand behind her to flip on the tape recorder. One finger rested lightly on the Stop key. "Okay, Brian. Lots of emotion. Let's go."

EXT. CITY STREET—NIGHT
To establish
EXT. PHONE BOOTH—NIGHT
Jarvis runs to booth, quickly punches out number, looks over his shoulder as if fearful.

JARVIS
It's me. Listen, plans have changed. She's going out of town. Meet me there, seven-thirty.

EILEEN (*vo., filtered*)
I can't. He'll . . .

JARVIS
We'll have a wonderful night, just you and me. And next week, we'll be together.

EILEEN (*vo., filtered*)
I—I want to be with you.

JARVIS
I love you. Don't disappoint me. I've got to go. Don't call me. Someone's . . .

Turnaround

★ ★ ★ ★ ★

She took two takes, then clapped her hands. "Brian, you are so good. Cameron will be blown away. I'll take the script and videotape to his office this afternoon."

Thursday morning Leigh's eyes glowed like a cat's as Brian walked to the garage with her. As she slipped behind the wheel, he tangled a finger in her dark hair. "Hell, I wish you didn't have to go to the damn production meeting."

Leigh smiled up at him, touched his cheek with her finger, drew it down slowly to his lips. "I could call in, say I was sick."

His eyes flared just for an instant. His laugh was hearty. "Not you, Leigh. You don't want them making decisions about your script without you there."

"As if I'd have any choice," she said dryly.

"Besides," his tone was rueful, "the guys'll kill me if I don't show up to play."

"Oh, yes, today's your regular game." Yes, she remembered that well. Every Thursday morning, Brian played doubles at the Beverly Hills Country Club. "And you're right. I can't miss this meeting." She smiled at him. "How well you know me." Yes, she was a fighter. Often if a studio bought a screenplay then changed its mind and the script went into turnaround, she used every contact she had to find the screenplay a new home. Soon he would know just how hard she was willing to fight for whatever belonged to her, including her life. "All day I'll be thinking about tonight. I'll see you at the canyon house."

She parked in the alley, waited until it was past time for Brian's tennis to start. In her office, she carried the tape player and the portable phone to a window overlooking the drive. She'd hear the Porsche if he returned early. She was taking no chances. Her lips moved in a cold smile. Brian thought he wasn't taking any chances. Ah, to be young and to live and learn.

She punched in the numbers.

A breathless voice, a sweet young voice, answered. "Hello."

Leigh pushed the button and the carefully edited tape ran:

"It's me. Listen, plans have changed. She's going out of town. Meet me there, seven-thirty. We'll have a wonderful night, just you and me. And next week we'll be together. I love you. Don't disappointment me. I've got to go. Don't call me. Someone's . . ."

"Brian, what—"

Leigh clicked off the phone.

Leigh took her time in the office. She found the sides, tucked one into her purse, tore the rest into shreds, flushed them down the toilet.

Leigh left the production meeting early, drove back to Beverly Hills. Brian wouldn't leave the house until after seven. He'd time the car wreck for around seven-fifteen. There would be a wait for the cops to come. But later, no one could ever suggest he'd been in Topanga Canyon. As alibis went, it was clever.

Leigh turned the Jag into their drive shortly after seven. She left the car running. The Jag was blocking the drive, but that wouldn't occur to Brian. She ran up the front steps, unlocked the door, flung it open, shouting, "Brian, Brian!"

He was coming down the stairs. He stopped and stared at her, his handsome face slack with shock.

"Brian, I've got the most wonderful news. I had a call from Cameron. He caught me just before I was leaving for the canyon. But that doesn't matter. You know how he is." She threw up both hands in exasperation. "He always has to do things at once. And his way. He'll audition you tonight. At his house. This may be your chance!"

She turned south on the San Diego freeway. Traffic was heavy. Finally, she reached 5 South, but rush hour traffic stalled them for more than an hour. "He lives to hell and gone." Her tone was irritated. "But he gave me directions. He's back in the hills down near Laguna. You concentrate on your lines."

Brian practiced.

Leigh listened in rapt admiration. Occasionally, she made a suggestion. She drove as dusk turned to darkness. She turned off 5, took a road into the hills, a twisting, hairpin road that skirted canyons. It was almost ten when she finally gave up. She stopped at the side of the road, got out her cell phone, scrabbled through her purse. "Damn, I thought I had his number. And it's unlisted. Oh Brian, I'm so sorry. I'll call first thing in the morning. I have his number in my Rolodex. Cameron's a good guy. He'll understand." A trill of laughter. "He knows I have the world's lousiest sense of direction."

Brian didn't laugh.

Leigh held the muscle relaxant tablets in her hand. One or two? One should be enough. Be damned awkward if there were an overdose. Using the back of a spoon, she ground the pill into white powder, scraped the powder into a wineglass. She poured in champagne, stirred, carefully set that glass at the front of the tray on the left side. She didn't fill the second glass quite so full.

She waited a few minutes, then carried the tray upstairs and knocked on Brian's door. She opened it.

Brian swung around, his face tight with irritation. He wouldn't keep those boyish good looks frowning like that. She noted his blue silk pajamas. Yes, she'd given him time to change. He'd tossed his gray slacks onto the sofa. "Brian"—Leigh stretched out his name like a dramatic festival tattoo—"I brought champagne to celebrate. Tomorrow will be the most unforgettable day of your life."

She handed him the glass on the left, picked up the nearby glass, raised it high. "To tomorrow and the new life of Brian Winslow."

The glasses clicked with a light chime. They drank.

In her room, Leigh changed unhurriedly from her silk tee and beige jeans into a long-sleeve black turtleneck, black jeans, black sneakers. She tucked money and a driver's license into her pocket. It took a moment to find a pair of gloves, since neither the society nor the climate required them. But there were soft doeskin driving gloves tucked in a winter coat she'd bought for location shooting in New York. She glanced at the clock. Just past midnight.

Brian's door was closed. She didn't bother to knock. She opened the door. He was sprawled on his back across the foot of his bed, mouth wide, breathing stertorous. She moved quickly, snatched up his slacks with her gloved hands. "Sweet dreams, little man." She checked the pockets, a tight frown thinning her mouth. Where was the sides he'd practiced? Not in the pockets. She glanced around the room, saw the sheet lying on the bedside stand. She grabbed it up, carried it to the bathroom, ripped the page into tiny pieces, flushed them away.

Leigh drove past the turnoff to the cliff road twice. On her third pass, reassured by the silence and the dark, she turned onto the narrow, rutted twisting road. Always before, the rustic, almost hidden entrance had appealed, the gateway to privacy and adventure. Now her heart thudded uncomfortably. Once on the road, she was trapped by anyone coming in after her. No one should come, of course. She'd considered parking along the road and walking up. But it was almost a mile to the house, and someone might see the parked car, note the license plate. If all went well, she could be up and down the road in a quarter hour at the most.

Leigh drove without lights, easing the car up the twisting road, using the moonlight as her guide. At the top of the grade she paused, studying the dark house. No lights, no movement. She turned into the drive, carefully turned and backed until the car was facing downhill. If she had to hurry . . .

She turned off the motor, listened to the swish of the pines and the crash of the waves far below. Her hands gripped the steering wheel. She should move now, this instant, hurry from the car, run across the graveled drive, up the steps to the redwood deck. Still she sat.

An owl hooted. What was that crackling sound? She jerked her head so quickly her neck hurt. Her heart thudded. Oh, God. She could scarcely hear above the roar in her ears. Slowly she sorted out the sounds, the crash of the waves, the sough of tree limbs, the rustle of shrubbery.

Leigh held tight to the wheel. She wanted desperately to turn on the motor and careen down the canyon, away from this pocket of dark and quiet, this isolated house and the malevolence that seemed so near. But she had no choice. There was no turning back.

She opened the door, slipped out of the car, leaving the door a little ajar. She forced herself to walk quickly. The faster she moved, the sooner she could be out of here. She

41

carried Brian's trousers in one hand, a small pocket flashlight in the other. She didn't need the flashlight. Moonlight bathed the deck, turning the dark windows to patches of silver.

The front door stood open. That's what Brian had planned, the open door and she stepping inside. One step, another, Leigh moved like a shadow across the deck. She eased open the screen door, stepped into the living room. She flicked on the flashlight and stared across the shining expanse of wood—she'd always been pleased with the white pine floors, such a dramatic contrast to the red cypress of the walls—at the body sprawled only a few feet away. The blood spatters were stark and ugly against the shell-pink dress and white wood floor. The young woman lay on her back, thrown there by the force of the shot.

Blond hair curved against a lace-white cheek. Dead green eyes stared emptily into eternity.

Leigh shuddered. She struggled to breathe, heard her own voice, high and stricken, "No, no, no . . ." She'd not realized how terrible this would be. She flung out her arms, the light of the flash dancing crazily around the dark room. Brian's trousers slapped against the door frame. She looked at the gray worsted slacks, then turned her head toward the murdered woman. Her hand steadied, light spilling over the still form.

That could be her body. That would be her body if she hadn't overheard Brian's clever plan. This woman had known. This woman had been willing for her to die. She owed her nothing.

Hands shaking, the trousers dangling in front of her, Leigh walked toward the body. Averting her eyes from the dead white face, she leaned forward, swiped the pants against that bloodied chest.

A click.

She froze. What was that sound? She jerked the flashlight around the room. Nothing moved. The dark shadows behind the furniture might harbor a thousand screaming devils of her imagination, but there was no one in this room except her and the forever still body.

All right, all right. God, how long had she been here? Too long. Time to move now. Fast. She hurried across the room to the wet bar, stepped behind, stuffed the trousers beneath the sink.

She didn't glance again toward the body. Everything was done now. Let Brian reap what he had sown. She clattered across the deck and down the stairs, ran to the car.

Three weeks later Leigh carried the *Times* to her favorite chair by the pool.

SCREENWRITER'S HUSBAND
CHARGED IN CABIN DEATH

Brian Winslow, husband of Oscar-winning screenwriter Leigh Graham Porter, was charged with first-degree murder today in the shooting death April 4 of Holly Fraser, a young actress he met while filming an unsuccessful TV pilot two years ago.

Winslow's attorney entered a plea of Not Guilty. Winslow is accused of shooting Fraser, 26, at the Topanga Canyon home owned by his wife. No motive has been established, and police said Winslow and Fraser had remained friends after the filming.

Winslow claims he spent the evening of the murder in the company of his wife. Porter has not responded to interview requests. However, intimates of the writer have said that Porter was shocked by her husband's statement. According to friends, Porter was home alone that evening and didn't see her husband. Further, Porter expressed surprise at his story of an audition for one of her scripts. She told a friend that she'd never written a script suitable for her husband. Porter is reported to have said that she didn't believe Winslow would shoot anyone. However, Winslow remains jailed, as he has been unable to post the $100,000 bail and Porter has declined to post bail.

Although police have not released details of their investigation, there is reason to believe . . .

Leigh dropped the paper on the wicker table, picked up her espresso, and reached for a script on the glass-topped table. The harder she worked, the easier it was to push away the memory of those dead green eyes.

The plain manila envelope was tucked into the mailbox when Leigh returned from the studio the next evening. She frowned as she picked it up. It was too light to be a script. It was amazing how often hopeful writers cornered her at cocktail parties, tucked scripts into the mailbox. What a bore. But this envelope couldn't hold much. Her name was written in a flowing script. That was all.

She carried the envelope into the kitchen, sniffed. Hmm. Rosa was such a good cook. What would it be this evening? She glanced at the note on the kitchen block. Dove casserole and rice. She poured a glass of Chablis, almost tossed the envelope into the wastebasket, shrugged, opened it.

A photograph dropped onto the pale yellow tiles of the cooking island.

Leigh's eyes widened. Her breath stopped. A hard pressure filled her chest. The wineglass slipped from her fingers, shattering on the red tile floor. Leigh stared at the picture, the telling, damning, hideous picture: the dark walls, the white floor, the dead girl, her open eyes, the blood that had welled across her pink dress, and Leigh leaning down, swiping Brian's gray trousers against the body. The flashlight pointed down toward the body, but Leigh's face was clear and distinct, her eyes hard, cheekbones jutting, lips pressed into a thin line.

Nausea welled in Leigh's throat. A wave of heat swept her. She crumpled the slick eight by ten photograph and shuddered. She'd thought herself alone with death, but she had not been alone. Someone watched, watched and waited, and when the moment was perfect, held the camera rock steady and pressed the button. There'd been no flash. But there need not have been, not with high speed film and the right lens aperture.

Fear washed over her. Where had this film been developed? Who had seen it? But there had likely been a casual explanation of publicity stills for a local playhouse. Who would ever question any kind of pose in this town? No doubt the film was taken to a one-hour photo shop and a false name given, the prints paid for with cash. Who would remember after time passed?

The negative.

A pulse quivered in Leigh's throat. The negative didn't matter. Any number of copies could be made from a photograph now. So, no matter how much she paid, there could always be copies in reserve.

Paid.

That was the point of this photograph, wasn't it?

Whirling, she grabbed the envelope, the unmarked plain manila envelope, ripped it open. Nothing. The envelope was empty. Reluctantly, she spread out the crumpled photograph, turned it over. Nothing on the back. In a frenzy, she ripped the photo into tiny pieces, carried them to the sink, hunted for matches. There had to be some matches somewhere—

The phone rang.

Leigh stared at the bright lemon portable phone.

Another peal. Another.

Stiffly, she reached out, picked up the receiver, pushed the button. She held the phone to her ear. She didn't speak. She knew who was calling, who had to be calling. It didn't matter when the envelope was delivered. The photographer—no, be plain, be honest, she told herself—the murderer, the friend Brian had asked to murder her, had only to park down the street, waiting until her silver Jag turned into the drive, allowing her time enough to find the envelope, open it, see the hellish picture.

The whisper was slow in coming. "Photography is an art, isn't it, Leigh?"

She stared at the Caller ID bar: *Unavailable.*

"Don't you like my picture?" The whisper was sexless, ageless, a wisp of sound.

Her throat was so dry, it hurt to talk. She pushed out the words, dropped them like steel balls into a cavern. "What do you want?"

"You get right to the point, I see. Very well. But I'll give you time to think about the future. Oh, say, until tomorrow. There's a pay phone at the Rite-Aid on Canon not far from your house. Be there at ten o'clock in the morning."

Leigh stared at her reflection in the shiny plate glass of the Rite-Aid. She looked old, her eyes bloodshot, her face pasty. She'd lain wakeful most of the night. When fatigue pulled her into sleep, she'd jerked awake at every sound, and in her mind a photograph expanded, grew larger and larger, until all she could see was dead staring eyes. She leaned against the plastic side of the pay phone, smelled that essentially California mixture of car fumes, gasoline, and eucalyptus, and waited.

How much money would he want? What else could she do but pay up? If she told the truth to the police, she was an accomplice to murder. A lizard slithered along the rock wall by the hedge. Accomplice? More than that. Though it seemed only fair. But the police didn't care about fair.

The phone rang. Leigh yanked up the receiver.

The whisper was as insubstantial as fog, but the words permeated her soul. "You're guilty of murder."

"No." The denial burst from her. "You were going to kill me. You were going to kill me!"

"You could have called the police."

Leigh felt her body shrink and tighten. That's what everyone would say.

"But you didn't." The whisper was silky. "Somehow you found out what was planned. I was waiting. I heard the footsteps running across the deck. As soon as she stepped inside, I shot. As you'll discover, it isn't easy to do. I wanted to get it over with. If I'd waited a minute, seen her better . . . But I didn't. Of course, after I shot, I had to be sure you were dead. Imagine my surprise—"

"Stop it." Leigh's voice rose. "Stop whispering!"

"Oh, I don't have much more to say." The whisper was even lighter, fainter. "The minute I saw the dead girl, I knew what had happened. I knew who she was, but it was too late. Too late for her and for Brian. But not too late for me. I knew you must have arranged for her to come. But I knew you wouldn't stop there."

Leigh's fingers tightened around the sticky receiver.

"I was sure you'd implicate Brian. That meant putting some kind of physical evidence in the house. I took a chance and went to get a camera."

Thoughts whipped in her mind . . . left and came back . . . how far could he live . . . he could have stopped, bought one . . . no way of knowing . . .

"How much do you want?" She tried to keep her voice even, but it cracked as she spoke. She was afraid, so damn afraid.

A husky laugh. "I don't want money, Leigh."

A car squealed out of the parking lot, the fumes choking her. Leigh didn't move. She stared at the black metal box.

"Brian and I had a deal. No one would ever suspect me of shooting you, and no one would ever suspect him of shooting a man quite unknown to him. I was to shoot his bête noir, he was to shoot mine. He was to have an unbreakable alibi at the time of your death. I will have an unbreakable alibi this coming Saturday night."

"You're out of your mind." She began to shake. She had sharp clear memory of Robert Walker and Farley in the classic *Strangers on a Train*. But this was so much worse. She'd never planned anyone's death. She pushed away the picture of the girl's dead green eyes. That hadn't been her plan. Holly died because of Brian and this nameless creature with the hideous whisper.

Soft laughter. "Aren't we all for living in La-La Land? But it's quid pro quo, Leigh. You'll do quite as well as Brian. Now," the whisper was brisk, "when you get home, go down to the alley. There's a backpack inside your gate. You'll find detailed instructions in it. Who you are going to kill and when."

"I can't." Leigh's chest squeezed.

"You can. You will." The whisper was cold and determined. "A final note, Leigh, don't try to be clever. You can't. There are too many people who want this man dead. His wife.

His son. His daughter. His ex-mistress. His business partner. And I've made it easy for you. You'll find the gun in the backpack. Zero hour? Saturday night, Leigh, nine o'clock."

The connection broke.

Leigh gripped the receiver. She struggled to breathe. Pay phone. The killer sent her here so she couldn't see the number on Caller ID . . .

Leigh scrabbled in her purse, her fingers desperately seeking coins. She found one, two, jammed them into slots, punched *69. There was a pause, a squeal, a recorded voice, "Call return service is not . . ."

Oh damn, damn, damn.

Leigh stared at the blue nylon backpack lying in deep shade next to the oleander. It held death. She didn't want to touch it, not ever. But she had to . . . She wore gardening gloves, carried the pack at arm's length into the garage to a worktable. She unbuckled the plastic snaps, pulled out a manila envelope. She left the gun in the dark interior. It was hard to open the envelope with her clumsily gloved hands. A studio portrait slipped to the cement floor. Leigh creased the picture as she picked it up.

Sunlight spilled through the window above the workbench. She studied the face. An Alan Alda type, but tougher, harder, with a sensuous mouth and combative eyes. Across the bottom, scrawled in a bold masculine script, was the inscription and name, *Love, Jake.*

She pulled two sheets of paper, both computer generated, from the envelope and a driver's license with her photograph. The name on the license was Ellen Vorhees and the address was in Long Beach. On one sheet was a map of an elegant backyard with a legend identifying sites, with a star by the Fortune Teller booth near the swimming pool. The second sheet contained instructions.

Leigh read swiftly, picking out the important facts. Saturday night the county bar association was having a fundraising carnival at a house three streets from her home. Jake Garrison was volunteering as a swami in the fortune-telling booth from eight-thirty to nine-thirty.

And:

The back flap of the tent will be unfastened. At nine o'clock, pull aside the flap, shoot Jake, drop the gun, meld into the crowd. You may be able to slip away down the alley. If not, the police will take names and IDs. You'll have one. But no one will ever find Ellen Vorhees. You will receive the photograph you desire in the next mail. Good hunting.

Jake Garrison. Attorney at law. Personal injury lawyer specializing in medical malpractice. Facts welled from his law firm's website, so many that Leigh didn't try to absorb them all. She found everything she needed to know about his wife, Ingrid; his son, Bobby; his daughter, Tina; his partner, Ray Porter. She found their ages, histories. And phone numbers.

Leigh tilted back her chair and stared at the screen. If she were the Whisperer, she wouldn't have included herself among the suggested villains.

Who hates medical malpractice lawyers?

Leigh shot a glance at the clock. She'd been at her computer ever since she got home from the pay phone, almost four hours. Her eyes ached, her head throbbed. The time, so little time, how could she find out in time . . . All right, all right. She had to narrow the search, set up parameters. She could rule out lawsuits against hospitals and HMOs. It had to be personal. Someone who had been damaged, perhaps irrevocably, by Garrison. Or, better yet, someone close to trial who might believe his death could make a difference. Yes, that was the route to take.

Turnaround

Leigh ended up with four names: a doctor who operated while high on drugs, a doctor who amputated the wrong leg, a doctor who misdiagnosed ovarian cancer, and a doctor whose liposuction patient died. Four names . . . Leigh rubbed her aching head and stared at the list. Abruptly, she jolted back her chair, ran down the hall to Brian's room. She grabbed the doorknob, flung the door open, hurried to the bath. Flicking on the light, she crossed to the medicine cabinet, opened it. She reached up, grabbed a handful of plastic vials.

Oh shit, yes. There it was. A painkiller after his knee surgery. Prescribed by Dr. Annabelle Smith. The same Dr. Annabelle Smith who had amputated a left leg instead of a right. Yes, yes, yes! Hello, Whisperer.

Leigh called Dr. Smith's home number at shortly after five. Voice mail picked up. Leigh didn't identify herself. If she'd found the Whisperer, no identification was needed. "Hello, Annabelle. I've been giving some thought to our conversation earlier today. I haven't yet informed Jake Garrison. I won't unless we can't make a deal. I suggest we get together at ten o'clock tonight at my house. You bring the picture and film. I'll have the backpack. Fair exchange. We both walk away with no hard feelings. See you then."

Ten o'clock came and went, of course. Leigh didn't expect Dr. Smith to respond to her summons. Not at the stated time. But she felt certain Dr. Smith would come very late, long after the appointed hour, when she should be deep in sleep. And easy to kill.

The house was dark and quiet. The only light came from security lights in the trees. It was just before three o'clock in the morning. Leigh waited in the deep shadow at the end of the patio, curled in a dark wicker chair. She had a good view of the back gate and the side yard. Her hair was tucked beneath a navy ball cap. She wore a black sweater, jeans, dark sneakers. She sipped a cup of strong black coffee, not that she was likely to drift into sleep. She felt oddly calm and perhaps a little exhilarated. This afternoon she'd been in a deadly box. Now she had a chance. If Dr. Smith was the Whisperer . . . Leigh shook her head impatiently. It couldn't be a coincidence, the doctor's trial set to begin next month and her name on Brian's medicine bottle. Dr. Smith was the Whisperer, smart, cunning, careful, dangerous, and a gambler. The Whisperer would come tonight, prepared to kill. Leigh sipped her coffee and waited, the gun heavy on her lap. Occasionally, she reached down to touch the heavy twine she'd tied to the switch that would turn on the patio lights.

The gate creaked. The squeal had to be unnerving to the doctor. Metal hinges scraped. A dark figure moved cautiously on the path, a small carryall in one hand.

Leigh watched, part of her mind at a distant remove, admiring the grace and stealth of the approach, part of her mind boring toward the moment when the lights would come on. Not yet. Not yet. Wait until the intruder was at a disadvantage. Leigh's hand gripped the twine. Wait, wait . . .

Enough light spilled down from the trees to illuminate the intruder's dark cap, black sweater, saggy black cardigan, shiny vinyl gloves, skintight black bike pants. No wonder she hadn't heard a car. Annabelle—surely they were on a first name basis now—had probably parked nearby. Her car must have a bike rack.

Annabelle stopped at the base of a tree with a limb that stretched over the second-story sun porch. She opened the carryall, pulled out a rope ladder. Dropping the small bag, she took a step nearer the tree, flung the ladder up. It took two tries before the hooks caught.

Leigh's hand tightened on the twine, yanked. Light blazed on the patio.

Annabelle froze on the rope ladder, halfway to the limb.

"Stay there." Leigh's voice was as sharp and hard as the click of a safety catch. She held the gun in both hands, aimed it.

Annabelle hung on the ladder, twisting to look down. The cap made her broad face look heavy. Burning dark eyes that slitted into fury. The long thin mouth quivered.

"Come down slowly. Yes, that's right. Put your hands up." Leigh was poised to shoot. She didn't want to. Not here. But if she had to . . .

The vinyl-gloved hands lifted, shiny in the lights of the patio. The hands of a killer.

Leigh watched those deep-socketed, furious eyes. "Don't move." The carryall—a blue canvas gym bag—lay near Annabelle's feet. "Shove the bag with your foot."

Cautiously, Leigh eased close enough to snag the bag with her foot. She felt the hardness of a gun, gave a quick glance, felt the tightness ease out of her shoulders. Triumph almost made her giddy. She was in charge now. She had the only weapon. Now to get Annabelle into the garage . . . Her mind shied away from the next moment. But she had no choice. A quick shot. She'd already spread big black garbage sacks on the cement floor. The rest would be hard, getting the body into the trunk, driving to a remote area of the San Gabriel Mountains, dumping the grisly load. There was a road near the Mount Wilson Observatory . . . There would be no connection between her and a body found there.

"Walk up to the garage. I'm right behind you." And in a hurry, a big hurry.

Annabelle slowly moved ahead of her. "I'll make a deal. I've got the picture—and the negative—in my car."

"Too little too late, Annabelle." They were at the side door to the garage. "Open the door." Leigh's hands tightened on the gun.

Annabelle grabbed the knob and pulled. "It's stuck."

Leigh prodded her with the gun. They were almost there, almost inside the garage. Impatiently, she pressed nearer. "Turn it—" Leigh never finished.

Annabelle's right hand plunged into her cardigan pocket and out and up.

Leigh glimpsed the needle, felt a sharp, hot prick in her neck. In her last moment of life, Leigh squeezed the gun, heard the shots, knew that Annabelle fell as she herself sagged into oblivion.

Secrets

Gretchen slid onto the hard metal stool at the soda fountain. She held tight to her nickel, enough for a cherry fausfade, her most favorite drink in the world, especially on a hot July day when the red liquid in the old tin thermometer on Main Street edged over a hundred and the breeze rustling the cottonwoods felt like hot molasses against her skin. She opened her mouth to order, knowing Millard would answer in his precise way, "Cherry phosphate, Gretchen." It was a favorite joke, and she would say again, emphasizing the sounds, "Cherry fausfade." He would smile his sweet, gentle smile. She would grin and say firmly, "It sounds like 'fausfade' to *me*," in the same tone as Miss Carstairs calling home room to attention.

Millard was there all right, slumped on a high wooden stool behind the cash register, but his round head topped by tight red curls rested on arms folded on the counter.

Gretchen darted a quick look toward the back of the drugstore. Mr. Thompson must be in back filling prescriptions. Millard's dad was strict as anything, and if he caught Millard asleep behind the counter . . . She reached out and pushed on Millard's shoulder.

"Wha-wha-wha—" Millard's head jerked up and his eyes were as dull and glazed as the rheumy old hog out at Aunt Lela's farm.

"Millard!" Gretchen's whisper was sharp.

Millard blinked. His round, freckled face looked bone

tired like pictures she'd seen in the newsreels of soldiers on Bataan before it fell. Grandmother cried the night they saw those pictures. They'd gone to the Bijou to see *Mrs. Miniver*. Gretchen knew Grandmother was thinking about Jimmy and hoping his face didn't look like that: dirty, with eyes dull as lumps of coal. Jimmy was in the South Pacific, and his last letter home didn't say much except thanks for the cookies and popcorn and he sure hoped the war would be over soon and he could come home. Gretchen and Millard had been friends for a long time, since Millard was seven and she was four, and they played together because their big brothers, Jimmy and Mike, were good friends and let them tag along when they took a .22 into the woods to pop tin cans.

Millard had turned sixteen last week, though he looked older because he was so big, already six feet tall and still growing. He'd be four years older for a little while until her birthday next month when she would be thirteen. She would start junior high this fall, and when she thought about it, she was pleased and scared.

Millard was always making funny drawings, and once he'd given her a picture he'd drawn of himself, a round pink face with bright red curls and big freckles and a grin as big as a carved pumpkin mouth. This afternoon, his skin was as white as library paste and his plump cheeks sagged. There was no trace of his sweet smile.

"Are you sick?" Gretchen whispered, keeping an eye on the door to the back of the store. She'd seen Mr. Thompson mad once, and the memory still made her stomach curl into a hard ball. Ever since the fighting in Italy got so bad and no letters came from Mike, Mr. Thompson walked with his head down and his shoulders bunched. He'd stopped coming over to the café for lunch. Gretchen could remember him coming in for lunch ever since she was a little girl. Mrs. Thompson taught math in the junior high. In the summers, she worked at the store, too. Mike had always jerked sodas, but when he went to war, Millard took his place, learning how to make brown cows and Hobokens and black-and-whites. And cherry phosphates.

The war had changed everything, turned Grandmother's little café from the Pfizer Café to Victory Café, sent Gretchen's mom off to Tulsa to work in the McDonnell Douglas plant, made Gretchen a girl-of-all-work, able to peel potatoes, wait tables, mop floors, wash dishes, carry out garbage, whatever needed to be done, whatever she could do to take the burden off Grandmother. In the hot summer afternoons, if they didn't have a late rush of customers, Grandmother insisted Gretchen go to Thompson's for her cherry phosphate, and sometimes she'd get a copy of the new movie magazine. Her favorite actress was Jennifer Jones, and she was from Oklahoma, too!

Everything should have been just like always, the whiff of the ceiling fans, the smell of ice cream, she and Millard reflected in the shiny mirror behind the counter with its rows of Coca-Cola glasses and sundae glasses. Instead, Millard blinked, his eyes dull, and his voice had a hollow sound like a long distance call from her mother.

"No. I'm okay. Cherry phosphate?" He thudded off the stool, moved to the fountain and the big spigots.

Gretchen nodded. Seltzer hissed into the tall glass, turning the thick cherry syrup into dancing pink liquid. Millard placed the glass in front of her. Before the war, his big brother Mike would have slapped down a paper doily and announced, "One cherry phosphate," and plopped the glass in the center of the white mat. But for the duration, there were no more paper doilies. Every month there was a paper drive and another for tin cans. She and Grandmother kept all the newspapers left by customers and washed each tin can and peeled off the paper. Usually Millard kept the marble counter sparkling clean. Today he didn't notice the spatters on the counter.

Gretchen sipped, wrinkling her nose at the fizz, savoring the tart cherry taste. "Are you worried about Mike?"

Millard's round face swung toward her. He rubbed his eyes. "We haven't heard from him for a month. My folks are scared." He yawned.

The door to the back of the store banged open. Mr. Thompson poked his head out, the overhead light shining on his bald head. His bony face was long like a horse. Big, black, tufty eyebrows creased into a dark frown above pale, cold eyes. "Millard!" His voice was sharp.

Millard hunched his shoulders. Big as he was, he suddenly seemed smaller. "Yes, sir."

"Come here." Mr. Thompson sounded like a man staring at a wall cloud in a dark spring sky. He lifted a thin hand to rub against his forehead.

Millard closed the door when he stepped into the back, but the arched window for prescriptions was open.

"Millard," Mr. Thompson's voice wavered. "You said nobody came in the store this morning while I went to the bank."

"I didn't see anybody." Millard almost sounded like his old, precise self except for his voice, hollow as an echo from the bottom of a dry well.

Gretchen gulped at her drink, then pushed the half-full glass away. She slapped her nickel on the counter by the cash register and hurried toward the front of the store, covering her ears to block out Mr. Thompson's angry shout.

The booths were full and the counter, too. Gretchen

worked fast. Somehow word had got around about meat loaf today. Often the butcher shop was full of empty trays, even if you had enough points in the ration book to buy. But today they had ground beef. Gretchen had chopped onions until her eyes watered and her nose itched, onions and green peppers and celery. Grandmother used fresh tomatoes for the sauce. The café had a holiday air. Talk was so loud, Gretchen strained to hear when she took orders. Everybody ordered the special, meat loaf with mashed potatoes and green beans (Grandmother added a dash of nutmeg to her beans), coffee or iced tea, and watermelon for dessert. Grandmother bustled from the kitchen to help serve, blond hair slipping from her coronet braids to frame her dumpling plump face, always a little pink and now flushed from the heat of the kitchen and the long morning's work.

Gretchen didn't try to lift a loaded tray. They were too heavy for her. Instead, she carried a plate in each hand and sped back and forth from the kitchen to the booths and the tables. Even though her legs were beginning to ache and she'd burned a blister on her left palm when she raised the lid on the big pot of boiling potatoes, she felt happy. Everybody loved Grandmother's cooking. Of course, the businessmen in town knew they could count on Grandmother. Gretchen saw the usual faces in booth three, everyone but Mr. Thompson. In booth one, even the serious-faced army officers from Camp Crowder were exclaiming over their lunch. Good food made everybody happy. Gretchen listened to the din of conversations, especially pleased when she overheard a compliment to Grandmother's cooking.

Booth one, the army men: ". . . best meat loaf I've ever . . ."

Booth two, a bunch of farmers over from the sale barn: ". . . always come here for lunch when I'm in town. Used to be called Pfizer's . . ."

Booth three, Mr. Kraft, the banker; Mr. Willet, the barber; Mr. Douglas, the insurance salesman: ". . . apparently Millard ran away last night . . ."

Gretchen was on her way to get coffee. She kept on walking, grabbed up the pot. She refilled the cups at booth one but strained to hear Mr. Kraft. ". . . Bert called to see if Julie knew where he could be. Millard's followed Julie around like a tail to a kite for years."

The other men nodded. The Thompsons lived on Jefferson across from the Krafts in a two-story white Victorian house. Jefferson was the best street in town. It had sidewalks and iron fences and big old elms. Julie Kraft was the prettiest girl in town, blue eyes soft as a spring sky and shiny blond hair that curled in a Ginger Rogers pageboy. All the boys looked at Julie, especially at Shady Grove Lake when she wore her Catalina swimsuit. Gretchen wished she could look like Julie instead of having straight black hair in pigtails and dark blue eyes and skinny legs. But that was as likely as she and Grandmother ever moving to Jefferson Street. Their street, Archer, was just a dirt road. An alley ran behind their house and the back of the Thompson house.

At booth two, Gretchen bent her head to listen to the businessmen in the next booth.

Mr. Willet swiped a piece of meat loaf through the tomato sauce. "Mighty good today." He gave a small belch. "Don't sound much like Millard. He's been in my Scout troop ever since he was little. Made Eagle Scout last year."

Gretchen reached booth three.

"Bert was real upset." Mr. Kraft held out his cup.

"What'd Julie say?" Mr. Douglas played golf a lot, and his face was as red as a summer sunset. When he walked down Main, he spoke to everybody he passed.

Mr. Kraft stared into the dark, hot coffee like it was a bubbling volcano, his jowly face as blank as the round stone statues in a *National Geographic*. "Julie," he spoke his daughter's name as if the syllables didn't fit his tongue, "don't say much anymore. Ever since that good for nothin' Lewis boy—" His thick lips pressed together tighter than a box turtle slamming shut his shell.

Mr. Douglas glanced at the banker with shrewd, kindly eyes and boomed, "Did you hear the report on the radio last night about the P-40s? They said . . ."

Gretchen moved to booth four, automatically refilled cups, stacked four plates, and headed for the kitchen. She looked up at the round clock behind the counter. At least another hour before she could hurry down the sidewalk to the drugstore. She worked faster than ever, her dark brows drawn in a frown. Millard run away? She felt shivery to her bones, like stepping out of the hot kitchen into a sleet-edged February wind.

The shivery feeling spread from Gretchen's bones to her heart when she looked into Mrs. Thompson's red-rimmed eyes. Gretchen stood beside the metal stool at the soda fountain. Gretchen heard the faint drip of water in the deep sink and the whirr of the ceiling fans and old Mrs. McClure's hoarse voice complaining to Mr. Thompson about the taste of the cough syrup he'd fixed up for her last week.

"Millard?" Gretchen was scared to ask, but she had to know.

Mrs. Thompson usually had a sweet smile, too, just like Millard's. Today her face was puffy and lopsided like a stepped-on pincushion. Her eyes filled with tears and her lips trembled. "He's gone, Gretchen. He's gone."

"But where?" Gretchen clung to the marble counter.

"We don't know. Oh, Gretchen, I didn't believe it. I didn't. Not my sweet Millard. Not until we found the money—"

"That's enough, Rose." At the end of the counter, Mr. Thompson bent forward like a black crow. "There's nothing to be said. Millard's gone. Good riddance. If your eye offends thee . . ." He turned away, tears edging down his cavernous cheeks.

Victory Café was closed on Sundays. Grandmother always fixed Sunday dinner, even though it was just the two of them. Gretchen wished she wouldn't. The kitchen table in its Sunday best was surrounded by ghosts. Every time Gretchen looked at the third seat on the right, she saw Jimmy, winking at her and sneaking a piece of meat from his plate to hand under the table to Walter, his springer spaniel. Walter died last March. Gretchen thought he died of a broken heart because Jimmy was gone, though Grandmother said he was twelve and old for a spaniel. They hadn't told Jimmy, and in every letter he asked about Walter, said to be sure and make hush puppies for him since Jimmy wasn't there to take him hunting and sit around a campfire.

"Ve haf chicken today." Grandmother still wore her navy silk dress from church.

Gretchen looked across the table and tried to smile. But she hadn't been able to smile this whole long week.

Grandmother knew, of course. "I'm sorry, *mein Schatz*." Her kind face looked unaccustomedly stern. "I would not haf beliefed it of Millard. He should not so treat his mama and papa. And to do such a bad thing! No more do ve talk about him. Here Gretchen, haf a leg I fix so fine for you."

"Millard wouldn't do anything bad." Gretchen's voice wobbled. Tears burned her eyes.

Grandmother's face softened. "I know. He vas your friend so gut. Ve vill not speak more."

Gretchen didn't go to Thompson's anymore in the afternoons for a cherry fausfade. She didn't mind working hard. She liked the crackle of grease on the grill and the smell of fried meat—when they had any—and stewed okra and tomatoes and, occasionally, apple pies. She liked polishing the tables at the end of the day and rolling clean silverware in red-and-white checked napkins and pushing the wheelbarrow with trash to the incinerator. That was the last thing she did every day. It was so hot now as the days rolled into August that the glazed sky steamed, and it hurt to touch the metal of the wheelbarrow. Gretchen kept on working and listening to the snatches of conversation, like turning the dial on the radio:

". . . ought to take John L. Lewis out and string him up to. . . ."

"Emma Whittle don't go anywhere now, not since they got word about Billy. Oh, you knew that, didn't you? Billy got killed at Kasserine Pass. She . . ."

". . . the murder of Sir Harry Oakes had to be an inside job."

". . . what will happen now that Mussolini's gone?"

No one talked about Millard, and every time someone played "Stardust" on the jukebox, she felt sad. "Stardust" was Millard's favorite song because Julie Kraft sang it at the Fourth of July picnic.

By the third week in August, the cicadas rasped so loud she couldn't hear the whine of the big trucks on Highway 66. It was Saturday night, and the pile of trash and garbage would take at least two trips to the incinerator. Little cracks and crevices ridged the yellowish dirt in the alley behind the café. Gretchen moved slowly. She'd started the day in a fresh white

Ship 'n' Shore blouse and pink pedal pushers. Spatters of spaghetti sauce trailed across the front of her blouse. When she mopped the kitchen, water from the bucket left a big wet patch on her pants. Maybe there would be time to ride her bike out to Shady Grove Lake for a swim before supper. But she was so tired. She shuffled toward the wheelbarrow leaning against the back wall. The alley was empty and Grandmother was already home, so Gretchen didn't have to act like she wasn't tired. Ever since her mother had gone off to Tulsa to work in the war plant, Gretchen had taken over closing down the café.

Gretchen stood on tiptoe to pull down the handles, careful not to touch the hot metal sides. She swung the wheelbarrow around and squinted against the sunlight glancing off the metal bed. When she dropped the legs next to the garbage pail, she took cotton work gloves from her pocket and pulled them on. She grabbed the edges of the garbage can, tipped it toward the barrow. The refuse slid forward. A cloud of flies swirled around her. She glanced at the wheelbarrow and saw a piece of brown cardboard stuck to the bottom of the bed with white adhesive tape. Slowly she righted the can, flapped her hands at the buzzing flies.

Her mind felt dull. But somebody had put the brown cardboard there, made it stay with bandage tape. Puzzled, she reached down, pulled away the tape, picked up the irregular piece of cardboard. Letters were printed on one side: m Beam. She turned it over. The message was simple:

Gretchen, meet me at midnight at the Fort.

There was no signature, only the drawing of a round face with tight curls.

Car lights flashed over the hill. Gretchen jumped into the ditch and crouched there until the car chugged past. It would be bad if anybody saw her out on Purdy Road and told Grandmother. But once she got past the Hansen farm, she didn't have to worry about being seen. She'd take the path that plunged into the woods. She held tight to a flashlight, but the full moon was so bright, she might not need the light.

The wavery cry of an owl made her skin prickle. She'd never come this way at night. Before the war, when she and Millard were little, they'd found a deserted shack near Piney Creek and made it into a fort. Millard pretended to be in the cavalry and she was a pioneer woman. Once they'd built a fire and made biscuits that were doughy in the middle and had black edges. Gretchen didn't think she would have liked being a pioneer woman, especially after Millard told her how the Indians sometimes swooped down and scalped everybody they caught. He said the movies never showed how the pioneers took the land away from the Indians. In fourth grade, Gretchen learned about the Trail of Tears and the Five Civilized Tribes who were moved to Indian Territory, pushed out of land the white man wanted. Lots of the kids were part Cherokee. Gretchen thought Gloria Walkingstick had the most beautiful dark brown eyes she'd ever seen.

The path curled around a stand of cottonwoods and dipped toward the creek. A soft light glowed in the open doorway of the shack.

Gretchen ran. "Millard?"

"Hey, Gretchen." He sounded like Millard. Almost. But his voice was kind of choked and happy and sad all at once. "You came."

She skidded to a stop in the doorway. Millard waited just inside. He was thinner, and his eyes were tired. His cream shirt had a stain on it—she'd never seen Millard that he wasn't neat as a pin—and his Levis looked grimy. The dirt floor of the shack had been swept, and there was a sleeping bag rolled up in a corner. A wooden crate held some bottles and cans.

They stared at each other, then both talked at once.

"Why did you run away?"

"You didn't tell anybody about the fort?"

And then were both silent.

Gretchen hated the emptiness of the fort. Maybe it had been fun when they were kids, but was this where Millard was staying? All by himself? With scraps to eat? And no books. Millard read books all the time.

Millard pointed at a log outside the door. "We can sit there."

They sat down, and the moon painted the trees and ground with cream.

"Millard, your mama is so sad." She stared at his round face and wished the light were brighter. His features were indistinct, and his hair looked dark, not red.

"But not my dad." His voice was bitter.

"Was he mad because you said nobody came that day?" Gretchen had been over it and over it in her mind, and she didn't understand. Why would that make Mr. Thompson so mad?

"I fell asleep. Once I kind of heard something and I almost woke up, but I was so tired. Later I thought about it, and I know somebody was there and it was somebody I knew. But I can't remember what it was that made me think so."

"You mean somebody came and you didn't see them? Were you afraid to tell your dad you were asleep? How come you were so tired?" Gretchen remembered Millard slumped against the counter and the way he'd trembled awake.

"Somebody came while I was asleep and stole a whole bottle of morphine tablets. That's a strong medicine. It's the kind people steal and sell for money."

Money. Gretchen heard Mrs. Thompson's voice, ". . . not until we found the money . . ."

Gretchen moved uneasily on the log, felt the ridge of bark against her legs. "You had some money."

"Yeah. I did. Money I worked for—"

She grabbed his arm. "Why didn't you tell your dad, explain that you were asleep, that you'd earned money?" She frowned. "How did you earn money, Millard?" He worked at the store all day in the summers and every day after school in the winter.

"The Blue Light." His voice was defiant. "It's—"

"I know." Actually, she didn't know much about it, just enough to cross to the other side of the road when she biked past the dance hall on her way out to Aunt Lela's farm to pick up eggs or honey or fresh vegetables. "Oh, golly." No wonder Millard didn't tell his father. Mr. Thompson was a deacon at the First Baptist Church, and he was real strong against dancing and alcohol. Everybody knew bootleg whiskey was easy to get at the Blue Light.

"They needed somebody in the band. Everybody's been drafted, and I can play the saxophone. I worked every night until midnight and then we'd clean up and I didn't get home until two and then I had to get up early . . ."

Gretchen was sure Millard played the saxophone real well. He played a lot of instruments, but he had to play the tuba in the band because he was big and strong enough to carry it.

She stared at the shadowed face. "Your dad thought you sold that stuff to somebody?"

"Yes." The single word bristled with anger and hurt.

Gretchen snapped off a piece of bark from the log, twisted it in her fingers. "You played in the band and you were tired. You fell asleep, and somebody stole that medicine. But Millard, if you'd told your folks, they might've been mad, but—"

"If I told them," and his voice was drained, "it would have meant I couldn't go to the Blue Light anymore. And I almost had enough money. I almost did! I ran away, but I was going to go home that night and get my money—I hid it in my sock drawer—but when I got close to the house, I heard Dad yelling at Mom, and he was saying I was worse than a thief, I was bad and I wasn't any son of his, not anymore."

"Millard, you should have told them. How could they know you didn't take money if you didn't tell them!"

"I shouldn't have had to tell them."

She understood. How could his dad have believed him to be a thief? But the stuff was gone, and there was money in Millard's sock drawer. "A lot of money?"

Millard was always quick. "Twenty-three dollars."

"Millard!" That was enough money to buy a new coat and shoes and a couple of dresses.

"I had to earn it all again." He jumped up, hurried into the shack. He came back with a wad of money in his hand. "I've got enough. It's for Julie."

Gretchen stared at the money. "But Julie's rich." Julie's father owned the bank and they lived in the biggest house in town and Mr. Kraft drove a black Cadillac, one of the last ones made before the factories turned to making tanks.

Millard thrust the money toward her. "I used to watch Julie at band practice and she—" He broke off, shook his head. "She's so beautiful." There was awe in his voice. He sounded the way Gretchen felt the day she and Millard came up over a rise and saw a valley blanketed by monarchs, and it was so beautiful her heart almost stopped.

"When Julie comes into the room, it's like a sunrise or the smell of wheat after the rain. So clean and good."

Gretchen knew about love, the way she felt when her mother called and told her how brave she was to help Grandmother, the look in Grandmother's eyes when Gretchen won the spelling bee, the long-ago memory of her father tucking her into bed and singing a lullaby. But this was something different.

"Julie loves Buzzy Lewis." Millard spoke in his precise way, reporting a fact. "Her folks won't let her marry him. He's going overseas pretty soon. If Julie had enough money, she could take the bus to Georgia."

The cicadas rasped so loud it almost sounded like the clack of train wheels.

"Gretchen," his voice broke, "please."

Gretchen loved the library, the musty smell of books, the shine of the hardwood floors, the big casement windows that were cranked wide in the summer, and the welcoming smile of Mrs. Parker, who helped Gretchen find all kinds of wonderful books, like *The Man in the Iron Mask* and *Treasure Island*. After the clatter and bustle of the café, Gretchen loved the peace of the library, the silence broken only by the snap of shoes on the floor and the rustle of paper and the whirr of ceiling fans. She went to the desk with her books: *Lad, a Dog, My Friend Flicka,* and *The Count of Monte Cristo.*

As she walked toward the fiction stacks, she searched the reading room, darted glances down the long rows. Julie Kraft stood on a step stool in the second row, shelving books. Sun slanted through a west window, turning her hair to gold.

Gretchen turned into the aisle, hurried up to Julie. Gretchen touched the envelope in her pocket.

Julie looked down. "Hi, Gretchen. Can I help you find something?" Her voice was kind of husky like June Allyson's. She looked directly into Gretchen's eyes, really looked, making Gretchen feet taller and older and special. Julie's light blue eyes had a dark blue edge. Her face was thinner than Gretchen remembered from school. Her pink cotton sundress didn't have a single wrinkle.

Gretchen looked around, then bent forward and whispered, "I have something for you from Millard."

"Millard!" Julie clapped a hand over her mouth. She glanced toward the reading room, but no one came. "Oh." Now her husky voice was low. "I'm so glad. Is he back?"

"No." The word felt as hard as a cherry pit in Gretchen's mouth. She pulled out the envelope. "He wants you to have this. He says it's enough money so that you can go to Buzzy."

Julie's face moved from shock to wonder to despair. It was like watching fireworks, the beginning flicker in the sky, the shower of sparks, the blinding brilliance, and then the fading clusters and light dimming to darkness. She stared at the envelope, her lovely eyes darkening. "They say Millard sold drugs."

"He didn't." No snake ever hissed harder. "No, he didn't, Julie. He's been playing in the band at the Blue Light. Somebody else stole the drugs. Millard had money, and he couldn't tell his dad how he got it because it was for you. He ran away and he worked more and now he has enough again."

"For me?" Julie pressed her hands together. "Millard did that?" Not fireworks this time, but the soft glow of moonrise.

"He wants you to be happy." More than he wanted to come home. More than he wanted to be in his room with its bunk beds and posters of the periodic elements and constellations and world map. More than he wanted to work behind the fountain and jerk sodas as good as his brother had.

Julie sat down on the step stool, buried her face in her hands. Her shoulders shook.

Gretchen reached out, touched Julie's arm. "He wouldn't want you to cry."

Julie lifted her face. Tears rolled down her cheeks. "I want to go so bad. I want to be with Buzzy. But I can't take the money. Please, tell Millard I can't take his money."

"It's not from drugs." Gretchen would have stamped her foot, but Mrs. Parker might hear.

Julie used her fingers to wipe away the tears. "I believe you. I told everyone that Millard wouldn't do that. And he could play in anybody's band. But," she sniffed, "it isn't right to take Millard's money."

"Because you aren't related?" If Millard was Julie's brother that would make it all right. Or even if maybe Millard was a girl. Or did Julie turn the money down because it wasn't right to ask other people for money? Not unless it was the bank . . . "You could borrow the money."

"Borrow—" Julie tasted the word like new food.

Millard wanted Julie to be happy. If he were here . . . Gretchen held out the envelope. "You can borrow it. And when you get there and get married—" when people were married, their husbands paid their bills—"you can send the money back to Millard."

Millard pulled the Coke bottles out of a tub with ice in it. "Want a Coke, Gretchen?"

"Sure." It was funny to drink anything after midnight.

He used the bottle opener, snapped off the caps. "How did Julie look?" He kept his tone casual except for the way he said her name, as if the syllables clung to his tongue.

"Pretty. She had on a pink dress. She almost didn't take the money—"

His head jerked toward her.

"—but finally she said she would borrow it. Millard, I've never seen anybody so happy."

He sat down on the log and looked at the water of the creek. "I wonder when she'll get to Georgia."

71

Gretchen knew he wasn't really asking.

He picked up a rock, tossed it into the water. "Will you come tell me if you hear?"

Gretchen frowned. "Millard, aren't you going to come home now?"

He drank some Coke. "I can't go back. I still don't know who took the morphine. My dad wouldn't believe me now, especially since I ran away."

"You can't stay out here." In the moonlight, the shack looked almost pretty, but the door was half off its hinges, and the windows were broken. "It will get cold. And you don't have any clothes. Or anything."

"I got a sleeping bag. Mrs. Hopper loaned it to me. She's real nice. She owns the Blue Light. But I'm not staying much longer. I've almost got enough money to go—" He broke off. "Don't worry, Gretchen. A lot of guys join up early. Sometimes recruiters don't even ask to see a birth certificate. I'll find one that needs to meet a quota."

Gretchen brought the pitcher of iced tea to booth three. It was like church; people always sat in the same places.

Mr. Douglas clapped his hands, good humored but exasperated. "Wake up, girl; we asked for coffee."

"I'm sorry." She hurried to the serving stand, used a hot pad to pick up the heavy pot. She better start minding her p's and q's. Even grandmother'd asked this morning if she had her head in the clouds. The heat had finally broken with a gully washer the night before and thunder that sounded like barrels bouncing down cellar steps. She couldn't stop thinking about the shack and how cold and miserable Millard must be. She would have been scared. And if he got wet in the night, how could he get any dry clothes? And school was starting next week. If only Millard could come home. . . .

She moved back and forth between the kitchen and the tables, bringing chicken-fried steaks and grilled cheeses and fried eggplant. They would sure be out of meat tomorrow and have to fix macaroni and cheese and maybe a big pot of navy beans.

If she could figure out who took the medicine, Millard could come home. He'd been too sleepy to wake up, but there was something that made him think he knew who'd come in. There must have been a sound or a smell he recognized. Somebody who came in often. Oh, maybe someone who got medicine a lot. Yes, it would have to be—

"We have bread pudding or Jell-O today."

—someone who'd gotten that medicine before. Otherwise, how would they know where the medicine was kept?

She looked across the room at the counter. Every day Dr. Jamison took the third stool from the left. He ordered chili and coffee in the winter, bean soup and iced tea in the summer. If the person who stole the medicine was a regular customer at Thompson's Drugs, they would come with a prescription from Dr. Jamison.

Gretchen rode her bike to the back door of the Jamison house. She wore her swimsuit under her clothes and had a towel rolled up in the basket. She'd told Grandmother she was going out to Shady Grove Lake. The doctor and his wife lived next door to the Krafts. She leaned her bike against an elm tree and ran up the back steps and knocked hard before she got too scared to try.

Mrs. Jamison, drying her hands on a dish towel, came out onto the screened-in porch. "Why, Gretchen." Her blue eyes clouded. "Is your grandmother sick?"

"No, ma'am. Please. Could I see Dr. Jamison for a minute?"

Her round face creased. "We're just about to sit down to dinner—"

"Matty, who's here?" His voice was tired. He stepped out onto the porch. Dr. Jamison looked like one of the Smith Brothers on the cough-drop box. His white hair was untidy, his mustache drooped, and long sideburns ran down his jaws. He hooked his thumbs behind his suspenders.

Gretchen said fast, "Dr. Jamison, I have to talk to you. Please. About some medicine."

Dr. Jamison's bristly eyebrows drew down.

"William—"

He waved his hand at his wife. "It's all right, Matty. Bring us out some lemonade." He held open the screen door, gestured toward the rocking chairs.

Gretchen perched on the edge of the smaller rocker. He lowered himself onto the big black one, looked at her soberly. "You need medicine, Gretchen?"

"No, sir." She started at the beginning, the day she'd gone to the drugstore for a cherry fausfade. She spoke loud enough for him to hear over the drone of big planes in the sky. Millard had told her the big army planes flew in formation.

Mrs. Jamison brought a tray with two big, cold glasses of lemonade. She placed it on the wicker stand and turned back to the kitchen.

Dr. Jamison listened without comment, sipping the lemonade.

". . . so you see, it had to be someone who came to the store all the time. Because Millard almost knew who it was. Maybe it was the sound of the footsteps. Or a smell." She closed her eyes. Sometimes Grandmother smelled like licorice, the candy she loved. Mom wore a perfume, Evening in Paris, and whenever Gretchen smelled it, she thought of Mom. She opened her eyes, looked at him hopefully.

"Anyway, I thought you might know who would steal that kind of medicine."

For an instant, there was a startled look in the doctor's light brown eyes.

Gretchen plowed ahead. "If you know who it could be, maybe you could talk to them and tell them how bad it was for Millard and if they'd just tell Mr. Thompson . . ."

"Do you know where Millard is?" Dr. Jamison's face was what Grandmother called a brown study.

Gretchen's hands held tight to the arms of the rocker. "I think I could find him," she said carefully. But she wasn't going to tell anyone about their fort, no matter what.

Dr. Jamison pushed up from the rocker, paced to the end of the porch. He stood with his back to her for a minute or more. Finally, he turned, took a deep breath. "I'll see what I can do, girl."

Gretchen hugged her secret to herself. Dr. Jamison knew who to talk to. She was sure of that. There had been that look in his eyes when she told him what happened. She hugged her secret and her hope. The next morning her grandmother smiled at her. "You haf a happy step today. I haf been vorried about you. Maybe it is that you are glad school is soon to start?"

Grandmother had arranged for Callie Perkins's mother to work in the café until Gretchen arrived after school. Mrs. Perkins was starting this morning so she could see how everything was done. They were standing behind the counter, Gretchen opening the cupboard with sugar and salt, when she looked through the front window and saw Dr. Jamison's dusty black car. Thoughts exploded in her mind like marbles hit by a lucky agate. Dr. Jamison didn't come downtown this early. Somebody else was in the car. He'd promised to do his best. "I've got to run an errand," she told the thin woman beside her. "I'll be back in a minute." She left Mrs. Perkins looking mournfully at the contents of the cupboard. Grandmother wouldn't be out in front—she was busy cooking. Mrs. Perkins could take care of things for a little while.

Gretchen darted out the front and saw Dr. Jamison holding open the front door to Thompson's. And she heard the tap of Mrs. Whittle's cane as she limped inside. Gretchen ran past the store, darted down the side street to the alley in back. Just as she'd thought, the back door was open. It was still too hot to close the doors, and some air crept past the screen doors.

"Bert, Emma wants to talk to you for a minute. I'll wait out in the front."

"Hello, Emma." The druggist's voice was kind.

"Bert—"

Gretchen edged near enough the screen door to peek inside. Mrs. Whiffle's fair hair, streaked with gray, drooped around her face. She didn't have on any makeup, and her big blue eyes looked dull as a mud-splashed car.

"I got to tell you the truth. Millard didn't take that morphine. I did. He was asleep that day when I came in. I was coming back to get a prescription for my throat. William said I couldn't have any more morphine, but I can't sleep, Bert. Not since Billy—" Her face screwed up like a broken doll and her voice washed away in a gulping sob.

Gretchen ran faster than a bull bucking a rider. She ran all the way even though it was still pretty hot, close to ninety-five. But she didn't care if she got hot and it hurt to breathe. Millard could come home. Millard could come *home.* She was so glad, but she pushed away the memory of those sobs. She burst out into the clearing near the creek and the shack. "Millard!" She didn't have to be quiet or . . .

Cottonwood leaves rustled in the ever-present wind. Cicadas still rasped, though their glory days were past. Birds chittered. The shack door was ajar. Even from the edge of the clearing, Gretchen saw the dusty floor, the slant of sun through the broken window, the emptiness.

"Oh, Millard." But no one heard except the birds.

Gretchen knew she had to hurry. What if Mrs. Perkins told Grandmother she'd left? Sweat slid down her back. Her pedal pushers stuck to her legs. But still she hesitated in the shadow of a huge old sycamore, looking across the road at the Blue Light. The long, low wooden building looked shabby, its paint dulled to a mustard brown, the tar-paper roof patched and uneven. The dusty parking lot was empty except for an old pickup truck.

Millard said Mrs. Hopper was nice. But Grandmother's friends looked the other way when Mrs. Hopper rattled into town to buy groceries. And she might not know where Millard had gone.

A side door banged open. A big woman with flaming red hair—but not a nice red like Millard's—stood on the low steps and flung soapy water from a pail.

Gretchen took one step, two, broke into a run as the woman turned to open the door. "Ma'am. Ma'am!" Gretchen skidded to a stop, near the wet patch with little soap bubbles.

Mrs. Hopper's skin was a tired white, but her mouth was bright as red neon. Huge eyes with thick black lashes cut a glance as sharp as a knife. "This is no place for kids." She pulled open the door.

"Please, Mrs. Hopper."

The woman's big dark eyes were as still as a pond at midnight.

"I'm a friend of Millard's. He said you were nice to him. He said you loaned him a sleeping bag. If you know where he is, please write him that he can come home, that his dad knows somebody else stole the medicine."

Mrs. Hopper pushed back a thick swath of dyed hair.

"People come and go," she said brusquely. She yanked open the door and stepped into dimness. The door banged shut behind her.

Every parking place downtown was taken on Saturdays. Despite the shortages and the coupon books, everybody came to town to shop, and the Victory Café was full from early until late. The roar of conversation was loud as bees buzzing around a hive. The jukebox blared "Chattanooga Choo Choo." The counter was full and so were the booths and tables. Gretchen and Mrs. Perkins worked fast. Gretchen was hurrying to the stand for a fresh pot of coffee when Mr. Thompson called out, "Gretchen."

She knew before she turned that he wasn't going to ask for ketchup or another ashtray, though the one on that table was full and she needed to change it. His voice was proud, like the principal reading the honor roll.

When she reached the table, Mr. Thompson held out a silver picture frame. She took it and stared at Millard in a sailor uniform with a little round white hat. He was her Millard, and yet he was different, thinner, and the look in his eyes . . .

". . . guess we have to accept it when our kids grow up. Stubborn young idiot wouldn't tell me what he was up to." Mr. Thompson's voice puffed like dough in hot grease. "Of course he was wrong to work at night. But he said he played in a band until he got enough money to go out to San Diego. He went through boot camp there and . . ."

The words rippled in her mind like Aunt Lela's pond on a March day, the wind kicking up little waves. You couldn't see through the surface of the muddy red brown water. You couldn't see the tadpoles and minnows and crawdads. Or even the water moccasins slipping by.

Gretchen held the frame and looked at an old young face that she'd once known so well. Words slipped past on the surface of her mind:

". . . mighty proud of him but his mama . . ."

". . . Julie will be home soon because Buzzy's shipped out. I guess I underestimated that boy since he saved enough money to send for Julie and marry her. . . ."

She handed back the frame. "I'll get some more coffee."

As she walked away, Mr. Thompson said, "Funny, I thought Gretchen would be interested. But I guess she and Millard are too far apart in age . . ."

She walked away with her secret that darted like a tadpole beneath the surface of the pond, like Dr. Jamison's secret and Mrs. Whittle's secret and Mr. Thompson's secret and Julie's secret and Mrs. Hopper's secret and Millard's secret. She picked up the coffeepot and moved slowly around the room, refilling the cups and looking at familiar faces and wondering about the secrets inside that nobody knew about.

A Settling
of Accounts

Part I
Kay
CHAPTER 1

The house looked as though it belonged, solid, substantial. Enduring. It looked as if it had stood there a hundred years. But Kay knew better. She knew it was a newcomer, a pretender to history.

She stood across the street from the row of duplexes. What were they called in England? Semi-detached villas? She wasn't sure. It didn't matter. They were nice houses, built all in the same manner, but, even so, each, like a uniformed child, was distinct from its neighbor.

The house directly across the street from her, the usurper, was stucco painted a carnation-pink. Lace curtains demurely masked the front bow window on the left. On the right, cheerful print curtains hung open, framing a table and lamp. The steps on the left glistened in the pale October sunlight. Had they been washed that morning? Rosebushes bordered the tiny yard. Red and white blooms, ragged now and past their peak, dotted the neat line of shrubs. The lawn that belonged to the right grew well (did anything not grow well in England?), but it was an informal yard, satisfied with a runaway growth of chrysanthemums and the rag-a-ma-tag litter of childhood, a soccer ball, a tipped-over blue tricycle, a red plastic bucket that had survived the seashore.

Kay stared somberly at the cheerful house and, much like

a cloud slipping across the sun or the quick shifting of a picture when a printed overlay drops in place, she saw another house, saw it as it had stood for two hundred years until Wednesday, September 11, 1940, saw the small perfect entryway, the glisten of the silver tea service on the sideboard in the dining room, saw the graceful curving staircase, the opening door from the library, and, standing in the doorway, she saw Lionel.

It was so clear, that moment out of time, so clear and perfect and real that she could see the rough weave of his gray-blue RAF uniform and the way it pulled in front because the jacket was a little small for him. He was smiling, his dark-blue eyes warm with laughter, and . . .

"Lionel . . ."

A red bus rumbled in front of her, blocking for a moment her view of the carnation-pink house, destroying utterly that vivid re-creation of bricks and wood and flesh. The bus lumbered past and once again she saw the carnation-pink house and the others like it, stretching in an orderly row down the street. They looked so permanent, so inevitable, so indestructible. But nothing is permanent or inevitable or indestructible. She knew that. Knew it well. Why then should it be so painful to look down this peaceful street?

She turned away suddenly, almost angrily, and walked up the street, her head bent, her hands thrust into the pockets of her raincoat.

She should not have come back to England. She never should have returned.

She walked quickly. Only someone watching closely would have noticed the slight limp, the almost imperceptible hesitation of her right leg. Usually, without thought or effort, she adjusted her stride so that no limp showed. It was only when she hurried or was tired that it became apparent. She walked one block, a second, a third before she slowed. By the time she reached the Embankment, she was managing a stroll and looking about. Then she saw the Thames sliding swiftly by and again, unexpectedly, memories darted bright and vivid as flames. The smell of the river was fresher in 1940, but there were other smells that she would never forget, oil and rubber and sugar and tea burning, smoke swirling upward in great black and brown and red plumes until the sky was a mass of writhing smoke and it seemed as though all the docks must be ablaze.

She sat down on a stone bench and watched the river flow by, and she might have been any American visitor resting for a moment by the vigorous old river, though she was a more striking woman than most. She sat on the bench with the unstudied grace of poise and confidence. She was a beautiful woman. As beautiful now as she had been in her twenties. Her face, with its deep-set, long-lashed violet eyes and high cheekbones, was as lovely and ageless as Artemis' on a Lydian coin. Her hair, coiled back in a bun, gleamed black as a magician's cape, only enhanced by wings of silver at the temples.

She stared across the river, her face composed, her hands loose in her lap, and fought the tumultuous spirit within her that was struggling to be free. She was astonished and a little frightened at the fury of the battle. It had been long years since she had truly felt anything at all. And she didn't want to start now. It was too late. Those years were over. Gone. Dead.

Dead.

Kay pushed up from the bench and turned toward the street. She stubbornly kept her back to the river as she waited for a taxi to roll by. When she hailed one, she stepped into it without a backward glance. She fumbled in her purse for the card with the gallery's address and gave the driver the number on Bond Street.

She leaned back into the soft upholstery of the stately taxi. She remembered the night that . . . No, she would not remember! She would not. This was Tuesday, October 25, 1966. She must cling to the present, resist the past. She would go to the gallery, see something of the items scheduled for auction, put her mind on the reason she had come to London, shut away memory and impulse and emotion, keep her mind firmly on today.

That was what she must remember, not to give way to impulse. Everything had gone so beautifully up to the moment this morning when the taxi driver had looked inquiringly back at her. Until then, she had fully intended to go directly to the gallery. She was reaching into her purse for the gallery card and then, abruptly, in a voice she scarcely recognized, she had given the address in Chelsea, the address she had given so easily and so often so many years ago.

That was a mistake, a grievous, wounding mistake. She must not do it again. She was in London on business. She would attend to that business, study the items Marjorie had marked in the catalog, pick up her tickets for the auction, attend the auction on Thursday and Friday. Then, on Saturday, she could start the long flight home to New Orleans.

Once again firm in her plans, she rested back on the comfortable cushions and watched the streets sliding by. She was still defensive, braced against the shock of any other sharp, unexpected memories, but she found no threat in King's Road. Its mélange of boutiques harbored nothing of yesterday. Even Piccadilly wasn't hurtful. The people and signs were so evidently of today that the backdrop of half-familiar buildings caused no painful stirrings in her mind.

The taxi turned into Bond Street. None of the elegant shops brought memories. When she knew Bond Street, the plate-glass windows were taped or boarded over and the crunch of broken glass underfoot had supplanted the hum of traffic.

She watched for the gallery and spotted it as the cab slowed. Gilt letters on the canopied entrance announced Durand Galleries, Auctioneers. Through windows on either side, silver glistened and crystal sparkled.

She stopped for a moment outside the gallery windows, studying the display. More than likely all these items were scheduled for auction. She hadn't had time to study the catalog carefully. It was only after Marjorie's accident on Friday that she had known she would be coming to the sale. And there had been too much for her to do before she left New Orleans on Sunday for her to prepare adequately.

Kay frowned as she pushed through the door of Durand Galleries. Perhaps it had been foolish to come at all. She hadn't, of course, wanted to come. But she had. And, now that she was here, she must concentrate on her job. It was going to be tough to make the right bids, to come home with the right buys, because she was outside her area of expertise. Certainly she mustn't make it more difficult by mooning about London, remembering things as they never would be again. She was not, she told herself brutally, a girl to be buffeted this way and that by emotion. She was Kay Emory of Emory and Richmond Antiques, New Orleans, LA, U.S.A. She and Marjorie had, all by themselves, built a firm that enjoyed a reputation for honesty, quality and reliability. It had been damn hard work, but it had been fun, too.

To run a successful antique shop takes many talents, including the instinct of a gambler, the competitive drive of a football coach, the knowledge of an antiquarian, and the luck of a pop recording star. It also helped to have a sense of humor and never to take either yourself or your clients too seriously.

On balance, Kay felt that she and Marjorie had managed very well. They were at the top now, and that was the toughest place to be. Because now, at this very moment in history, was the most exciting time to be involved in the antique trade, but it was also the most difficult. The market had expanded fantastically and the sale prices had to be seen to be believed, but the number of available artworks, whether a client wanted a Degas or Tibetan carved ivory, had shrunk and shrunk until the bidding on what was left was both fierce and frantic. The coming auction would likely follow the pattern so familiar now, bidding that careened out of sight and a narrowing of the market even further into the hands of only a few houses.

But Kay's frown fell away as she stepped inside the gallery because she immediately felt at home. It was not that all galleries are alike. Far from it. Some are sumptuous. Some austere. But all possess an atmosphere of pride, a pride that verges on arrogance. The loveliest, costliest, rarest artworks in the world passed through these halls or others like them. And those who work in these kinds of galleries feed on the value, the sometimes incredible value, of their offerings. Checking this special form of egotism is another necessary talent of buyers, and Kay knew how to do it well. Much better than she could handle the formless but sharply painful pricks of memories struggling to be acknowledged.

The gallery foyer was charming, a shining pegged oak floor, a worn Persian rug in its center. Sunlight streamed softly through a skylight. She looked up, admiring the ornate wooden balcony that ran around three sides of the room.

A supercilious young man materialized suddenly at her elbow. "May I be of service, madam?" The accent was English but the attitude universal. She wished with a glint of humor for an avalanche of artworks to glut the market and instill a little of the old need-to-please. But the age of miracles is past.

She introduced herself. "I am Kay Emory of Emory and Richmond in New Orleans. We have corresponded with you about the auction Thursday and Friday. However, you were expecting my partner, Miss Richmond, but she has been taken ill and I have come in her place."

Had she identification? Letters? Miss Richmond's authorization? Because, of course, she did understand that this was to be the sale of the century, well, if not of the century then certainly of the decade, and they had to be very careful whom they admitted. Not, of course, that Miss Emory appeared in the least unsuitable, but care must be taken. If she would be seated, wait a moment, they would check their files. . . .

Kay nodded, surrendered her passport for identification. She wondered how much of this was care and how much was calculated to produce that state of mind so desired by auctioneers, the frantic desire to bid, bid, bid before it all went to someone else.

As she waited, Kay looked around the foyer, at the elegantly framed artwork, and noted the archways to the left and right. They more than likely led to galleries where many of the items would be on display. The auction room was probably upstairs.

She was not, to be truthful, looking forward to this auction. If it weren't for the fact that Damon Fetherlee, one of their oldest, most valued customers, had a passionate love for Louis XIV miniatures, she would have refused to come. European art was Marjorie's bailiwick, had always been. Kay's expertise ran to pre-Columbian and Colonial artifacts. She and Marjorie made a first-rate team, each taking full responsibility in her own area. But Marjorie's broken leg had abruptly and violently upset their settled routine. On Friday

Marjorie had slipped on spilled soap powders at the supermarket. It was that pointless and unexpected. So now, the next Tuesday, Kay stood in the elegant London gallery in Marjorie's place. Kay didn't have any illusions that she was anything but a lamb among wolves. All she had was Marjorie's catalog with cryptic marginal notes and instructions to come home with the miniatures unless they went for more than eighteen thousand.

Kay had looked at the catalog on the long flight to London. She would study it again before the sale. Thinking of it, she opened her handbag and pulled it out, a thick booklet with pale-blue cardboard covers. The miniatures were described on Page 14. She flipped the pages and once again read the brief technical descriptions. Absorbed, she didn't hear a door open above her.

The balcony ran around three sides of the second floor. The door that opened so softly was not, from the outside, easily seen. Its frame merged with the heavy Italian wood of the wall. It opened slowly, just wide enough for a watcher to look down into the foyer, down at Kay.

Kay finished reading. She snapped shut the catalog and, once again, looked around the foyer. The light from the skylight fell softly on her. Her black hair gleamed like a raven's wing. She lifted her chin, looking up, and the lovely line of her cheek and throat was as clear and unmistakable as a Dürer drawing.

She had no presentiment. But she was, abruptly, aware of some other presence, of someone watching her. She looked first toward the door through which the young man had disappeared with her passport. But it was closed. Then her eyes sought the archways and found no one. She looked up toward the balcony and she was just too late. The discreetly cut door in the Italian wood wall was closing. Closed.

Her faint sense of unease fell away, supplanted by a ripple of irritation. Where was that supercilious young man? There were, after all, limits! How long should she be expected to stand here, awaiting his pleasure?

The door opened then and the young man hurried into the foyer. She looked coldly at him, but he was, surprisingly, full of apologies, the words rushing one over the other. "So sorry to be so long, Miss Emory, very sorry indeed. Had a little difficulty with our file, but everything is in order, we have indeed corresponded with Emory and Richmond, Miss Richmond has attended many of our sales, and we are so sorry to know she is ill and do hope she will make a quick recovery . . ."

Kay thanked him and tried to quell the onrush of words. "I'm sure she will, and I know she will appreciate your kind wishes. Now, if you have the tickets . . ."

The young man didn't wring his hands, but the effect was the same.

"Would you mind awfully, Miss Emory, if we delivered them to you? I assure you they will arrive in good time, but, you see, we have been so careful, especially careful, to issue cards that can't be duplicated. There will be so many incredibly valuable pieces (his voice rose here) and we can't afford to take any chances and, you see, once we pass out cards with a name just scratched through (his hands flew up in dismay), why, anything could happen! So," and now he was brisk, matter-of-fact, "we will reprint your tickets, the tickets for Emory and Richmond, and deliver them to you."

He turned then, moving to a desk at the side of the foyer. "If you will give me your hotel?"

She was tucking her passport back into her purse. She told him, of course, and managed to keep any expression out of her voice, though she thought it all a foolish lot of bother.

Surely this was carrying security a step too far?

He wrote down the address, nodding, "Yes, that's just off Russell Square."

"Yes." She was turning to leave when he called her back.

"Would you like to see the auction items? They are on display in the Red Gallery."

She almost said no. She wished, abruptly, to be out of there. Instead she smiled and accepted. A good view of the sale items could be an advantage, and she would need every possible advantage. Perhaps the eighteenth-century portrait plate would be on view. Marjorie had tried to describe how to gauge its worth. ". . . if it has a peach tone, a kind of soft glowing orange underlay, then it's good, Kay, very good, but . . ."

She found the plate midway down the gallery. It was in a display case with seven other plates. All fine china. Kay studied the portrait and its background for a long moment. Then, shaking her head, she moved on. Was that a peach tone? She couldn't tell.

When she had circled the gallery, she debated crossing to the Blue Gallery, then decided against it. Once outside on Bond Street, she savored the sharp chill of the air. Thick gray-black clouds hid the low-hung afternoon sun. She was ready for a good brisk walk. She turned to her right. She would pause at one shop window and then another to admire porcelains, jewelry, even, a surprise here, Toltec sculpture. She saw Sotheby's, that most famous of auction galleries. It wasn't long before she reached Oxford Street and, looming off to her right, was one of London's larger and finer department stores.

Kay hesitated, stood for a long moment with the polite pedestrians curling around her like water eddying past a rock, then she pulled her raincoat tighter about her and crossed the street toward the store.

She loved department stores. They were everywhere more fun than a circus, more interesting than a political rally. To wander through a department store in a strange city was as revealing as opening a friend's medicine cabinet or reading someone's diary—and much more acceptable. Which floor would house the toys? And what would they be? Where were the household goods? And ladies' coats? What was popular here, cloth, fake fur, vicuna?

She pushed through the main revolving door and breathed in the smell of the store, a warm mixture of cloth and leather and a faint scent of perfume. She was smiling, happier than she had been all day.

Later, she would wonder—if she hadn't gone to the store, if she had returned straight to the hotel . . .

CHAPTER 2

Leather goods were on the first floor along with men's suits and overcoats, women's jewelry, gloves, scarves and cosmetics. Kay was tempted by the array of men's gloves. That pigskin pair would make a perfect gift for John. She stood by the counter, touching the gloves, and realized with a sense of shock that this was the first moment she had thought about him since she left New Orleans. A smile flickered on her face. John wouldn't like that at all! He was so confident of his charm and magnetism. Charm and magnetism which he undeniably possessed. He was a year or so older than she, as fair as she was dark. He tanned a most delightful golden tawny in the summer. He played vigorous, aggressive tennis. He was a very successful surgeon, a widower and her lover.

How long was it now . . . But her mind shied away from dates and tallies. He had been puzzled that she wouldn't marry him. So many others had tried so hard to interest him. He had, in fact, been offended, but she had ruffled his short crisp golden hair, and suggested gently that it was foolish to try and improve upon perfection. They were both free. They could enjoy each other and they did, they did, yet there was nothing to cage them, nothing to disrupt their quite comfortable lives, he in his stately home, she in her old and elegant townhouse not far from the shop. He was not, for all his cleverness, a very perceptive man. In the end, he was flattered by their arrangement. It saved him from many difficulties, the necessity to rearrange his property, the bother of making a new home, the jealousy his grown children would have felt.

Kay saw him as he was, arrogant, vain, unimaginative but,

also, clever and virile and incredibly handsome. She did not love him. But she enjoyed him.

She had never loved anyone but Lionel.

Her hand tightened on the gloves, crushing their softness. The thought had come without warning and she felt an acute wave of nausea. She had not permitted herself to think of Lionel, to remember him in many years. Since long before she met John. To think of them at once in her mind, to recall Lionel's sturdy unlined face, then to picture John's knowing, experienced, faintly malicious gaze made her feel tawdry and old—older than time.

She stood by the counter, clutching the gloves, and she was oblivious to the gentle stir and rustle around her, a clerk near enough to touch but half turned away as she helped a young man select a muffler, shoppers moving along the aisle behind her, the tap-tap of an elderly woman's cane. She was caught up in a dizzying rush of feeling, sorrow and an odd sense of shame which was absurd.

So the bump at her elbow and the murmured apology scarcely registered. She didn't even turn to answer. She managed a muttered, "That's all right."

She stood stiff and straight, her face pale, her violet eyes strained and staring.

"May I help you, madam?"

The clerk's face was soft and wrinkled and kindly. She wore a shapeless black dress, or perhaps it was navy, and she was frankly bulky and matronly.

Kay looked at her and thought, a little wildly, that the clerk looked so old and . . . shapeless. Why, the two of them were probably near in age, but what a gulf between them, what a difference in life and style and viewpoint. What were the odds that the woman facing her had been young and plumply pretty in 1940? And that she had listened in London to the heavy pulsating rumble of German bombers?

Kay almost asked. Her mouth opened and the words almost tumbled out, then, desperately, swallowing hard, she forced a meaningless smile instead.

"Is anything wrong, madam?" The clerk's kind face furrowed in concern.

Quickly, Kay shook her head. Somehow she managed to speak. "Nothing. Nothing at all." She swallowed once more and concentrated every effort of her will on the next sentence. "I was looking at these gloves." And she looked down and was shocked to find them twisted and lumped, her hand a rigid fist.

The clerk looked too and her gasp of dismay yanked Kay fully back to the present, to this old and stately store.

Kay had always been able to think fast. She acted without letting a pause grow. As naturally as though a prospective buyer would always crumple gloves, she shook them, laid them on the glass counter top and smoothed their backs.

"These will suit perfectly. Do you have a box?"

The clerk nodded quickly, so grateful that no confrontation would be necessary that she blossomed into chattery uncharacteristic speech.

"Madam will find these gloves to be of the finest quality, the very finest quality. And would there be anything else that madam would like to see, anything at all . . ."

Kay waited impatiently as the clerk accepted her money and boxed the gloves. She would throw them away, she never ever wanted to see them again, she couldn't possibly give them to John. She took her change and put her billfold in her purse and snapped it shut. Grabbing up the sack and slipping the purse over her right arm, she tucked her left hand in her coat pocket. And stopped even as she began to turn away from the counter.

A Settling of Accounts

She was a fastidious woman. In every way. Her townhouse was a poem in soft grays and yellows. And she couldn't abide dirt. She would tell the maid if she found dust on the mantel or the feathery spiral beginnings of a web in a corner or smudges on the door panels. A soiled dress went immediately to the cleaner's. Her jackets and suits were always immaculate. Her purse was neatly compartmented, mirror, comb, lipstick, compact, keys, billfold, checkbook, cigarette case, lighter. Nothing extraneous, no sloppily dropped receipts or used stubs or extra pens.

And she didn't, of course, carry lumpy rocks in her raincoat pocket.

She caught her breath sharply when she pulled out the necklace. Bright red stones winked and glistened. The price tag dangled from the clasp, which was nicely worked in white gold. She stared at the necklace. Where had it come from? How could it possibly . . .

"Madam, if you will come this way, please."

He was short for a man but broadly built. He stood in front of her and, as she looked up, one of his pudgy hands took the necklace, the other gripped her elbow tightly.

"That isn't mine," she said quickly.

"I know that, madam. Please, if you will come this way. You are blocking the aisle."

There was a veneer of courtesy but it was as brittle and meaningless as a model's smile. And there was nothing but disdain in his eyes and the thin tight line that was his mouth.

Dimly Kay was aware that the clerk who had helped her was watching, one hand against her lips. A shopper had stopped to watch with greedy, avid eyes.

The enormous shock washed over Kay then and it left her shaking and frightened. She tried to speak and she couldn't force any words. It was the stuff of nightmares and she was helpless. She didn't resist when the man moved close beside her and none too gently pushed her along the aisle toward the back of the store. It was a hideous walk. The chandeliers glittered, the prisms flashing in the store lights. Kay felt her face flame and it was a sickening mixture of shame and terror. Once, years ago when she was a girl at school in Paris, Sister Marie Anne had held her elbow in just such a grip as she hurried Kay down the long hall toward the Reverend Mother's room and then, as now, heels had clicked on a wooden floor and there had been the same violent disbelief that it could be happening to her, to Kay Emory. Then, as now, she had been innocent of any wrongdoing. How vividly she remembered that long-ago winter morning, the smell of soapsuds in a wooden bucket as they passed one of the lay sisters scrubbing the floor and Kay drawing breath to tell the Reverend Mother that she had not drawn the crude and blasphemous scrawl on the blackboard even though Jeannette said so! Until this moment, she had forgotten that humiliating memory, pushed it far down into an inner recess of her mind.

There had been so many memories to suppress and, soon enough, that winter morning's embarrassment had been a minor one.

Her captor, call him what he was, led her to a freight elevator. When they stepped inside, she shook free of his hand. As the door slowly closed, she said breathlessly, sharply, "I did not steal that necklace."

He didn't even look at her.

Somehow that steadied her. His contempt, his cold indifference stiffened her back, quieted the uneven thumping of her pulse.

She was, after all, Kay Emory.

The manager's office reassured her, too. At first. It was such a small, bare room, a linoleum floor, an old common desk, brown painted walls. There was only one window and it was masked by a drawn yellow shade.

A secondhand junk dealer would have a better office at home.

Then the young man behind the desk looked up and his narrow, clever, hard face jolted her. It belonged in a slick Fifth Avenue office.

"Yes, Fredericks?" His voice was not quite a rasp but near enough to make the breath catch in her throat again.

Her captor, Fredericks, held up the garnet necklace. It dangled from his pudgy hand. She stared, repelled but fascinated, at the faceted stones, bright blood-red, held between a stubby thumb and forefinger, slowly swinging back and forth.

"In her coat pocket."

The young man's cold, dark eyes swung to Kay.

She stared back at him. Her eyes didn't fall. Slowly she nodded. "But I did not put them in my pocket."

The young man's mouth twisted in a humorless smile. "A pixie did it."

"I doubt that," Kay said evenly.

"Then . . ."

"I can't explain it. But I am not a thief." She opened her purse, began to fumble for her passport, for letters . . .

The manager shook his head. "I don't care who you are." He studied her and there was a flicker of curiosity in his eyes. "Obviously, you are American. You are well-dressed. If you steal for money, you're good at it. But you probably just steal for . . . what is it you Yanks say? . . . for the hell of it."

"No." Her violet eyes studied him in turn. "Let's be clear on it. The necklace was in my pocket, I found it there. Pulled it out! I wouldn't have done that if I'd stolen it, would I?"

When he made no answer, she yanked her head sideways. "Ask him."

Kay and the young hard-faced manager both looked at the pudgy short man.

Would he lie? Kay wondered coldly.

"Perhaps she saw me coming," Fredericks answered obliquely. The manager continued to look at him. Fredericks shrugged. "That's right, then. She had them in her hand, was pulling them out of her pocket."

That gave Kay hope, gave her strength to struggle.

"Don't you see?" Kay asked quickly, "I had made my purchase, a pair of gloves, and I had paid and I was turning to go. I tucked my hand into my pocket and, of course, I knew at once that . . ."

The manager made a slicing motion with his hand. It wasn't a rude gesture or harsh, merely impatient. He saw, he understood, that was enough said. He was already lifting his phone, dialing. "Bates, who's in jewelry now?" He listened, then said abruptly, "Send her up here."

As they waited, silently, he lit a small cigar and looked back down at a column of figures and began to make quick small checkmarks.

Kay had his measure now. He was abrasive, hard, bright, impersonal. She had wedged a tiny seed of doubt. She had a chance.

She moved then, crossed the tiny space to sit in the chair across from the desk. He looked up, watched briefly. She opened her purse and pulled out her cigarette case. She ignored both of them and lit a cigarette, and the sharp acrid taste was as frankly sensual and bracing as a drink.

It didn't take long for the jewelry clerk to come. Kay almost despaired when she saw her. She was young, not yet twenty, young and willowy and rather breathtakingly beautiful until you noticed the emptiness in her eyes and then, at second glance, she looked almost commonplace and drab.

There was the faintest edge of interest in her voice when she spoke to the manager. "Mr. Bates said you sent for me?"

"Yes, Miss O'Connor. Come here."

Miss O'Connor dutifully crossed to stand quietly in front of his desk.

My God, Kay thought, a cow would show more curiosity. And her reputation and freedom balanced on what this . . . this creature had seen.

But the girl surprised all of them.

"Miss O'Connor," the raspy-voiced manager asked, "have you seen this woman before?"

The willowy girl half turned to look at Kay and, for the first time, a hint of animation touched her, gave color to her cheeks, a spark of light to her eyes. "Oh yes, sir, Mr. Morton, I did so see the lady, yes, indeed, sir, I did."

Kay had a little trouble with the girl's accent. It was a distinctive twang with an odd lilt to the vowels.

The man behind the desk was curious now. He asked gently, "When did you first see . . . this lady?"

"Ow, the minute she came in the store, sir, I noticed her and I knew right off that she was an American. You can always tell, sir, can't you?"

When he nodded, she continued, oblivious to the depth of interest in her prattling recital. She didn't notice how tensely Kay leaned forward, the better to hear, or the way Fredericks hunched his thick neck into his shoulders, defensively, or the intent look in the manager's eyes. She was only interested in what she had seen.

". . . such a lovely purse, really. Anybody would know it's alligator and . . ."

The two men looked at Kay's purse, and she did herself

and thought how odd that this purse should save her, distinctly odd, because she almost didn't buy it—alligator is an endangered species and she felt a pang of guilt, but it was truly lovely, the way the grained leather glistened in the light, it had a smooth and glowing beauty, and she had bought it.

". . . her shoes match. Don't you see? Perfect shoes and purse, and I thought how it is that Americans always have the most beautiful things." The girl stopped, then continued almost plaintively, as though someone had scolded her, "But you know it's true, Mr. Morton. They always do."

"Sometimes," Mr. Morton said heavily. "Now, Miss O'Connor, tell me what happened when this lady came to your counter."

The beautiful empty-faced clerk looked surprised, then shook her head. "She never did, Mr. Morton, she never did."

"Then how do you suppose this ended up in her coat pocket?" And the manager held up the gleaming bright-red garnet necklace.

The clerk's shock was painful and obvious. Her white face paled whiter. "But it can't be. It can't," and her voice rose with every syllable. "I counted every one of them after the man looked. Every one of them, and he helped me so I'd be sure . . ."

When they had the girl's story, it was pitifully little to go on, scarcely more than a signpost dimly seen on a fog-shrouded road.

But it was something.

And it was for Kay the first hint of rationality since her hand had tucked into her coat pocket.

No, Miss O'Connor didn't remember what the man looked like. He was pretty old.

"As old as your father?" Morton asked. Kay looked at him with growing respect. She had not in the least thought him a fool, but he was a very clever man indeed.

Miss O'Connor thought. "Older than Dad. I just mean he wasn't so old he looked real old." She frowned, trying hard now to remember. But there was nothing distinctive about the man to help her recall.

Nothing like Kay's alligator purse.

A man. An older man. Wearing a homburg and a dark overcoat. And dark glasses.

"It was a man in a homburg who called my attention to the lady," Fredericks said slowly but not, give him credit, grudgingly. More thoughtfully.

The floorwalker was trained to remember faces, to look and recall. But the man had spoken to him quite quickly, as if discharging a distasteful duty yet determined not to become involved. He had then turned away. Fredericks had almost moved after him, but it was just then that Kay had finished her purchase and started to leave. Fredericks had followed her and watched her reach into her pocket and stop and pull out the necklace.

They were all quiet for a moment. Then, once again, it was the raspy-voiced manager who had a question.

"Was he an American?"

Kay had just drawn another cigarette from her case. She looked up over the flame of her lighter and she watched Miss O'Connor and Fredericks very carefully indeed.

"No," Fredericks said. Miss O'Connor shook her head at almost the same instant. Then both of them looked uncertain.

"But I don't think he was an Englishman. At least, not English-born," Fredericks said slowly.

Kay and the manager looked at Miss O'Connor.

She shook her lovely head. "I don't know, I'm sure. But he spoke like a gentleman."

CHAPTER 3

The music was muted. Piped in, of course. Strings and a saccharine piano. The atmosphere deliberately light, pastel walls decorated with painted parasols, pink-topped tables. A very civilized bar. But Kay didn't feel the least bit civilized. Or soothed.

She stared at her drink. Her second drink, to be precise. The scotch glowed like amber, tasted smooth and faintly sweet. Abruptly, she picked up her glass and drank it half down.

If she could only stop trembling inside.

They had not quite got so far as apologizing at the store. It was too bizarre, too little explained. But they had realized that it wasn't enough for the police. The clever, hard-faced young manager had dismissed Miss O'Connor and Fredericks. When he and Kay were alone, he said, "What do you say we call it even?"

She had stared at him, not quite understanding.

"We'll forget it happened," he said impatiently. "I'll put the necklace back. You go on your way."

"Someone put it in my pocket." She was stubborn now and beginning to be angry. There had not been breath for anger before.

He shrugged. "Right enough. Someone did. Perhaps it was you." She started to speak but he ignored that. "Perhaps it was a confederate who got the hell out when Fredericks nabbed you." His eyes were intent on hers. "Or perhaps it was the man who spoke to Fredericks. And, if it was, then you'd best be casting about in your mind, Miss Emory."

She looked at him steadily.

He nodded slowly. "For that means a grave enemy to be sure."

The background music slipped into "Wunderbar." Kay stubbed out her cigarette. Her throat hurt. She had smoked too much today.

A grave enemy. What an odd phrase. It was only as he said it that she heard the Irish lilt to his voice. Sure, and he was Irish with that dark, hard face and clever mind. And the Irish are always dramatic.

A grave enemy.

Once again that uneven breathlessness fluttered in her lungs, that frightful trembling.

She would have said, until today, that she had not an enemy in the world.

All the way back to the hotel, that lilting phrase had echoed in her mind. In the hotel dining room, as she forced herself to eat the veal and peas and round new potatoes, she looked around the rectangular room at the several dozen tables with snowy damask cloths, at the diners, couples, some families, two large tour groups, several singles like herself, and it was such an ordinary, everyday, predictable collection of people, and all the while the three little words throbbed in her mind and nothing could ever be ordinary again.

A grave enemy.

She fled the dining room, leaving her dessert untouched. She almost passed the bar, almost went straight up to her room and then, abruptly, she turned into that civilized, airy, light bar. She drank her first drink almost in a gulp and waited impatiently for her second. But the scotch didn't touch that hard core of tension inside her. As she realized it, she gave a little sigh and sat back against the leatherette seat. Slowly she opened her purse and drew out another cigarette and lit it.

She inhaled deeply, then watched the smoke swirl and spiral.

Stop running, Kay, she told herself. Stop and think. Think.

The necklace hadn't walked into her pocket. Someone put it there.

Why? There's an easy one, Kay. To get you thrown in jail. Or whatever the English do to shoplifters.

And why would anyone want her in jail?

For the hell of it?

Slowly she shook her head. Her eyes narrowed in thought, she sipped at her drink, slowly stubbed out her cigarette. Oh no, it had to be something important, a compelling reason. Something damned important, in fact, because someone had run a risk. Someone—call it the man who alerted the floor-walker—he had filched the necklace, running the risk of being caught by the clerk or, more likely, by the sharp-eyed floor-walker. Risk one. Then he had to stash the necklace in her pocket. And how could he be sure she wouldn't turn and cry out, "This man is molesting me!"? But she had made it easy for him, standing there lost in thought. Risk two. Even then he wasn't through. He had to walk up to Fredericks and tell him about the supposed theft. Risk three.

But it had almost worked. If that empty-faced, silly little girl hadn't noticed her, if the manager weren't clever and suspicious, she would right now be in a London police station. Would she be behind bars? Or could she post bail as one would at home? Or would she be trying to call the Consulate, which would probably be very cold and hostile, embarrassed that a well-to-do American was being had up for shoplifting?

Once again that sickening breathlessness swept her. It had been a near thing. Very near indeed.

If she hadn't at that point been so tired, her mind buffeted by so much in one short day, the nearness of her escape would have signaled a warning, as clear and distinct and harsh as the brass bells that clang for a fire alarm.

But she was very tired. And she hadn't managed to eat much of her dinner. And she didn't usually drink whisky. She liked a sherry after dinner, occasionally a daiquiri. She took another sip of scotch, warm, smooth, rich scotch, then jumped a little at the deferential voice beside her.

"Miss Emory?"

She looked up, startled, wary, alert, then was embarrassed at her jumpiness. It was only Timothy, the nice young bellboy who had taken up her luggage yesterday.

Could it have been only yesterday? Monday morning?

She smiled at him and wondered if her smile was the grimace it felt.

"Telephone for you, Miss Emory."

She looked at him rather as if she had never heard the word before. "Telephone?" she repeated uncertainly.

"Yes, miss."

She looked around.

"In the lobby."

She knew no one in London. So it must be . . . As she began to slide out from behind the small table, she looked at her watch. It would be midday at home. What could be wrong! For surely only an emergency would warrant a call. Marjorie looked as sturdy as a small oak, wiry, brown-skinned, tough. But, had the fall been too much for her? Was she seriously ill? Or had something happened to Julie?

Kay was hurrying now, her heels clicking across the marble floor.

Or to John?

At the lobby she stopped, at a loss, until Timothy pointed to the rank of telephone booths. "The first one, Miss Emory."

That, of course, should have signaled something to her, also. But too much had happened today. She rushed to the booth, not even bothering to pull the door shut behind her, and grabbed up the receiver which lay on its side on the little metal shelf beneath the coin box.

"Hello. Hello."

There was no sound, nothing on the line, echoing emptiness.

"Hello. Hello," she said sharply.

Nothing.

She jiggled the hook, once, twice, again. An operator finally came on the line and asked in a bored voice whom she was calling. Kay explained, her voice thin. There was an instant's pause. "Apparently," the operator replied, "the party calling you hung up."

Could the operator check, see if there had been a long-distance call, an international call, to this number? The operator could and, while Kay waited nervously in the small hot booth, listening to the odd squawks and buzzes on the open line, the operator did. Kay waited five minutes. Ten.

"Madam, no international call has been recorded for that number."

"Thank you, operator." When she had rehung the receiver, Kay stared at the coin box and realized abruptly that no one could have called her from home at this pay-phone number. They would have called the hotel number, the desk number, not the number of a pay phone in the lobby.

So there was no lost long-distance call. No emergency at home.

She stood in the doorway of the booth and felt a prickle of unease down her back, like the ruffling of a cat's fur when a finger lightly touches its spine.

Who could have called her?

A Settling of Accounts

She looked across the shining gray-and-white squares of marble flooring toward the desk. She hesitated, then crossed to it.

The clerk looked up. "Yes, madam?"

"Are there any messages for me? Miss Emory in 706."

He checked the rank of pigeonholes, then turned back to her, shaking his head. "No, Miss Emory."

"Thank you."

Nothing there. No one on the line. What an odd, pointless episode—except *someone* had called her, someone had dialed a number and asked for her and there was no one in this entire gigantic sprawling metropolis . . .

She was walking back toward the bar now.

Yes, there was one person. The young man at Durand Galleries. Then she was impatient with herself. Once again, if he had called, it would be to the hotel number, asking for her room to be rung. Not a pay phone in the lobby.

The bar was as brightly lit, as antiseptic as before. Two men at a nearby table looked up, watched her for a long moment, ready to be interested. Ignoring them, she sat down at her small table. The ice was almost melted in her glass, which was about half full. She picked it up absently and took a sip, then realized she was, suddenly, very thirsty and she drank it down in three swift gulps, then grimaced at the bitter taste. The soda must have gone flat. She looked up and caught the bartender's attention. When her fresh drink came, she drank a good third of it.

Perhaps the call had been a mistake altogether. Certainly it couldn't be important. If anyone truly needed to speak to her, wanted to speak to her, they would call back. So dismiss it. She had other things to think about.

Didn't she indeed, she thought wryly. A small matter. A frame-up. That's what it was called in the movies when she

109

was young. The George Raft movies. Funny the things you remember, the unconnected bits that your mind could unexpectedly produce, like gay-colored scraps from a long-forgotten ragbag. George Raft. Odd how clearly she could picture him, short, saturnine, standing squarely in a doorway, the narrow, colorless black-and-gray doorway, the square, undistinguished furniture, a slinky girl with a short white fur wrap, an orchid pinned . . .

The onslaught was sudden, devastating.

One instant she was seeing in her mind the projection from narrow strips of aged celluloid. The next instant, the images were dissolving, whirling into blurry splotches that fast faded into shapelessness. She reached out clumsily, clutching at the table edge. Her hands, lumpy and unmanageable, knocked against her glass. It tipped over and the drink spread onto the table. The glass began to roll. She saw it going, lunged to catch it and fell sideways from the banquette seat and realized with incredulous horror that she was tumbling onto the floor.

She heard voices but she could not understand what they said. She tried desperately to get up. Everything moved, the floor, the shoes, giant bulbous shoes that surrounded her, the glass ceiling. Her hands and arms and legs were like lumps of sticky clay. She tried to talk. Her tongue moved against her teeth but the sounds were nonsense, thick and slurred and meaningless.

Worst of all was the fear, the wild, sickening rush of fear. What was happening to her? She tried to think, her mind struggled to answer, but words and colors and shapes swirled faster and faster, she was sick and fainting, but still she tried to reason, she held grimly onto consciousness even as the dizziness grew and grew until it was a thick gray wave sweeping her farther and farther away.

A Settling of Accounts

She didn't feel the hands that gripped her, pulled her up, the arm that supported her, the brisk voice of the desk clerk. "No need for alarm. Let us pass, please. Everything will be all right."

Kay was vaguely aware of movement. She kept trying to speak, tried so hard.

The desk clerk supported her on one side, the cheerful young bellboy on the other. It took them only a moment to hurry her across the lobby and into an elevator.

The clerk punched the button. He held a passkey in his hand. As the cage rose, he looked at Kay derisively. "She doesn't look a drunk."

The bellboy shook his head slowly back and forth. "She had a phone call. Just a while ago. She seemed all right then."

The clerk shrugged. "They can fool you."

The boy hesitated, then asked diffidently, "You don't think we ought to call Dr. Symonds?"

The clerk looked at him in surprise.

The bellboy flushed a little, then said determinedly, "She might be sick. Sometimes people can't tell the difference. She seemed like such a nice lady."

The clerk grimaced with all the world-weariness of four years in the hotel business. "Peters, a lot of nice ladies are drunks."

CHAPTER 4

Sick. Sick. Sick. She had never in her life been so sick. Kay leaned over the lavatory and her hands on the basin trembled from weakness. Her head hung down and she breathed shallowly, trying not to vomit again. God, she couldn't stand to be sick again. But she was. Again and again. It did stop finally. She washed her face then, her face and hands, and rested for a long time, sitting slumped on the edge of the bath. When she had strength to stand, she shuffled into the bedroom, moving like an old, old woman. She made it from the bathroom door to a chair midway to the bed. She had to stop and grip the chairback and wait for waves of faintness to pass. Then, grimly, she lurched the rest of the way to the bed and fell onto it. She lay atop the spread, too weak and miserable to pull it down. She began to tremble then from cold, the cold of shock. Even when she did manage to twist the spread loose and pull it over her, she was cold, so cold, as cold as wind howling over snow, colder than ice-blanched bones. Finally she sank into an exhausted, nightmare-ridden sleep.

It was midafternoon before she woke to a throbbing headache and a sense of panic. What had happened, what . . . She shivered and drew the beige chenille spread closer to her.

Drugged, of course. That was the only possible explanation for that abrupt, frightful collapse.

She remembered vaguely, as if in a dream, being brought to her room. And, after that, nothing until she found herself, sick and shaken, in the bathroom.

Kay pushed the spread away. Her mouth crinkled in distaste as she looked down at herself, at her soiled and rumpled dress, a yellow silk. She had slept the night in her clothes. She struggled to sit up. More recollection now, of that heaving sickness and the quivering weakness in her arms and legs. So, hideous as she felt now, it was better than it had been.

And she was thirsty. She reached for the glass at her bedside, and the tepid liquid tasted wonderful. She felt decidedly better. Well enough to get up.

She bathed and dressed, pulling on a soft cashmere dress of a rich chocolate-brown that lent a touch of color to her face. She dried her hair and brushed it and pulled it back into a chignon. Eye shadow and a touch of rouge and a pinkish-red lipstick.

She studied the mirror. She was still pale, but she looked better, much better. She didn't look like a raddled old drunk.

There it was, the night's horror faced. A raddled old drunk. She stared at the mirror and saw the Kay that she knew, weary, yes, but the familiar, sharply drawn features she had briefly checked every morning all her life. Only this morning, there was something new.

Fear.

She looked deep in her own eyes and knew that fear stared back at her.

It had been many years, half a lifetime ago, that she had lived with fear. But she recognized it at once.

Fear is not a good companion. But sometimes fear is welcome. It is not comfortable to be afraid. But it can save your life.

She rang room service, ordered coffee, tomato juice, toast. She didn't want the toast, her stomach curled at the thought, but she needed food, must have food. When the order came, she signed the check, then she double-locked the door and settled in a comfortable chair to drink the coffee and smoke and, finally, to eat a little toast and down the tomato juice.

And then she was ready to face her fear.

It was time to be afraid, wasn't it?

Stolen goods planted in her pocket, a drug dropped in her drink. Yes, it was time to be frightened and, more, it was time to fight back.

The police.

Her hands began to shake and, very slowly, she reached for another cigarette and lit it. And still they trembled.

The police would not help her. They might listen, but what would they think of her story—the garnet necklace in her pocket, falling down drunk in the bar?

She blew cigarette smoke in gentle spirals and poured another cup of coffee.

Her eyes narrowed. But she had spotted the common thread that linked those two happenings. Kay Emory was publicly humiliated twice, found out as a thief, on view as a drunk.

So someone wanted Kay Emory's image tarnished. Damn messy, in fact. Now, why should anyone want that?

Kay rubbed at her forehead. It was still hard to think. Her head throbbed steadily. But she *had* to think. It was to someone's advantage to embarrass her.

Why?

That was the stone wall, the impenetrable barrier. There was no one, to her knowledge, that she could in any way threaten.

To her knowledge . . .

She hunched forward in her chair, intent, sensing the teasing, elusive tip-end of the thread that could unravel the whole.

To her knowledge . . . Grab it, hold it in mind! She must be a danger to someone. Someone here in London, of course. She threatened someone because she had come to London.

London was the focal point.

In all the years in New Orleans, she had never been the victim of any kind of harassment. Never. But she comes to London and, twice in one day, utterly bizarre things happen to her.

She had taken the night flight to London, arriving on Monday morning. Tired, she had slept most of that day, had not left her hotel. Tuesday was her first day out in London. She had, on impulse, gone to that old address in Chelsea to took at a house gone these long years, then, pushing memory away, hurrying into now, she had gone to the gallery.

The gallery.

That was her first real contact with London. The Durand Galleries.

Kay sipped her coffee. It was cold now but she drank it anyway, then poured another cup.

That supercilious young man at the Durand Galleries? She shook her head. It was madness, it verged on delusions of persecution to imagine that bony, effete young man skulking after her down Bond Street, trailing her to the department store and setting her up as a shoplifter.

Dear God, why?

She lit another cigarette and was impatient with herself. The girl, that lovely, empty-headed clerk, had said the man was older than her own father.

So, not the young man at the gallery.

Kay leaned back in the chair, stared blindly at the ceiling. That would have made it too easy, the young man at the gallery.

And she shivered because somewhere out there, nameless, faceless, anonymous in the millions, was an enemy. How could she put features to that face? She was totally at his mercy. Her mouth twisted. But obviously he had no mercy.

He didn't care what he did to her, what it took, to achieve his purpose.

There it was again. His purpose. What earthly good could it do anyone to discredit Kay Emory?

The darker horror washed over her then, the frightening specter of mindlessness. What if it were aimless, pointless persecution by an unbalanced mind? What if . . .

The sharp ring of the telephone was so unexpected, so shocking that she whirled in her chair and her coffee cup clattered off the little table and rolled onto the floor and coffee spread in a darkening stain on the gray rug.

She stared at the telephone and it rang again.

"Answer it, Kay."

She said it aloud, and the sound of her own voice, tight and controlled though it was, reassured her, gave her strength to control a trembling hand and reach out to the receiver. "Hello."

"Miss Emory?"

"Yes.

"This is Charles Henderson of Durand Galleries. I've brought round your tickets. May I bring them up?"

"Tickets?" she repeated warily.

He paused. "Yes. I said we'd deliver them when they were redone."

Yesterday, at the gallery, she had given her hotel to this young man so that he could bring the new tickets, her entree to the auction. She had thought then that it was a lot of bother, really overdoing the security nonsense.

Had it been much more deliberate than that? Was it a clever way to find out where she was staying in London?

"Don't you remember?" He sounded puzzled now.

"Yes, I remember," she said quietly. Oh, you bastard, I remember. "Leave the tickets at the desk," she continued crisply.

"But I am supposed to deliver them personally . . ."

"That will not be convenient. Leave them at the desk, Mr. Henderson. Thank you." And she hung up.

The phone rang again in a moment. She watched it and smoked. It rang four times and was silent.

Mr. Henderson was not her enemy. The young department store clerk had been too definite that it was an older man who looked at the jewelry, admired the flashing red stones of the garnet necklace. Someone older. A contemporary of Kay's.

She smoked and thought. Nothing was clear yet, but there was a hint of a pattern.

If the clever, careful attempts to compromise her were part of a rational plan, then they must have some connection with what she had done in London.

She had arrived, come to the hotel, driven to Chelsea, gone to the Durand Galleries.

And she was expected to return to the Durand Galleries. To spend, in fact, all day Thursday and all day Friday there.

That was her reason for coming to London.

The auction? Could she in some way pose a threat to someone at the auction? But she wasn't in a violent competition for a rare piece of art. In fact, none of the purchases she was likely to make could possibly matter to anyone else. There was no secret to this type of auction, no great coup to be made. Everything was listed, evaluated, its worth known within a few hundred dollars by everyone coming, agents, collectors and auctioneer together.

And certainly no one with whom they usually competed in a civilized fashion would be worried by her attendance. She was out of her element. This was Marjorie's domain. Marjorie attended all the English auctions. And those in Paris and Berlin.

117

Kay had not been to London since 1941.

And no one had expected her. There had not been time to notify the gallery that Miss Richmond was not coming, that Kay Emory was coming in her place.

Kay swallowed but her throat was dry and she felt an aching, fearful emptiness in her chest. Her mind refused to face the dark imaginings that began to stir in her inmost thoughts.

But she knew she must return to Durand Galleries.

CHAPTER 5

Once, many years ago, half a lifetime ago, she had lived with danger, the exhilaration of hairbreadth escape, the depression of gray, tension-filled hour succeeding hour. She had managed, one raw spring day, to climb aboard a train and walk unflinching between two burly SS men and not attract their notice when every nerve end shrieked with fear and hatred.

So it wasn't hard for her to slip from the hotel, walk briskly to the Underground and take one train, then get off and double back on herself until she was sure no one followed. It took no thought to pause at a sidewalk boutique and buy a purple-and-gray checked scarf to wind around her head and a pair of huge triangular-shaped sunglasses. These and her reversible raincoat, turned from its usual lemon to the inner lining of beige, transformed her appearance.

She had the cab drop her off just past Claridge's and she walked the few blocks down Bond Street to the gallery. She walked more slowly as she neared it. She could see the shop clearly now, iron railings and the small square grillwork canopy, glass windows and the gleam of silver and the sparkle of crystal in the late-afternoon sun. The gallery was midway down the block and had only the single front entrance. There would, of course, be tradesmen's entrances in a rear alley and, almost certainly, a garage opening for trucks.

But surely the staff came and went the front way. It was hard to picture the fastidious Charles Henderson picking his way down an alley.

So she should, from the proper vantage point, be able to

see whoever came and went from the Durand Galleries this afternoon. She didn't dwell on what she would do if no familiar face appeared. If she could not find the source of her danger, she would again be defenseless—and terribly afraid.

She walked slowly past the gallery on the far side of the street, and all the while she was looking for a place to stand and watch where she would not be noticed. There were enough pedestrians to hide her, but too many for her to keep the canopied entrance always in view. And if she stopped, the foot traffic eddied around her and she became noticeable at once. If she paused to look in a window and glanced back over her shoulder, she had to strain to look beyond pedestrians and the cars and buses.

A dozen people could have walked in and out of the gallery without her seeing.

She crossed at the end of the block onto the gallery's side of the street, and the closer she came to it the harder it was to stroll, and she could feel the faint film of sweat on her hands.

The sun's rays had slipped a little lower and now there was only a faint glow to the clean, bright windows. She walked past them, her head turned a little to one side, and she walked very deliberately so that no trace of limp showed.

She looked to the opposite side of the street and saw the small three-story office building that faced the gallery. Gold lettering on the second floor advertised a dentist and a lithograph office and an assurance company.

She walked on to the corner, crossed and turned back down the block. At the little office building she turned in, and it was, as she had thought, an entryway into a small foyer and hall with offices opening off on either side. Nothing barred her from the narrow stairs that wound to the second floor and more offices.

As she gained the hall, the door opposite the stairs opened

and a woman shepherded three small children ahead of her. Kay glimpsed a small waiting room before the door swung shut. A dentist's office. The woman and children brushed by her and started down the stairs.

Kay looked to her left. The hallway ended at a window. From it, she could see the gallery entrance perfectly.

And no one, of course, would see her.

She looked back down the dimly lit hallway. The dentist apparently absorbed the front half of the narrow building. Something called Inventors, Ltd., occupied the first office this side of the hall. Reams and Porter had the two back offices, and Cole Agency occupied the remainder.

Six times in the next two hours, Kay played a little charade. Someone would come up the stairs or an office door would open. Then she would turn to the door nearest the window and stand by it, her purse open, as if she were looking for a key. She acted it out, secure in her knowledge of the Englishman, who firmly believes in leaving his neighbor to his own devices. Had she asked for assistance, she would have been answered courteously. But, so long as she didn't stop someone, they passed her by, eyes averted. Centuries of shoulder-to-shoulder living have conditioned the Londoner to minding his own business, if at all possible.

When the hall was empty again, she would swing around to her window post and once again watch the entrance opposite.

She was not impatient. She had learned patience in a demanding school, the winter of 1941.

1941. Twenty-five years ago. A quarter of a century. A long time, yes, but it didn't seem long enough for all the changes, for the difference between 1941 and 1966. Or were the changes in her, in the way she saw the world around her? Had life always been as uncertain, as ill-defined as it was now?

She watched the gallery door but her thoughts ranged in time and, slowly, to herself, she shook her dark head. No, and the no was as definite and sharp as a chisel against stone. No. She did see things differently, certainly that was true, but it was also true that everything had changed incredibly.

In 1940 and 1941, you knew the enemy. There was never any doubt about it. In 1966, neither enemy nor friend was sure or certain.

In 1940, you knew what was ugly and hateful. You could stand in London on a fall night and hear the hum of the bombers, like a horde of angry bees, catch their uneven rhythm, and watch the flash of tracers and red-smudged, oily fires licking at the sky.

You knew.

Life was uncertain—God, yes. For so many, the hours were running out like the relentless ebb of the sea. But some things were absolutely sure. Hitler had to be fought. There was no question about that.

In 1966, life was still uncertain. But in so many more respects. Nothing was sure, including government. Everything was suspect.

Kay watched the crowds hurrying along the sidewalks. The evening rush was underway now. People going home, to warm fires or to empty rooms, to love or to loneliness, to all the imaginable conditions of man. How odd that she should stand here, this Wednesday evening, October 26, 1966, watching people she would never know as they hurried by, their shoes clicking on the pavement, their coats pulled tight against the early-evening chill. She had come a long way to be here and she wondered, as she had before, how much of life was fortuity and how much an inescapable turn of the wheel.

It was harder, the longer she watched, to suppress memories she had successfully repelled for so many years. So many things reminded her as she looked down from the window. A double-decker red bus lumbered past, and she remembered the one that had been blown over onto its side into a bomb crater and the way it was squeezed in the middle, like a child's toy stepped upon by mistake. A tall, slender man in a homburg paused beneath a street lamp to glance at his watch. His curling white mustache reminded her sharply of Lionel's older cousin, she could not now remember his name, and that it was he who had taken them to the party the night she met Sir Derek Houghton. That was in June 1940, not long after she and Lionel's sister, Betty, had fled France. The war, of course, had started in September 1939, but that was the long year of the Phony War. At the party, Lionel had been irritated because Sir Derek kept talking to Kay, interested in the time she had spent in France, interested in how well she spoke French.

Over that quarter of a century, Kay could hear her own voice, so much lighter and warmer then, as she had laughed and explained, "But you see, Sir Derek, I grew up speaking French. I'm from New Orleans and . . ." She had explained about her family, descendants of a French trader, Philippe Robards, and how her father, Jean Emory, had visited a branch of his mother's family in Provence and met there a distant cousin, Angelique Varney, and taken her home to America, a beautiful young bride who would be Kay's mother. "And I have spent several summers with Grand'mère . . ." And Kay had talked on to Sir Derek, taking an innocent pride in her family, in her French heritage, in how well, of course, she spoke French. And she had laughed up at Lionel's scarcely concealed jealousy. . . .

She had forgotten that scene, Lionel's dark-blue eyes hurt and furious all at once and the way his jaw had jutted and the stiff silence as they walked to the Underground that night.

Forgotten or, more likely, refused to remember. Because, if she had not prattled on and on to Sir Derek, if she had not spoken French so well, if . . .

So many ifs that had, in the long run, mattered so much more than they should have.

Kay stared somberly down at the entrance to the gallery. No, that was not a scene she would have remembered by choice. And now, standing here a quarter of a century later, she remembered so vividly the color of the dress she had worn that night. It had been blue, almost as blue as Lionel's eyes . . .

Her hand snapped open her purse and the click was loud and metallic. She pulled out her cigarette case, lit a cigarette and drew sharply on it.

She had not smoked, that fall of 1940.

"Stop it, Kay. Stop it."

She listened to herself and yet she was pulled to remember. It was so easy, like slipping back into bed on a cold morning, pulling up the thick warmth of covers and drifting down into dreams.

But there would be no warmth in remembering. It would only bring grief, reopen wounds so painfully healed.

Stubbornly, with the very great discipline that had saved her before, she closed the doors in her mind, one by one. She was Kay Emory, a woman, not a girl. A successful antique dealer. This was Wednesday, October 26, 1966. She was in London. Alone in London.

Her mouth curved a little. What quirky tangle of thought had prompted that last? Of course, she was alone.

Completely alone.

She had come to terms with that, these past years. And it was not simply a matter of loneliness. Nothing quite so easily tagged. She was not especially lonely. There was John. And she had friends, her partner Marjorie, others.

It was the fact of being the only Emory of her generation left. The only one. Of all that family created by her father and his French bride, only she and Julie, the daughter of her sister Amalie, survived.

She stood in the narrow hallway, it was chilly now, the warmth of midday long fled, and watched the gallery and thought back to the years before she came to England for the first time, back to the years when she was in the middle of a rollicking, vigorous family. It was like picking up cameos, still and perfect, studying them for a moment, then laying them gently back in cotton-lined boxes. These memories didn't ache. But, as the sunlight slipped farther down the street and the great lamps began to flicker on, she felt very alone.

How odd to be alone in London, remembering faces crumpled to dust. Only in her mind now, perhaps, did some of these faces have substance. Did anyone else ever think of Robert? He was the brother nearest her in age. He was bombardier on a plane shot down over Africa. Or dark, sardonic Jean, who loved boats and sailing and who had died in a submarine somewhere in the North Atlantic? Did someone else in some faraway city remember the way he had laughed, his face immobile for so long you would think the joke had passed him by and then, abruptly, he would throw back his head and laugh so hard that you had to join him? Did anyone ever think of Jean?

Robert. Jean. Louis.

She had never liked her brother Louis. He was the youngest of them all. Too young for World War II. Louis always managed to snag the cream of everything. He had been, she knew, startlingly handsome. Thick black hair and fine dark eyes, a high-bridged nose and full mouth. He had been quietly aware of his looks and always used them. But his handsome face and winning smile masked a heart as shriveled and empty as a cornhusk. Louis never cared for anyone but Louis.

He was killed in a company plane crash. An ice storm. A small plane that never should have left New Orleans to fly north into that kind of weather. Kay heard later, heard and, unhappily, believed, that it was Louis who had insisted on the flight, ordered out the pilot and his own young assistant because Louis was determined to reach Hot Springs that weekend.

A woman he wanted to see.

And whatever Louis wanted, he would have. Always.

The pilot left behind him four small children. Louis's assistant was a new father.

Oh Louis, what a burden to bear.

Louis himself had still been a bachelor. Why buy a cow, he had said . . .

Robert. Jean. Louis. Amalie.

The minutes trickled by and Kay stood at the window and the shadows began to slip across Bond Street, soft and gray as smoke.

At least someone would remember Amalie. Julie was ten when her mother died.

It had seemed terribly unfair to Kay that Amalie should have been stricken with cancer. Busy, happy Amalie, so eager to live, so brimful of plans, so confident that good things were going to happen today and tomorrow and always. When the end was near, it was almost more than Kay could bear, to visit her, to see her strong athletic sister shrunken into a pitiable heap of bones with eyes so sunken they seemed to lie in deep hollows.

Robert. Jean. Louis. Amalie. Kay.

Once, not so very long ago as men measure time, they had lived in a sprawling, three-story, white frame house and it had always been busy and noisy, the front closet filled with coats and skates and balls, hockey sticks, stilts, golf clubs, tennis rackets, riding boots.

And now, of all that ferment and life, only she and her sister's daughter Julie survived.

The survivors.

The afternoon was slipping into evening now, the street lamps alight, the car headlights bright and sharp.

Kay shivered. She had spent the afternoon with ghosts, seen faces long dissolved into dust. She felt ghostlike herself, a stranger in a strange city, drawn back into a past that no longer existed.

But it had once existed. It had once been as real, as actual as the wooden floor where she now stood, as the gray pavements she watched, as tangible as that black canopied entrance to Durand Galleries.

Real and a world and many lifetimes away from London, the London of 1940–41 or of 1966. She had not wanted this long afternoon to watch that gallery door and think of London, of the London she had known and the ghosts she could re-create here. It had been better by far to recall people and places that were part of her life—but not the core of her life.

The core of her life.

Kay drew a deep breath. She felt desperately unsettled, frighteningly closer in time to the Kay of twenty-five years ago than the Kay of today.

She should not have come here to watch and try to find the cause for those two disquieting, more than that, those two threatening incidents. She should, and suddenly she knew it, knew it in her bones, she should have gone to the airport, changed her ticket, left London, left England behind forever.

She should have let herself be driven away. Because some encounters permit no retreat, no withdrawal, only a final accounting.

She edged her tongue against dry lips and yet still she stood, staring down at that elegant entryway. Then she blinked, her tired eyes narrowed. The lights in the gallery had flickered off. Beyond the plate glass, she could dimly see the smudged shape of a man. He reached up and pulled down a shade.

Durand Galleries was closed.

She had, finally, to vacate her spot at the window because the small building was closing, too. She stood on the pavement opposite the gallery for a long moment before she turned and began to walk toward the Underground.

She had not recognized anyone who had come out of Durand Galleries that afternoon.

Was she wrong? Did the ugly, frightening incidents have nothing to do with her visit to the gallery, the one place she had contacted in London? Or was it only that she had not chanced to see a face she knew?

In a sense, she was coming home free tonight. She was not committed, yet, to any course of action. She could get up in the morning, call the airline, change her reservation, go home to New Orleans.

Marjorie would understand. In fact, Marjorie would never press her for any explanation.

Kay hurried down the steps into the Underground, merging into the thick throng of homeward-bound Londoners.

She stood in a clean, bright car, held to a strap and swayed to the rhythm of the train. The wheels rolled to a solid swinging beat and the question thudded in her mind, What was she going to do? what was she going to do? whatwasshegoingtodo? whatwasshegoing . . .

CHAPTER 6

The late Duchess of Arbyford, the Lady Sybil Willingham, had collected china, silver, paintings, Russian samovars, jewels and cats, crowding artworks and animals into a dingy, ill-lighted and poorly heated castle in a remote corner of England, not far from the Scottish border. Lady Sybil had died eight months earlier, leaving no issue, and decreeing in her will that her estate should be liquidated and the proceeds used, after death duties were satisfied, to endow a shelter for homeless animals.

The executors of the estate, a local veterinarian, the vicar and Lady Sybil's solicitor, had dickered with the leading London auction houses, and Durand's had won the lot, much to the surprise of Sotheby's and Christie's.

Kay was sitting almost in the center of the salesroom. The gilded chairs, arranged in semicircular rows, were nearly all taken, and it still lacked fifteen minutes before eleven when the auction would begin.

Kay held the catalog loosely in her lap. There were seventy-three lots scheduled and the sale would run at least today and Friday. Paintings were coming up first. This had tipped the scale. She had slept poorly, still debating whether to cut and run, change her ticket, fly home and skip the auction.

But nothing threatening happened during the night and, at breakfast, drinking the fairly decent coffee and reading the catalog once again, she had realized that the French miniatures would surely be up by early afternoon—and they would be a sure and profitable resale to Damon Fetherlee. She had, after all, come a long distance. She would do her job, then immediately fly home. Perhaps even leave tonight.

So she came to Durand Galleries and showed her lavender ticket at the door to the second-story salesroom, was checked off a list and shown to her seat.

She felt more comfortable with every moment that passed. It was all so familiar, so predictable, the air of tension and excitement, the rustle of catalogs, the uneasy scraping of chair legs, the careful eyes of the well-dressed men and women who studied each other without seeming to.

Was that the Greek shipping magnate, the one over there in the dark glasses? Surely that blonde was the comedienne with the lead in *Tonight Came Yesterday!* Was the rumor true, that an Arab sheik was determined to buy all the Chippendale? Was the Renoir a fake? Did the catalog hedge just a little on its pedigree?

Voices rose and fell, the words indistinguishable, a soft hum, muted but electric with anticipation. Do you suppose . . . I wonder if he . . . It can't be genuine though it's . . .

Kay smiled. This compact, special world was familiar and safe. She would bid, do her best, hope another collector of miniatures wasn't here, and then her job would be done and she could leave London behind. Forever. And not think of a past which was so much better left unrecalled.

As for the frightening things which had happened to her in London, there was no real reason to suppose they had any sort of focus at all. Perhaps she had been the mistaken recipient of the stolen necklace. And her collapse in the bar, perhaps she was the victim of a particularly virulent virus.

The telephone call?

Everything could be neatly disposed of, if she didn't think about the telephone call. But even it could be explained. A mistake on the part of the bellboy. Emory was not an unusual name.

So she sat at ease in the spindly chair. The air of excitement mounted as the great bank of lights along either side of the small stage flashed on. The lights were for the closed-circuit television cameras which would beam the sale down into other salesrooms to those not fortunate enough to possess lavender tickets and entree to the actual auction. The television viewers, however, could bid, and their bids would be called on microphones into the main salesroom. It was Kay's experience that every bid from a closed-circuit viewer pushed the bidding higher in the main salesroom, a boon to the auctioneer, a bane to buyers.

Five minutes before eleven now, and all the seats were filled and the two double doors at either end of the salesroom were closing and uniformed guards standing beside them. (Art thieves had yet to raid a gallery, preferring instead to steal into French villas and old churches at night, but Durand's intended to take no chances.)

Kay was rereading the catalog entries of the lots Marjorie had marked. There were only four, which didn't seem enough to justify the long trip to London, but any one of these, if bought at a decent price, could bring in a substantial return. London catalogs, of course, were always less explicit than their counterparts in New York. And they took a little careful reading to understand all the implications. If a painting were attributed to a painter by full name and date and suggested place of origin, a buyer could count on the fact that the house itself felt it had the genuine article. If, however, the painting were attributed to a painter but no date or place were given, the house felt a little less sure of authenticity. And, if the painting were listed only by the last name of the painter, the house was only suggesting that the work was of that school.

Caveat emptor.

The pedigree of the miniatures seemed perfectly sure, and

that enhanced their value considerably, of course. There were four of them, all done on enamel and attributed to Petitot. She studied the reproductions in the catalog, four small but perfectly detailed portraits. One fascinated her especially, Le Comte Philippe Augustin. His dark, bold eyes stared at her across the centuries, impatient, peremptory, but with a hint of laughter. He had not faced the artist squarely but was half turned, as if he were moving forward, in a hurry, going somewhere now. That, of course, was the fascination of miniatures. They were the photographs, the newspaper snapshots, of the seventeenth and eighteenth centuries. To hold one was to look back, across the span of years, and know that you saw a real face, that you looked at a man who had laughed at jokes, reached out for love, sworn in anger. For an instant, you could hear footsteps behind you.

Absorbed in the reproductions of the miniatures, Kay didn't look up when a door opened at the back of the room behind the dais. The man who came through the door caused another rustle and stir in the audience. He nodded gravely at several among the front rows and, once again, whispers and soft-voiced comments sounded like the flutter of pigeon wings. The woman sitting beside Kay tapped a man in the next row on the shoulder. "That's Durand," she whispered. "He always puts on a good show."

Kay heard that, realized the chief auctioneer must be at hand, but still she didn't lift her head. She was reading the description of the fourth miniature. ". . . believed to have been executed in 1674 when Le Comte's youngest son, Pierre, was seven. This miniature is considered one of Petitot's finest and is . . ."

It was the voice that Kay heard first.

The words were innocuous enough. She had heard them a hundred times.

A Settling of Accounts

"Lot one. And what am I bid, ladies and gentlemen, for this celebrated work by Hogarth? Five thousand pounds? Yes. Do I hear six thousand?"

It could not be . . .

She shook her head and, defensively, kept on staring at the catalog, though the words were suddenly meaningless, strange black marks that wavered in front of her eyes. But no matter that she did not look up, her ears still heard.

"Eight thousand pounds, yes. Do I hear another bid? Do I . . . Yes, ten thousand pounds. Ladies and gentlemen, this is an exceptional painting. One of Hogarth's finest to be offered in recent years. Do I hear . . . Fifteen thousand pounds. Eighteen thousand. Eighteen thousand. To the gentleman in the fourth row. And now ladies and . . ."

She lifted her head finally.

She had never imagined seeing him again. She had never in her bleakest nightmare envisioned coming face to face with Edmond. And there had been nightmares, where once again she was cradling that old broken form in her arms and praying that the labored breathing would stop and Grand'mère would die and be free of the pain. That nightmare, yes, and the hideous dream where once more she smelled the sweet fragrance of orange blossoms and watched blood well and spread, bright and red, staining the sharp white of the oyster-shell drive.

But in no nightmare had she dreamed that Edmond lived. After the war, she had written to the mayor, not telling the story, only asking if the friends she named had survived. The answer had been no. The doctor, the priest, the countess, all were dead. Like Lionel and Grand'mère. And she had, in that letter, asked if anything were known about the whereabouts of Edmond Lorillard. When she received the reply, that Edmond Lorillard was reported killed in the spring of 1942, she had considered the account closed.

For long years now, she had accepted the deaths of them all, known that only she survived . . . But Edmond had not died.

She looked across the rows in front of her, above the plumed hats, to the dais and the man standing behind the black lectern. He held an ivory gavel, poised to strike. He bent forward, waiting for another bid.

She never doubted that it was Edmond. Older, yes, but unmistakably Edmond. Black hair, thickly curled, fashionably long, lightly touched now with streaks of gray. That broad, curved forehead and slightly hooked nose and thin yet somehow sensuous mouth.

"Handsome as the devil, of course!" She could hear Lionel's lazy drawl, so lightly contemptuous. Lionel had never taken Edmond seriously.

Handsome as the devil. Evil. Evil with a handsome face, a warm voice, hands outstretched.

The gallery assistants were carrying the next painting out, placing it on the stand in front of the dais.

Edmond was speaking, the bidding beginning.

Kay stood. She pushed back the flimsy gilded chair. Edmond stopped for an instant. He looked down, his black eyes locked with hers. There was no surprise in them. None at all. He knew who she was. He had expected her. There was no surprise in those brilliant black eyes. And no fear.

He looked without surprise, without any expression at all, then, quickly, he continued his spiel, called for bids.

Everything made sense now, made the best of sense. Had it shocked him when she walked into his gallery on Tuesday? Had it opened a door long barred and shut? Had he looked for a moment into the face of retribution, thought it inescapable after years of comfort and success?

He knocked down the second lot, opened bidding on the third and, once again, those dark eyes touched hers. But he didn't pause now, he didn't falter in his rapid-fire patter. Because Edmond wasn't worried that she could harm him.

She stood and knew those around her were watching with short, curious sidelong glances. She almost raised her hand, her lips trembled.

She almost cried out their names, those long dead names that had not sounded on anyone's lips for so many years. She almost cried out, "Lionel. Grand'mère. Pere Lombard. Docteur Morisant. Countess Rakovsky."

Her lips parted. A hand touched her arm. She flinched and turned to look into the face of Mr. Henderson, and its soft fullness was flushed. "Miss Emory, please!" and the whisper was a hiss.

She jerked her arm away, looked once again at Edmond, saw those dark eyes, those dark, empty eyes, then she moved unsteadily, blindly, struggling toward the aisle. She stumbled over feet, murmuring, "Excuse me, please, excuse me. So sorry." She pushed past Mr. Henderson and fled up the aisle, not caring that faces turned to watch, not hearing the hush that fell. To escape—that was her instinct.

CHAPTER 7

Once outside the gallery, she dashed across Bond Street, ignoring a traffic policeman's whistle. She half ran, half walked, paying no attention to her direction. All she could think of was to get away, as far away as possible.

Edmond. Edmond alive.

And the anger grew, the terrible anger.

She ended up finally at Park Lane and looked across the broad thoroughfare at Hyde Park. The park—what safer place could she find?

Safer? Was that it? Did she fear Edmond? A bitter voice cried inside, she'd damn well better, hadn't she? Edmond had always done her injury.

She thought of that as she crossed into the park and turned up a graveled path, pale-brown stones neatly spread. She still walked but more slowly now, for her leg was beginning to ache. Mark that up to Edmond, too.

She stopped when she reached the Serpentine, that big odd-shaped lake in the heart of Hyde Park with room enough for boaters and bathers, for children to skip rocks and sail wooden chips, for swans and ducks.

No swimmers now, of course, with the late-October chill sharpening the gentle breeze off the water. A swan curved past and the sun touched his glistening white feathers with the sparkle of a diamond.

It was peaceful here. Not even faintly could she hear London's traffic. She might have been miles deep in a country estate, she and the shining green water and cool air. But there was no peace in her heart.

A Settling of Accounts

She dropped onto a stone bench and pulled her raincoat closer. The stone was cold to touch. She shivered and realized that she was very tired—and that her leg was dangerously close to giving out. She lit a cigarette, drew deeply on it, welcoming the acrid warmth of the smoke.

It had not, of course, been a mistake that the necklace was thrust into her pocket in the department store. And a strange virus had not sickened her. No, her drink had been drugged. How easily it had all been done—and how cleverly. But then, Edmond had always been clever—and feline, leaving no trace behind him.

Had he seen her come into the gallery on Tuesday? Or had young Mr. Henderson, as a matter of course, taken to his boss the request for new tickets and the passport with her face and name?

Had Edmond's hands trembled at all when he looked at that passport picture? Had he been frightened?

(Did he know true fear? The stomach-wrenching, slimy hollowness of fear? Damn him, he should!)

He must have looked down at her picture and known that he had only hours until she would see him and tell the world that he was Edmond Lorillard, not . . . What had the woman in front of her called him? Durand?

Kay reached into her raincoat pocket and drew out the crumpled, bent catalog. She opened it. Yes. Henri Durand, President and Chief Auctioneer, Durand Galleries.

You have to have capital to start a gallery. And she knew how Edmond had come by his.

All these years, safe, rich, respected, and then, abruptly, he looks down at a passport picture.

He had thought quickly, moved quickly. It must have been easy to follow her up Bond Street and into the department store. All the way, he must have been scheming, planning, hunting for an answer to his dilemma. And then she had made it so simple, standing there at the glove counter, lost to the present, fending off the past.

He had planted the necklace, alerted the floorwalker, then hurried out into the evening. He must have waited outside the department store and been chagrined when she came out, a free agent. He wasn't satisfied. He wanted Kay Emory utterly discredited.

She had returned to the hotel but he had not needed to follow her. He knew the address. She had given it to Charles Henderson at the gallery.

Had he come to the hotel, no definite plan in mind but ready to take any advantage?

If only she had gone directly to her room after dinner! If only she had not gone to the bar. The evidence of the bartender, the bellboy, the clerk, all of it would be damning. Who would believe she was anything but a drunk?

But if she had gone directly to her room . . . Kay shivered again. Edmond might have thought of something worse.

She had gone to the bar. It was easy for him to go into one of the rank of pay telephones, ring the next one, ask the answering clerk for Miss Emory, then to hang up his receiver. There were three huge potted palms that screened one corner of the lobby. He could have watched her progress from the bar to the booth, then moved quickly into the bar, stopped beside her table and looked about as if hunting someone, then dropped the drug into her drink, turned away and hurried out into the night.

Clever Edmond. Clever, heartless, cruel Edmond.

Edmond. She saw his face once again, that older, harder, sharper face, and it merged into the face she remembered so well. Handsome as the devil. Yes, he had been, yes.

And she was swept abruptly by unbearable anguish. It was

anguish she had felt before and suffered through and survived, but seeing him again, the shock of that encounter, swept the years away and it was as if no time had passed, as if Lionel were just now dead and she was young Kay Emory, far from home, desperately frightened, injured and wild with grief.

She never knew how long it was that she huddled on that bench by the Serpentine, what measure of time passed before the trembling stopped and her eyes once again focused on the clear, cold, green beauty of the water. Not long, as men count time. Perhaps an hour. But time enough for old wounds to open and throb. Time enough for an implacable decision to be made.

Edmond would pay. He would not, this time, be clever enough.

The violet eyes that stared at the water were steady and merciless and very thoughtful.

If she went to the police, if right this minute she went to Scotland Yard and said she knew of a man who was an impostor, who lived under an assumed name—and who was a murderer, she would excite interest.

Murder was murder, whether it happened last night or twenty-five years ago.

She could tell the police that Henri Durand was Edmond Lorillard and that he was a murderer.

They would ask where the murder happened, and when, and who was the victim.

Victims, she would answer.

She could tell them all of it, but when they started to investigate, it would all come out, the necklace in her pocket at the department store, the drunken collapse in the hotel bar—and no one would believe anything she said.

A troublemaker, they would say. Or they might be kinder.

A middle-aged spinster. Deluded. Confused. An alcoholic, haunted by imaginings.

Given time, given an even mildly sympathetic listener, she could perhaps persuade that she was not an alcoholic. (But wouldn't the natural suspicion remain that she was a secret drinker, this once found out? Her friends in New Orleans would confirm that she never drank too much. But would that prove anything?)

But by the time she could marshal that kind of support, no one would be willing to listen at all. The police would have long since dismissed her story as fanciful, hysterical.

Clever Edmond.

She pushed up from the marble bench and walked stiffly to the path.

More serious yet, even if the police did not reject her outright, even if she could come to them as an unimpeachable witness, she had no proof. None at all. Only her word, her eyes, to testify. And that against a respected businessman, owner of a thriving London gallery.

No proof at all. No proof here. Or in France. Those who had known, who could stand and point an accusing finger, were long since bone and dust. And there would be no record left from Vichy France.

Only she and Edmond knew.

She walked more swiftly, ignoring the ache in her leg. She had never even told her family the truth of it. She had been ill so long and she so obviously had not wished to talk about what had happened to her. They had been kind and gentle and they had not asked.

"Surely, Miss Emory, you must have told someone at some point in your life?" a policeman would ask.

She would, helplessly, shake her head. She had never told anyone because it was too painful to talk about. It had not been, for her, "war experience," the kind of snapshot memory to be pushed on family and acquaintances. She had, instead, painfully, slowly, with a great deal of agony, managed to forget. No. No. That wasn't true, either. Nothing was forgotten. But all of it was put away, shut deep within her, a part of herself never to be shared. Because she wasn't, after 1941, a sharing person. That, too, was lost.

Edmond had destroyed much, including Kay's youth. She had been, the fall of 1940, so young, so in love, so open to life. So sure, really, that everything would come right. The world was exploding around her, but she had never doubted that she and Lionel would be all right.

"Papers, Miss Emory? A diary, perhaps?"

Those who have lost confidence in life do not keep diaries.

No, she would go empty-handed to the police. There was not one shred of evidence to support her charge. Nothing at home. Nothing in France. Nothing, of course, here in London because . . .

Sir Derek Houghton? He had remembered how well she spoke French. It was he who had called her, set up the interview.

Kay walked slowly onto a bridge and stopped at its center to look out across the lake. Slowly she shook her head. Sir Derek must have been almost seventy then. Impossible to imagine him still alive. Had Sir Derek kept a file? Surely he had. But that file would long ago have been marked closed. Perhaps even destroyed.

No, there was no one in all of England.

Angus Moray. His face came clear in her mind, was so vivid he might have stood next to her. Huge, capable Angus Moray, Captain, Territorial Guards, detached, to SOE. Angus had trained them, that hurried preparation, trying to prepare for all kinds of eventualities, what script was in use, the curfew, which roads were prohibited to all but the military, thousands of facts they had tried to learn so quickly. And, in the end, none of them had mattered. It wasn't a little fact that tripped them up. They made no mistakes except the gravest possible. They had not judged friend from enemy.

But Angus, good-humored, patient Angus, if he had survived the war, would not be an old man. In his mid-fifties, perhaps.

She hurried off the bridge, struck off down the nearest path and didn't slow until she was out of the park. She found a call box and quickly, quickly riffled through the pages of the directory.

Michaelson. Minton. Moran. Moray. Alan. Albert. Andrew. Angus.

Her breath caught at the address. Was it the same? She thought so, but she wasn't sure. God, was it possible after all these years!

CHAPTER 8

It was the rush-hour Underground. Kay waited on the packed platform, inched her way forward, was lucky and slipped into a car. She clung to a strap. She welcomed the crush. It was, somehow, comforting to be so close to others, to feel their warmth, the edge of an elbow in her back, the pressure of a briefcase against her leg. All of it, at the same time, quite impersonal, undemanding. It was two stations to Piccadilly Circus and she was sorry to leave the refuge of the car, to begin the slow struggle up, climbing steps, moving on a wooden escalator, finally pushing into a rickety lift to spill out into the bright cold night and the noise of Piccadilly Circus.

Neon lights flickered red as a matador's cape. Lights swirled and curved as cars swept around Eros's base. The last time she had stood here, not a light had shone, not the faintest glimmer. Lionel had a weekend pass in July. They had gone to a play and come out to a London shrouded in the blackout and made their hesitant way to the Underground, narrowly missing being run over by a lightless bus. It had almost seemed a game, hand in hand with Lionel, laughing when they bumped into a tree or post.

Abruptly, Kay turned toward the welcoming lights spilling out of the Lyons Corner House and hurried inside to warmth and the smell of frying foods and sound of clattering dishes. She hesitated, the restaurant here was full and a line waiting. She turned and walked up the stairs to a more expensive restaurant and many empty tables.

She ordered sole and a half bottle of sauterne, then leaned thankfully back against the hard banquette seat. It was dim and uncrowded. She would not need to hurry her dinner. Or her thinking. And she needed both food and careful thought. It was important, her pulse quickened, it was very important that she proceed correctly.

Because Edmond was clever and dangerous.

Right now she should be safe enough. He must feel confident that she had run away, perhaps even started home to America. He must, right now, be pleased with the success of his stage management and, surely, a little disdainful of that fleeing figure, stumbling so clumsily to the aisle. She reached into her purse, pulled out her cigarette case and the folded gallery catalog with Angus Moray's address and telephone number scrawled on its cover.

She ate her dinner and slowly drank the light golden wine and, for the first time in twenty-five years, consciously, deliberately, grimly recalled memories she had always before fought to suppress.

Memories are willful, not subject to push-button recall. You remember in still photographs, not motion pictures, and looking back is like turning the black pages of a scrapbook and catching glimpses of yourself in sharp bright colors, your face unguarded, unaware of what will come. Defenseless.

So many things blurred in her mind. She couldn't pluck the words said on a certain evening, or even, odd to realize, remember sometimes what day of the week something happened. Instead, there were these moments out of time, memory's snapshots.

She did remember the day of the telephone call that started it all. For that was an unforgettable day, surely, to all Londoners. Saturday, September 7, 1940. The day that Hitler ordered London bombed. It was what everyone had feared, even before the war started. All the long months they had waited in dread and the bombs came.

A Settling of Accounts

Kay sipped her sauterne. She didn't now remember what they had done early that Saturday, where they had gone. She didn't remember hearing the sirens. Their first warning, hers and Betty's, had been the uneven, heavy throb of the bombers, the sound that would become familiar to southern England. She didn't remember either how they had reached their duty stations, both were ARP volunteers. The raid began about five in the afternoon, and the soft-blue cloudless sky was soon crisscrossed by vapor trails. The target was the dock area, of course. The fires began on the docks long before sunset. The call for an ambulance was relayed to their sector and Kay set out with her driver, clanging toward the East End. She leaned out the window to watch, and she was afraid that all of London would soon be afire. The eastern third of the horizon was an angry orange with spirals and columns of black and oily-brown smoke twisting, curling, swirling, rising to join into a billowy, moving curtain of flame-shot smoke.

"We can't go there," she thought, then realized she had said the words aloud. How could any living thing survive in that maelstrom of fire? But they did go. They careened around bomb craters, humped over sidewalks to pass broken, burning gas mains, backed and turned and crept, thumping over fire hoses, trying one way, then another, and somehow they did reach the East End. The nearer they came, the more little groups of bombed-out people that passed them. The people clutched sacks, pushed baby carriages piled high with what they had salvaged. Dazed and dirty, they all were filthy from the smoke and the bomb-thrown dirt.

Kay was sure she would never have had the courage to drive that ambulance on and on into the moving sea of fire, but nothing daunted her driver. Once, flames danced a hundred feet high on both sides of the street and there was an unceasing roar as the fire fed on itself, but the ambulance chugged on, and then the docks were just to their left.

They found the Anderson shelter where the injured had been taken. They piled in a mother and three little girls, one unconscious, and turned to seek their way out again.

The fires were so huge, so ferocious that the heat scorched the side of the ambulance, but they rode on until they were free of the fires and delivered those wounded to a hospital.

They made three such trips that night, and it was such an unreal world that she was scarcely afraid. You just couldn't believe in flames that high, in blocks and blocks of buildings ablaze, a world where night was lit like a day in hell, a reddish wavering light.

Every so often throughout the long night, fire engines in the unfamiliar colors of other cities would pass, hurrying to help. London was fighting for her life.

Above the crackle and roar of the flames came the endless crump of exploding bombs. She didn't even realize, close to dawn, when the raid ended. She was far too tired to care. She started home, it was midmorning on Sunday, and could scarcely believe that most of London, almost all that she saw of it, looked just as it had yesterday once she was away from the docks.

The coiling smoke, the firemen still fighting those immense block-long blazes, all of that was behind them as the ambulance began its homeward run. She saw clear skies, untouched blocks, and the despair that had touched her during the night began to fade.

Bad as the night had been, London still lived.

Once back to the small immaculate house in Chelsea, she took only time enough to be sure that Betty, too, was safely home, then, shaking her head to breakfast, Kay started up the stairs. All she wanted in the world was a bath and sleep.

Lionel's mother called after her.

A Settling of Accounts

"Kay, there was a telephone call for you last night."

Another sharp picture, now, of herself standing on the landing and the sunlight sparkling through a stained-glass window, of herself turning a little to look dully down at Lionel's mother.

A telephone call. What could it possibly matter? But Kay was too polite to say so. Somehow she found the strength to stand there one more minute and to nod and say thank you before turning to stumble on up the stairs that seemed to grow steeper with each step. She plodded to the bathroom and stripped off her dress and knew she could never wear it again. It was filthy! Stiff with dirt and sweat and smoke. She almost fell asleep in the bath, and she never gave another thought to Mrs. Neal's message. After all, what could it possibly matter?

That night the bombers came again and once more the East End was ablaze, and now those bombed out Saturday were bombed out from new hiding holes. Kay and Betty once again worked the night through and came back to Chelsea in the early morning, gray-faced, filthy, exhausted. They hadn't wanted to go home but Mr. MacDougal, their warden, insisted. "And don't come back until tonight." He'd paused at that and smiled grimly. "I'm only thinking they'll be back and I'll need the two of you then."

Kay and Betty had scarcely reached the house and bathed and gone to bed when the sirens blew again. The heavy, hesitating rumble of the bombers sounded. A daylight raid.

Kay was too tired to care. She only burrowed deeper in her bed. But Mrs. Neal tugged at her covers and called to her. "Please, my dear. Bring a comfort and come down to the cellar."

The girls straggled downstairs and joined the rest of the household. Kay couldn't get back to sleep. She sat in the shadows between the wooden steps and the furnace and leaned back against the wall.

Lionel's mother talked that morning in her gentle voice with its soft Scottish burr. She talked to her daughters, Betty and Alice, and to their guest, Kay, and to the cook and the two maids, Annie, young and away from home for the first time, and Bridget, plump and cheerful and an unashamed forty-five.

Words hung in the dim air. Desultory conversation, all to pass as pleasantly as possible an interrupted morning. She hoped that Betty's Frank would get leave and be able to visit before he was transferred out of London. She encouraged Alice to sign up for another class in still lifes (they would manage the transport somehow). She complimented Mrs. Prentiss upon last night's lemon trifle (such a delicate lemony flavor). She smiled as Annie proudly responded that it was she who had stood in line at the greengrocer's (oh, it was all of two hours, ma'am) to get the lemon that Mrs. Prentiss had used. She gently patted Bridget's hand when the maid's cheerful voice quivered and fell away as a bomb fell near enough that the house seemed to shake itself like a dog flicking off water. "Oh, ma'am," Bridget cried, "my Alfred's pump company is to Bermondsey!" and both maid and mistress listened to the roar of the planes, and Kay knew they must be picturing their targets.

At least, Kay thought, head raised, listening to the continual, dreadful, numbing roar, at least if they are bombing London, perhaps they aren't attacking the sector stations now. Please God, keep Lionel safe!

She was ashamed of that small private plea, but at the same time she couldn't squash the hope that Lionel might not, at least at this moment, be in it. She had been glad, though she had hidden it well, when his hand was hurt, for it meant he couldn't fly. And she knew, as all England knew, that the RAF losses mounted day by bloody day as young fliers scrambled out of their huts and raced across shell-pocked fields to rev their motors and lift their planes up to meet the Germans, always locking with the fighters, trying to pare away the German supremacy, hanging on day by day, hour by hour.

Kay listened to the bombs and wondered what Lionel was doing now, this moment. He had insisted, his shattered hand tightly bandaged, on rejoining his squadron even though he couldn't fly.

"Why did it have to be my bloody right hand?"

Oh Lionel, how lucky you were! The machine-gun bullets had shattered the Plexiglas of his cockpit, so near his face. Yet only one bullet had hit him, and that one in the back of his hand, just behind the middle knuckle. Painful, disabling, it had knocked the stick out of commission, so he had bailed out and drifted down in the Channel to be picked up in only a few minutes by a sailboat. On shore, he was taken to the hospital where they operated, but he stayed only two days, then insisted on getting back to Kenley Field.

"You can't fly," they told him.

He'd shrugged. "I'll help out in Ops. Do something." And, at the back of his mind, he weighed his options, copilot, navigator, if his hand didn't come right.

Lionel, are you all right? Are you all right . . .

Another bomb exploded nearby. Once again the house trembled. They all looked up, scarcely daring to breathe, and it was very quiet in the cellar. The single bulb gave a little spurt, then faded away, and now the only light came from two narrow, shallow windows high in the cellar wall. A match scraped, a candlewick caught and the pinpoint flame of light danced in the drafty air, throwing sharp-angled shadows against the brick wall.

Mrs. Neal put the candleholder in the center of the floor. "I must remember to set by a store of candles . . ." She paused and, for the first time, her gentle voice was thin and strained. "Bombed by candlelight." She clasped her hands together and turned to Kay. "Oh my dear, we have kept you with us too long, been too selfish. We should have sent you home to America at once when you and Betty came from France!"

Kay reached out, took those soft, plump hands in her own. "Oh no, please no. Don't send me away. I can't leave . . ."

Her own voice failed, for there was nothing so definite as an engagement between her and Lionel. It was all a beginning, tentative, electric, tantalizing, and yet more certain than anything had ever been in her life. But she would not announce that she had stayed in England because of him. She had pleaded concern over her grandmother, still, of course, in Nice. And insisted, moreover, that she was determined to stay in London and help in war work, and she and Betty together had joined the ARP.

But in her heart she knew, and when Lionel's mother squeezed her hands in return she realized with a start that Mrs. Neal knew, too.

It was then, before Kay could say more, that she heard, so faintly, the peal of the telephone.

She lifted her head, listened hard, trying to hear above that hated, heavy, hesitating rumble of the bombers, and she was sure that she heard it again.

The telephone. She dropped Mrs. Neal's hands.

Perhaps it was because her every thought was of Lionel that she was so sure it was news of him.

Something had happened to Lionel!

She was sure of it, hideously sure, and the thought spun her around and to the stairs.

"I hear the telephone," she cried breathlessly, already starting up the steep wooden steps. "I'll go. It might be important."

They called after her, but she didn't stop. Once upstairs, the cellar door closed behind her, she hesitated an instant, for there was a dry dusty smell and she saw with a sick shock that a blast had blown in the lovely fanlight above the door and there was dirt everywhere in the hall.

Then the telephone shrilled again, loud now, demanding.

She turned toward the back of the house, hurrying to the little alcove beneath the stairs where the telephone had been added years earlier.

"Hello."

A voice began to speak, but the connection was so scratchy that it was almost blotted out. Then bombs fell so near that the whole house swayed. Dishes crashed down in the kitchen just beyond and she couldn't hear anything on the line.

Was the connection broken?

"Hello! Hello! Are you there?"

"May I speak to Miss Kay Emory? Do I have the Neal residence? I should like . . ."

The voice was faint but clear now. Kay pressed the receiver so hard against her ear that it ached.

A call for her! Something must have happened to Lionel!

"This is Miss Emory. Who is calling?"

"Miss Emory? Miss Kay Emory?"

She wanted to scream at the far-off disembodied voice. For God's sake, what had happened? Please, what had happened! Her hand tightened on the receiver. "Yes, yes, this is Kay Emory."

"Miss Emory, this is Derek Houghton. I don't know if you will remember the occasion of our meeting. It was, if you recall, a cocktail party at . . ."

"Lionel," she interrupted sharply, "are you calling about Lionel?"

There was an instant's pause, then the cultivated voice replied, "No, not at all. I haven't seen Lionel recently. I hope everything is going well for him."

"Yes," Kay said quietly, and the relief washed over her and left her so weak that she didn't listen as he spoke again. Yes, of course, she remembered Sir Derek and how long she had talked to him and how it had irritated Lionel and how, just before they reached home, she had slipped her hand in Lionel's and said obliquely, "I'm sorry we went to that party." Lionel didn't answer, then she added, "I would much rather have been alone with you."

He had looked down at her then, his dark-blue eyes still distant, then his broad mouth softened. "I think you're what's called an artful baggage. And don't worry, we damn well won't go to any more useless parties." The laughter left his voice. "My God, Kay, we don't have time to waste."

And here was Sir Derek calling her, talking as politely as at a garden party, his modulated voice rising and falling, and now stopping.

She realized abruptly that he was waiting for her response and she had heard scarcely a word that he'd said.

"I'm sorry, Sir Derek, I couldn't hear you. There's so much noise here. The bombers."

"Yes, indeed. The end of this raid's not in sight yet. Sorry to have called you at such a noisy moment. I tried to get you Saturday but you were out. The thing about it, though, is that there really isn't a moment to spare—if, of course, you would consider helping."

"Helping?"

"And the devil of it is, I can't explain it over the telephone. If you would be free on Wednesday morning, a coworker of mine would like to interview you—about some war work. Of course, I know you are a Yank and so I don't have any right to ask you to pitch in. But I thought, with your French background, that you might be willing to take part."

Sir Derek Houghton. What was it someone at the party had whispered? Hush-hush, that's what they'd said and nodded at Sir Derek.

So Kay had an inkling, but she didn't hesitate.

"If you can use me," she said quictly, "I will help."

CHAPTER 9

"Bonjour, mademoiselle, comment allez-vous?"

"Bien, merci. Et vous?"

"Bien. Entrez-vous, s'il vous plait."

She hesitated for an instant, looking up again to check the flat number, because she had never seen the narrow-faced man who had opened the door. Sir Derek had not, of course, said that he would be here, but somehow she had expected to see him. And it was ten o'clock on Wednesday morning, as he had specified . . .

"C'est bon, mademoiselle," and the sharp-featured man nodded and told her reassuringly that she was at the proper place.

Kay stepped inside. It was a small apartment and it did not look lived in, although it had an air of occupancy. Cigarette smoke hung in a faint bluish cloud. A man's hat was hung on a chair by the door. A desk sat near one window. The man walked to it and Kay, a little uncertainly, settled in the easy chair in front of it. Light spilled through uncurtained windows and dust motes danced in the air as he rustled papers on his desk.

"Maintenant, mademoiselle, vous avez des parents en France, oui?"

That was the beginning, his query as to what relatives she had in France. They talked for almost two hours, all in French. He asked question after question, patiently, quietly, persistently.

He was especially interested in how much time she had spent in France and she told him, two summers with her grandmother in Nice, 1938 and 1939, and then the winters of 1938–39 and 1939–40 in Paris completing her secondary schooling. She had lived with the Deschamps, friends of her grandmother. It was then that she had met Betty Neal, an English girl attending the same school.

He had fastened on that quickly. Did Betty speak French as well as Kay?

Slowly, Kay had shaken her head. Betty's French was passable but she spoke it with such a decided English accent. No one would ever think she could be a French girl.

"Unlike you," the thin-faced man murmured. Kay felt a quick flicker of pride.

It was then that he asked if she knew anyone else who spoke French well.

The implication was clear enough certainly, anyone who could speak it well enough to go to France and pretend to be French.

"Oh yes," Kay said quickly. "Lionel."

The man looked at her questioningly and she added quickly, "Lionel Neal, Betty's brother."

She told how she had met Lionel when he came to Paris to do graduate work at the Sorbonne, having completed his studies at Oxford in French literature. She told so many things, how well Lionel spoke French, that, if it weren't for the war, he would be a language master, how Lionel had left immediately for England when war was declared in September of 1939 to join the RAF. (He had learned to fly on weekends while at Oxford.)

"Oh, RAF." He laid down his pen as if that precluded any further interest in Lionel.

Kay grieved for years that she spoke up, quickly, eagerly. If she hadn't told the man, if . . .

"But he's grounded now. A hand wound. And they don't

think he'll be able to fly again."

The man's eyes, tired gray eyes, flickered with interest and he picked up his pen and began to write again.

Finally, the questions were over. He ignored her for a long five minutes as he read over his notes, reviewed what he had written. When he finally looked up, he studied her face for another long while and then, only then, did he speak to her in English.

"You have been very patient, very cooperative, Miss Emory. I appreciate that." He lit another cigarette, watched her closely. "You realize, of course, the point of these questions?"

She had nodded.

"Do you realize also that, should you decide to help us, your chances of returning to England are no better than even?"

He would not take an answer, that morning. Instead, he gave her a telephone number. She was to call it only if "you choose to throw your lot in with us."

Once away from the dingy little apartment, walking briskly toward Bayswater Road, it all bordered on the fantastic, that she, Kay Emory, had been invited in ever such an obscure fashion to become a secret agent.

But there had been nothing obscure about the warnings he gave her. Odds no better than even. Likely to die, die horribly.

And she could not tell anyone about this invitation. "Quite secret, you know." She must decide alone, unaided.

She could not even tell Lionel.

"If you should choose to ring us up, Miss Emory, then we'll help you make your arrangements, inform your acquaintances that you have decided to return home to America. If you like, we could have a message come, an emergency requiring you to return."

She was near the Queensway station when the siren sounded. Another raid. She hurried down into the Underground, caught her train. All the way, she heard the man's thin, precise voice, what he had said, in French and in English.

She clung to a strap in the crowded car and scarcely noticed the stations they passed, was oblivious to the crowds, greater on the platforms than in the cars, Londoners dodging bombs.

A decision only she could make.

The hardest part would be to leave Lionel.

But women all over the world were saying good-bye to the men they loved.

What would he think of her? He couldn't help but be disappointed in her, if he thought she was running home to America to be safe. Even though he and all his family had urged her to go home.

Then the man's words sounded again in her mind. "So few English can speak French without immediately being spotted as foreigners."

She spoke such easy, fluent, unaccented French. They needed her.

She was tired when she reached her station. She walked slowly up and out of the Underground. She scarcely even noticed that the raid was over. She was oblivious to her surroundings as she walked the eight blocks to the Neal house.

It was that afternoon, even before she reached the house, that she began to lose her youth. For she was saying good-bye to Lionel in her heart with every step she took.

This was Wednesday. Would she have at least a week? Surely they would give her that much time, to pack, to say good-bye.

She was turning the corner when she smelled smoke. She looked up and saw the fire truck and the hose snaking from a hydrant and then, beyond it, thin gray wisps of smoke curling from the wet and smoldering blackened humps of debris that had been the Neal house.

"Oh no, no, no . . ." and she began to run.

It was she, of course, who had to call Kenley Field, get word to Lionel. She talked to his squadron commander.

"They were in the cellar, all of them, Rescue thinks. No. No one survived."

Unthinkable words. Unbearable imaginings. She woke, that first night, screaming, trying to reach Betty, but bright yellow-orange flames swirled around her and Betty crumpled, her hair aflame, her clothes . . .

At the funeral, she sat beside Lionel and a plump aunt from Bournemouth, Mrs. Neal's sister. Lionel's father was at sea. She listened to the short and lovely old service and tried desperately not to imagine the contents of the three plain coffins.

Everything happened so quickly after that. She said good-bye to a rigid-faced Lionel when all she wanted to do was hold him in her arms and try to ease his sorrow. Instead, they spoke quick sentences and there were odd, uncomfortable pauses. Once they both started to speak together, then each abruptly fell silent. It was all wrong. It was almost time for him to go when she said baldly, "I must go home, Lionel. To America."

His head jerked up. He started to speak, then he shook his head a little. "Yes," he said quietly, "you should go home."

If only he would ask her to stay! If he only would. But he didn't.

He didn't even kiss her good-bye, there in the drawing room of the family friends who had taken Kay in. Instead, he lightly touched her arm. "I'll try to come up and see you off. Let me know."

And he was gone.

She walked out after that to a nearby call box and rang up the number she had been given.

All she felt that night was a great emptiness. No tears. Not even any fear.

Her departure for "America" was set for Friday. Somehow Lionel wangled leave and he saw her off at Paddington. (Victoria was still closed from that massive Wednesday raid.)

Their conversation was disjointed, meaningless. "Do you have your tickets?" "Yes." "You'll write." "Yes. You will, too?"

The train was called.

She half turned, then swung back. "Oh Lionel."

He took her in his arms then and held her so tightly that a gilt button on his jacket gouged at her cheek.

"When the war is over . . ."

She lifted her face to his. "I'll come back to you, Lionel."

She didn't cry until he was gone. Then, clutching her handbag, and the small case that held the few things she had bought for her "journey," she hurried through the station to catch a taxi and the tears ran silently down her face.

She had a different address this time. A house in Mayfair. She must have known, when she paid off the taxi and moved to the bottom of the steps, that she was leaving behind life as she had known it.

Yes, young as she was, she knew that. But she had no idea, no inkling at all, that she would mount those steps and make her first encounter with the duplicity which was to become a way of life.

CHAPTER 10

"Madam, would you care for dessert? An ice, perhaps?"

Kay came back a long way to look slowly up at the waiter. He bent near her table in the proper deferential manner. She looked at him curiously, his raven-black hair and sallow skin. He was so patently Italian and she wondered what trick of fate had fetched him up in London's West End to spend his days serving strangers, asking carefully prescribed questions in a ritual as formalized as a dance. "Vichyssoise or soup du jour, madam?" "Wine with your dinner, sir?" "Cheese or fruit, madam?"

He had a mole on his right cheek. One shoulder looked a little lower than the other. An injury? Or an awkward way of standing? He waited patiently, his dark eyes unreadable. Was he bored? Happy? Eager to finish his shift? Did a willing wife await him or an empty cheap apartment?

"Dessert, madam?"

She nodded. When he turned and walked away, she could see that one shoulder was indeed lower. She had not, she realized with an odd shifting sense of excitement, been so aware of anyone or anything about her in years.

It hurt, yes, to remember so vividly, almost to feel again all her yesterdays, but, at the same time, there was an eagerness, an awareness that had been lacking all those long numb years. And perhaps it is better to hurt than not to feel at all.

Alive now, she could remember how alive she had been that sunny Friday afternoon in 1940 when she rang the bell at the narrow brick house in Mayfair. Excited, yes. Uncertain but determined. Drawing in a quick shallow breath as the door began to open.

A manservant welcomed her.

"Miss Emory? Yes, this way please," and he ushered her down a dim hall and into a room on the right, a comfortable man's room with a sturdy desk and heavy brown curtains and books in shelves along three walls.

And the first person she saw was Lionel.

She must have stumbled a little in her shock, raised a hand in surprise. Her stunned disbelief was mirrored in Lionel's broad open face.

"Kay!"

"Lionel!"

"You'll do well, the two of you. You've passed your first test with flying colors."

They both looked round and that was the first time Kay saw Angus Moray. He sat in a huge leather chair but still he filled it. He was watching them kindly enough but those pale-green eyes were sharp, too, and measuring. Kay was to know that look well in the next nine weeks.

Nine weeks.

Nine happy weeks.

Odd to remember them like that, those long tough days, learning how to kill and bomb, run and hide, anything and everything that might give them one more day's safety in the shadow of the Gestapo.

They were happy days because Lionel was near. She knew, deep inside, that it was the glimpse of his wheat-colored hair in the moonlight on a night march, his quick comforting touch on her elbow when they paused midway across a field with the angry chatter of machine-gun bullets above them, that gave her the courage and the strength to last it out, to do anything they asked and do it well enough.

The nearness of Lionel and, as well, the comforting, rock-solid dependable presence of Angus Moray.

Angus was their conducting officer. It was his job to shepherd new recruits through their hasty training, then see them off to France.

Seven started out together at Wanborough Manor in the gently rolling country not far from Guildford. The elegant mansion was an odd backdrop for the trainees and their instructors, three sergeant majors. But anything seemed possible, the fall of 1940, and no one thought much about the strange juxtaposition of elegance and violence.

Each morning began with a two-mile cross-country run. Then the morning was shared over in map reading, with especial emphasis on topography. They learned to shoot Sten guns and Thompson submachine guns.

And always, right behind them, guiding, encouraging, supporting, was Angus.

At the end of three weeks, they were told without comment that they would have a week's leave in London and were given the address of a "safe" hotel where rooms were booked for them under new names. They weren't, of course, to reveal anything of what they had been doing to anyone.

It was a week apart. Kay and Lionel didn't talk about the war or about France or about the Blitz. There was, every night, the familiar squall of the sirens. Bombs fell. People lived or died, buildings flamed. But they moved that week to their own song and the world didn't intrude. It wasn't even necessary, would somehow have diminished their happiness, if they had tried to put it into words. But they knew, both of them, that when the War was over . . .

Of the seven who started out together at Wanborough, five met again at the isolated country home on Scotland's bleak western coast. No one mentioned the two who did not come, an older Frenchman who had a slight but persistent cough and a bouncy blond former schoolteacher who had shown too distinct an interest in one of the sergeant majors.

The five weeks in Scotland made Wanborough seem like scout camp. So much to learn and so little time. Each night when she tumbled exhausted into the narrow camp bed, Kay was grateful for the thick sweeping oblivion of heavy dreamless sleep. She didn't want to think. To think was to imagine —and there were too many frightful possibilities.

They learned elementary Morse, how to set up explosives, the best way to demolish a train engine, how to sabotage the lines. They learned how to hide plastic explosives, soft, buttery-yellow and doughy. The best PE had no smell at all. Often enough, they didn't have the best, but PE with a rank almondy odor that caused a headache if worked within an enclosed space. It wasn't frightening to work with, however, unlike black powder, because PE could be thrown, set on fire or dropped and still it would lay in a bland harmless lump. It took a sharp explosive charge to set it off.

Angus was pleased the wet and rainy afternoon that Kay set out with three lumps of PE and managed to place them so carefully that a "work" party never found them and they went off in fine order, crumpling a trestle like wind-thrown matches. Good marks.

And, of course, they learned how to kill in silence.

To creep through the thick grass around the side of a gentle hill, to slip from a thorny bush along a gray stone wall to a clump of trees, thin wire loop in hand until she was hard upon the sentry post. To wait until the soldier moved away, his back to her, then to jump up and run quietly and drop the thin wire loop over his head—if he'd worn German gray, he'd have been a dead man.

No, she didn't want to think too hard.

Five weeks in Scotland. By their end, she, her four companions and Angus knew one another full well.

Kay knew many things about all of them, knew that the French girl Lisette was utterly nerveless, that good-humored Peter pulled on his right ear lobe when he was uncertain, that Jacques smiled when he threw a grenade, that Lionel wore a particularly stolid and pedestrian expression when daring the most dangerous feats, and that Angus loved them all and drove himself the hardest, trying his best to equip them for their tasks.

Another leave then. The second week in December and they were once again in London, a London with boarded-over windows, white-painted curbs and trees, blackened ruins, bare-shelved stores, and weary-faced men and women hurrying down gray streets. Christmas not far away and all the news was grim. She didn't remember that week clearly. She thought perhaps it rained most of it. The only sharp, clear picture she had was of Lionel standing with his back to her, looking out a window.

Then another country manor, this one near Beaulieu in the southern New Forest. And, once again, Angus Moray led and bullied and praised them.

"Marie, how much do you tell a subagent?"

Kay's name was now Marie Deschamps—and she must never forget it. She knew the answers and she understood full well the cost of just one mistake.

"There is no second chance in the field."

Angus told them that, over and over and over again. He told them just what they could expect if the Gestapo got them.

You were to cling to your cover story, Kay knew, tell it over and over, never admit anything. Never.

But, if you had to talk, if you couldn't bear more pain, at least hang on for as long as possible. One day or two could save your friends. If they knew you had been picked up, they would immediately leave their present address, move to a new house, cut all ties with the circuit, contact London, and perhaps even take an escape line out of France.

You were supposed to hang on as long as you could.

There was no sound at all in the chilly room the morning Angus told them all of this. Not the faintest whisper of sound. They sat, the five of them and Angus, in the morning room. She and Lionel were together on a hardwood settee. Peter leaned against the rough stone of the fireplace. Lisette sat, hands clasping her crossed knees, and watched, her face unmoved. Jacques smiled.

"*Je suis Marie Deschamps. Je suis Marie Deschamps. Je suis*" . . . Kay broke off, shocked that she had spoken aloud, then shocked the more that no one took any notice at all, except Angus. Each of the others sat immobile, and Kay wondered sharply what faraway and frightening thoughts possessed them.

Angus looked at her and she saw both sorrow and pride in his pale-green eyes. "You'll do fine . . . Marie."

Had he been fey, had Scottish second sight?

She remembered that moment so clearly. A pale shaft of January sun slanted through a window to touch his ginger-colored hair. His reddish eyebrows bunched in a frown but his look was as warming as a kiss.

That moment and one other. When they said good-bye. He spoke briefly to each of them, handing them up into the back of an enclosed lorry. As he took her elbow, he bent to her face. "God bless you, my dear," and brushed her cheek with his lips.

Even now, twenty-five years later, she remembered the bristly sweep of his mustache against her cheek.

Angus would remember her.

Once again she looked at the address she had scrawled on the auction catalog. She pushed back her dessert, left it untouched.

It was a short taxi drive to the number in Mayfair. After she paid off the cab, she stood for a long moment staring up at the small house, clearly visible under a street lamp. Was it the same house where she had first met Angus Moray? She was unsure. She had come here that one time only.

A manservant opened the door to her ring. She hesitated an instant. Should she ask for Captain Moray? No, no.

"Mr. Moray? Mr. Angus Moray?"

"Mr. Moray is not in, madam."

"Do you expect him soon?" She should have called, of course. Angus could be anywhere and surely there was a Mrs. Moray.

The manservant hesitated.

Kay rushed ahead. "Please, it is very important that I get in touch with Mr. Moray. As soon as possible."

The manservant seemed to withdraw a little, though he didn't move. "I'm sorry, madam, but Mr. Moray is not expected in London until Tuesday."

Next Tuesday, and this was Thursday.

"Would you know where I might be able to reach him?"

"No, madam. Mr. Moray is on the Continent on a camping holiday. He had no fixed itinerary."

Something of her urgency must have touched the man. "I'm sorry," and he sounded sorry. "He arrives at Heathrow just past ten Tuesday morning."

Kay nodded and started to turn away.

"Whom shall I say asked for him, madam?"

She turned back. "Tell him Kay Emory needs him. Tell him that please." And she gave him the name of her hotel, then once again turned to go but paused. "May I leave a message?"

A Settling of Accounts

The manservant's hesitation was almost imperceptible, then he nodded and held the door for her. He led the way down a short hall and into a room to the right. He turned on the lights.

Kay stopped in the doorway. Brown curtains, books, a desk, an Aubusson carpet. The same room. The very same room. She looked to her left. Lionel had sat just there. She walked to the chair and reached out. Just there.

"There is paper and pen on the desk, madam."

"Thank you." She sat at the desk, found the paper. She stared down at it for a long moment, then began to write: "Dear Angus, Do you remember when the jackals were at England's throat? Do you remember Wanborough Manor and Arisaig and Beaulieu? Do you remember Lionel Neal and Kay Emory? You tried in those days, you tried with every fiber of your heart, to arm us against the enemy. You helped us in every way you could. Angus, I need your help now . . ."

She bit at her lip, paused, then wrote again and her pen raced across the paper. She filled the rest of the page, read it over once with somber eyes, then signed it.

The manservant waited in the hall. She gave him the folded sheet. "Thank you."

All the way back to the hotel, she wondered if Angus would still care that brave men had died because of a traitor. She wondered if years and time had eased that pain, had transformed their brutal anguish into anecdotes. "I knew a fella . . ."

She walked from the tube station toward the hotel, unhurried now, comfortable in the shadowed streets. She felt confident. She had made a beginning and she would not turn back. She could count on . . .

She stopped and reached out to catch onto an iron fence for support. Was her imagination spinning out of control?

Had the shock and pain of the day destroyed her balance? Surely that could not be . . . but it was. She would never, could never, mistake Edmond. He stood on the opposite corner and he was watching the hotel entrance.

Waiting for her?

Why else?

Why?

He had done his damage, hadn't he? She was discredited, no danger to him. But he could not be sure, the more he worried, that he had done enough. The guilty flee and, so often, they are pursued.

Had he somehow discovered that she hadn't run home to America? But, of course, all he had to do was call the hotel. She should have come back, checked out. Such a simple thing. She should have thought of it.

Only one mistake in the field. But this wasn't the field. Her thoughts tumbled. Field of honor, yes. Yes, Edmond, you are right to fear.

Almost as if he sensed her thought, felt her presence, he turned and looked, and across that dark street they stared at each other.

Then Kay, sharply, quickly, desperately, turned and began to run.

Part II
Julie
CHAPTER 11

Elbows up. Elbows up! Dammit. Her lungs ached. Ached and burned. Pain and suffering, that's what makes a swimmer. But is it? And why should she care? She wasn't swimming any more. But she had told herself she was going to finish a thousand. What was a thousand, anyway. Only forty laps. Elbows up, Julie!

Did she think she would have all the answers if she did a thousand? Would that make everything all right? Oh, damn Greg, damn him. Damn everything. Six beat kick. Six beat kick. That's right, Julie, you can do it, six beat kick.

She swam through the water, elbows high, kick strong, legs straight, flutter, flutter. As the bulkhead neared, she curved down, twisted, thrust her foot against the wall to make her flip turn and churned up the pool.

Stroke, kick, breathe. Stroke, kick, breathe. Soon it was the old familiar burning struggle, it hurt to swim, but she would, she would do it, she would.

Twenty-nine laps now. Six beat kick. Six beat kick.

Her mind was free of the water, at a distance from that disciplined driving force that moved on and on through the water.

She had told him no. Then, at the last minute, as his face tightened, the sulky look that she dreaded, she had quailed.

"Not this weekend, Greg."

169

He had shrugged. "Look, Julie, I'm not a little kid. And I'm not playing games. With you. With anybody. Either you care for me. Or you don't. It's that simple."

But it wasn't that simple at all. At least, not for her. Was it for anybody? But it must be, mustn't it?

He started to turn away and quickly, too quickly, she said, "I have to pick up my aunt at the airport."

He'd paused. "Yeah. Well. You can call me." And he was gone.

Six beat kick. Six beat kick. Stroke harder, faster. The wall was coming up . . . now the turn. The water foamed and she was starting another lap. Twenty-six to go.

What was wrong with her? She loved Greg. Didn't she? And she felt the familiar sweeping warmth as she pictured his face, the long length of him, the way his mouth curved when he smiled.

And yet . . .

Her lungs ached intolerably now. But she would do a thousand, do it or drown. She was slowing. How long had it been since she had worked out in a pool? At least a year. College teams were for men. So she'd hung up her cap. But today she felt a desperate need for the cathartic body-straining struggle of a workout. The women's pool was empty, this late-fall afternoon. Only she, laboring now, and a bored senior lifeguard, who didn't once look up from his textbook.

Elbows up, Julie. Keep on going.

Everyone said it was love that counted. The relationship. Not words. Empty vows. If two people loved each other . . .

Marriage is a sacrament.

Her stroke faltered. She could remember so clearly the earnest frown on the priest's face in confirmation class and how bored she had been and how the words fluttered like lazy butterflies, skipping and floating, insubstantial, unimportant sounds. So long ago.

So indelible.

Was that it? Was she a prisoner to her Catholic childhood? But she was an adult now, free, ready to make choices based on . . .

Someone else's demand?

She stroked more slowly now and the water slipped smoothly along her. She was warm and tired. Fifteen more laps.

Very tired. But she would finish what she had begun. That was the rule and you could never break it. If once you stopped, if once you gave in to aching muscles and breathless lungs, why you would always be weak, ready to fail, sure to fail.

Five more laps.

Maybe if her mother hadn't died so long ago . . . But did anyone ever ask their mother that kind of question? No, for surely the answer was certain. Mothers wanted things to be perfect for daughters. And safe, of course. No, even if her mother were alive, this would still be Julie's problem. Dammit, it shouldn't be a problem at all.

No one to ask. Her friends? Those who did would say, by all means, those who didn't . . .

And the only family she had was her aunt, Kay. If she weren't so tired, so absolutely macaroni-limp, she'd laugh at the idea of asking Kay that kind of question. Kay was so . . .

Elbows up, Julie. Two more laps. Two more. You can always do two more laps.

When she was finished, she rested in the water for a long moment, then wearily pulled herself over the gutter to the deck. She slipped off her cap. Her pale ash-blond hair shimmered free. The ends were damp, of course. She shook her head a little and her hair swung loose.

"Very nice." His voice was unexpectedly deep and soft. She had forgotten the lifeguard, slouched in the canvas chair. She looked up, startled, then smiled at the admiration in his eyes. She knew quite well it wasn't her swimming he was complimenting. He apparently had looked up from his book, after all.

"Who'd you swim for?"

"The Dolphins," she answered.

He mentioned his old team and, in a moment, they had discovered mutual friends and it was all very cheerful and fun —and nonthreatening. When he asked her name, she told him—and she knew he would call her.

She wondered as she drove away from the campus, down a narrow road with cypresses crowded close to either side, why she had encouraged him. She was committed to Greg. Wasn't she? Fish or cut bait. It was at that point. And that, of course, was why she had run away this weekend. She wasn't ready to make a decision. She was grasping for delay. But no decision would be a decision. Greg had made that clear. So this weekend could be the most important in her life.

Kay probably would be surprised to see her at the airport, though she had left Julie the flight number and arrival time.

Julie glanced at her watch and pushed a little harder on the accelerator. When she had checked, just before leaving the campus, the airliner was expected to be on schedule. She made it to the airport with fifteen minutes to spare. She parked, then hurried toward the terminal. It would be silly to come all this way, then miss Kay. And Kay never loitered. She would be early off the plane and on her way, crisp, elegant, self-possessed.

Suddenly, sharply, Julie envied her aunt and then, as quickly, didn't envy her at all, and wondered, in confusion, what prompted both feelings. She had never before contrasted herself with Kay, and why should she start today? But this seemed to be the day for a good many feelings, not all of them admirable.

She reached the gate where Kay's plane would unload. She glanced down at her watch. Kay's plane should even now be gliding down through gray Louisiana skies. For the first time, Julie wondered how Kay's trip had gone, if the auction had been worth the long journey. And, for the first time, she wondered, a little absently, why Kay hadn't stayed over a bit once in England. This wasn't, after all, her usual trip. In fact, she never did go to England or the Continent, did she? Julie didn't wonder very hard. It was a stray peripheral thought. The core of her mind still tugged at the problem, the single overwhelming, unresolved question.

What was she going to do?

She sat in a red plastic chair near the arrival area, a small gray-eyed blond girl, and in the anonymity of the airport she looked fresh and vulnerable and very pretty. One hand opened and shut the clasp to her purse. Click. Click. Click. She had once, at camp, when she was twelve, had a horse run away with her, and even now she could remember the sudden plunging emptiness as the horse galloped wildly down the trail. She had clung to the saddle horn and hunched down like a beetle holding to a wind-tossed leaf. She didn't remember how they had caught up with her, who had reached out and grabbed the bit and forced the horse to stop. But she had never forgotten the feeling of being out of control, of being absolutely helpless, caught up by forces she could not manage.

Voices echoed over loudspeakers. Shoes clicked on the terrazzo flooring. A child cried. And Julie watched the passengers begin to stream into the arrival area and she felt that same sense of helplessness.

But she wasn't helpless, damn everything! It was *her* life. Whatever she chose to do, it would be *her* choice. That was the frightening thing, of course, because it was time for her to strike out on her own, make her own decisions.

Something she had never done before. Was it the orphan's will to please? Was it a soul-deep ache for approval? Or was she basically bent, lacking courage, as deformed as a five-legged calf?

Click. Click. Click.

Her father had died in Korea. She didn't actually remember him. She had his picture. And her mother's. She always tried to remember her mother the way she was before the sickness came. She had died when Julie was ten. Her father's parents had taken her in, and in a gentle, distant way they had loved her and been very kind to her, but those years, those growing-up years, had been a kind of exile. She had never felt at home in Houston, and every summer she had come home to New Orleans and stayed with Kay.

Always and ever, Julie caused no one any trouble. She was cheerful, obedient and always agreeable. When it was time to go to college, Kay had urged her to come back to Louisiana. Julie had jumped at it, never even thought of striking out on her own.

So this weekend would prove whether she was only a reflection of others. But it is all right to draw strength where you can. That, of course, was why she had come to pick up Kay. Julie admired her aunt, admired especially Kay's cool surety in an uncertain world.

And, another first thought, she wondered if Kay . . . whether Kay . . . And she realized abruptly how little she knew of her aunt. As a woman. As a person. For Kay was beautiful and feminine. And there was that handsome doctor who was always somewhere in the background. Click. Click.

Click. Julie snapped the clasp shut so hard that her fingers tingled and her hand dropped away. John, that was his name. Julie frowned. He was a widower, wasn't he? Why hadn't Kay married him?

Once again she saw Greg's dark, intent face and heard his tight, angry voice. "I'm not a kid. And I don't play kid games." Never a word about marriage. Or love. For all of that was meaningless, in the new view. All that mattered was honesty, nothing hinging on empty form.

Marriage is a sacrament.

She pushed up from the chair, walked nearer the ornamental railing. Julie craned for a better view of the incoming travelers. She started forward, thinking she saw Kay, then stopped when the woman came closer and, obviously, wasn't Kay at all. Julie's eyes skipped here and there in the crowd and she felt the first beginnings of puzzlement. Kay was always among the first off a plane. But not today.

Julie waited until every last passenger came through before she accepted the obvious. Kay had not been on that plane. She was turning to go, uncertain what to do next, when a rumpled stewardess, traveling bag in hand, coat over her arm, came tiredly through the door.

Julie moved forward. "Please, could you help me?"

The stewardess was tired. There had been an especially offensive drunk in first class and a sick baby in tourist. The captain had been even more unpleasant than usual. She had a date tonight but already she could feel the telltale signals of an oncoming migraine. She almost walked right by Julie without even hearing her. It was the tag end of a soft "Please" that reached her, and she stopped and turned blankly toward a small blond girl and saw, because she was kind, the worry in those steady gray eyes and the hand reaching out that said so much more than words. So she listened and zipped open her bag and pulled out the passenger list.

"A 'no show.' "

When she was gone, Julie was more puzzled than ever. No show. That meant that somehow Kay had missed her flight for she had not canceled her ticket.

Kay did not miss flights.

Oh well, of course she could. International flights often ran late. That was the explanation. Her flight was late into New York and she had not made her connecting flight. The thing was to check on the earlier flight.

The ticket agent was very helpful, very efficient. It didn't take another ten minutes to discover that Kay's international flight had landed at Kennedy in good time for her to have made the connecting flight to New Orleans. It took a little longer to find out that K. Emory had also been a "no show" in London.

Julie stood uncertainly by the ticket desk. She looked up at the round clock faces all in a row, telling the time in New Orleans and in Shanghai, in Tel Aviv and in London. It would be getting dark in London now, shadows lengthening in gray streets.

A departure was announced over the loudspeaker. Then the modulated voice began to page Mr. Ralph Evans. A telegram for Mr. Ralph Evans at Continental Airlines.

A telegram. That was the answer. Kay would surely have sent some word. Julie swung around and began to hurry. There would be word at the shop or the house. Everything was all right. Of course it was.

CHAPTER 12

Julie was positive there would be a cablegram. So positive
that she shrugged away the uneasiness that had settled on her
when she knew that Kay had missed her flight.

Julie called the shop first and talked to Carole Stewart,
Kay and Marjorie's young assistant.

"No word from Kay at all?"

"Why no, Julie. She told me she would get home today but
probably wouldn't come to the shop until Monday." Carole
asked quickly, "Is anything wrong?"

"No," Julie said slowly. "It's only that I would have
thought she would send us some word if she were staying
longer in London."

"Perhaps we'll hear later today."

"Yes. Call me if you do get word."

Julie drove to Kay's house. But there was no cablegram
there, and really that wasn't even likely. Then, a flare of hope,
she called her dorm to see if there were any messages.

But there was no word anywhere. Uneasiness slipped into
worry, and worry bordered on fear.

Some people can be counted on. Kay was one of them.
And she didn't do unexpected, thoughtless, worrisome things.

Julie paced nervously up and down Kay's living room. It
was already dark outside, the early dusk of October. Light
spread from a cheerful rose-shaded lamp, glistened through
the crystals of chandeliers. The only sound in the pale-yellow
and gray room was the muted ticking of the ormolu clock and
the oft scuff of Julie's shoes on the thick gay carpet. Surely
Kay would get in touch with them, perhaps call . . .

177

Julie looked at the telephone, then at the clock. It was long past midnight in London.

It didn't take long to put the call through.

"A call for Miss Kay Emory?" the desk clerk asked.

It seemed to Julie there was an odd pause after the operator said yes.

"I don't believe . . ." the crisp English voice began, then it broke off. There was a silence and, finally, "I will ring, Operator."

Across an ocean, Julie heard a flat buzz and knew it was sounding in Kay's room. She could imagine the sleepy voice, knew how it would lighten, hear Kay's soft laugh . . . Buzz. Buzz. Buzz. Buzz.

It was ringing in an empty room, had to be ringing in an empty room.

"There doesn't seem to be any answer," the operator said. "Do you wish to leave a number for the party to call?"

"Yes," Julie said quickly, "yes."

When that was done, when once again she was alone in Kay's own living room, Julie looked again at the clock. Almost six o'clock in the evening in New Orleans. It was eight hours later in London. Two o'clock in the morning there. Where in the world could Kay be at two o'clock in the morning?

Something had happened to Kay.

Julie's hand darted out to the telephone. Greg, she would call Greg. She picked up the receiver, began to dial, then stopped in midnumber and slowly pressed the cradle bar. What good would it do to call Greg? She hung up the receiver and jumped to her feet. Marjorie would know what to do. It wasn't too late to go to the hospital. She would go and ask Marjorie what to do.

The hospital was old and had been built haphazardly over

the course of a hundred and fifty years. It took a while for Julie to find the right annex, the proper floor. There was everywhere the distinctive hospital smell, mop water and antiseptics, medicines, bland food, and, underlying it all, the unmistakable odor of sickness. She knocked gently on the closed door, then opened it and looked in. She could see a row of beds, four perhaps, each separated by white curtains suspended from rods.

A woman slept heavily in the first bed. Julie could see a mass of dark-brown hair. That would not be Marjorie. Julie found her in the third bed and was shocked at how small she looked, propped up against the thick hospital pillow. And her hair, always so carefully blued and coiffed, straggled down over her ears. A faint flush reddened her cheeks and she looked up at Julie with pain-dulled eyes, then, recognizing her, struggled to sit up straighter and reached a hand to pat ineffectually at her hair.

"Julie, how nice of you to come. Afraid I've been asleep. I seem to have caught a cold, you know how it is, one thing happens, then something else hits you too, but, child, it's so nice of you . . ." and she broke off to cough rackingly, and Julie remembered that Marjorie always smoked one cigarette after another. A cold with bad lungs and weak from her fall —why, Kay would want to be here. Marjorie was really sick!

Julie poured some water into a glass and helped Marjorie drink and the coughing eased. The older woman lay weakly back on her pillows. "Such a time," she murmured, and then, once again, she began to struggle to talk.

Julie quieted her. "Oh Marjorie, don't try to talk, please. You must rest. Here, let me help you," and the girl plumped the pillows and refilled the water jug and sat and talked quietly until Marjorie began to get drowsy. And didn't mention Kay at all.

On the drive back to Kay's house, Julie thought of the handsome doctor. But she couldn't presume to go to him. It would suggest a knowledge on Julie's part that would be an affront to both of them. Wouldn't it? The girl shook her head. She just didn't know, but she had a basic instinctive feeling that Kay wouldn't want that.

So that left it all up to Julie.

She parked in the narrow enclosure off the alley that ran behind Kay's townhouse, locked the car, and hurried into the empty, dusty house. Odd how a house could lose its life and color in such a short time. Kay had been gone a little less than a week, but the house already felt vacant and lifeless.

Julie continued to worry as she got ready for bed. Nothing was resolved. It still came to the puzzling, almost frightening fact that Kay had not come home when she was expected and, more, had not notified anyone of a change in her plans.

And nothing Julie had done had cleared the air at all. She snuggled under the sheet and thin cotton blanket and bunched up her pillow behind her head. All right, maybe she hadn't come up with any answers, but she had done everything she could. The ball was in Kay's court now, since the message had been left asking Kay to call New Orleans.

That's what would happen. Kay would get the message and call tomorrow. Everything would be all right.

Julie woke early. She turned her face to look at the alarm on the bedside table. Seven-ten.

Just past three o'clock in the afternoon in London.

Why hadn't Kay called?

Julie was awake now, thoroughly awake, and plunged right back into yesterday's worry.

It took a little longer this time to get the call through.

A Settling of Accounts

Sunday morning in New Orleans. Sunday afternoon in London.

It was a replay of the evening before, except there were more noises in the background and the answering voice was different.

"A call for Miss Kay Emory?"

Julie waited, holding the telephone receiver so hard that her hand ached. She wanted to hurry them. Perhaps Kay hadn't received the message. Desk clerks did make mistakes. Should she leave word again if there were no answer?

Buzz. Buzz.

Julie took a deep breath. They were ringing Kay's room. She willed an answer. Be there, Kay. Lift the receiver. Oh Kay, where are you?

Buzz. Buzz.

Julie's shoulders slumped and she expelled her breath in a sigh.

Buzz. Buzz.

"Operator, please, let me speak to the desk clerk."

There would be a charge, of course, did she understand that?

Yes, yes.

But once she had the clerk on the line, it seemed another futile attempt on her part.

Yes, the impersonal clipped voice replied, the message requesting Miss Emory to call New Orleans had been placed in her letter box, was, in fact, still in it. Along with her room key.

"But, if she went out today, left her key, then why wasn't the message given to her?"

The bland, impersonal voice gave way then. "Because she hasn't been back to her room since Thursday! We've had no word from her—and her reservation was good only through

Friday night. We've held the room for her, but we can't do it much longer. We will have to put her things in storage."

"Not since Thursday?" Julie repeated sharply.

"Right. Now, miss, what shall we do with her belongings?"

"Have you called the police, done anything?"

"Heavens, no! Had there been an accident, the police would have been on to us. And a hotel can't call the police merely because a guest stays elsewhere. But it's a matter of the reservation. We can't continue to hold the room for her."

"Hold it," Julie said quickly.

"But, miss, who's going to pay . . ."

"I will. Hold the room . . . hold it for me. I'll pay everything that's owed. And leave Miss Emory's belongings there. I'll see to everything."

It was only after she had hung up that she realized what she had done. She breathed rapidly and her hands shook a little with excitement and fear.

She was going to London.

CHAPTER 13

She shrugged away the offer of headphones for the movie, refused a cocktail. Lights were being snapped off now, up and down the length of the huge airplane, as people tried to settle into sleep. The flight wasn't very crowded. The two seats next to her were empty. She lifted up the armrests, curled up with a pillow behind her head and a blanket tucked over her feet and knees. It was odd how cold the plane was near the floor. Of course, only inches away was the bitingly cold thin air thousands of feet from the earth. Incredible to realize that she was actually suspended high above the earth in a moving metal container. It all seemed unreal, the small movie screen with the brightly colored pictures, all animation, no sound, the darkened oval with the high seat backs and slumped figures of sleeping travelers. Impossible to believe that she, Julie Fremont, was somewhere high over the Atlantic Ocean, on her way to England.

Someone in a seat behind her shuffled a deck of cards, over and over again. Snap, snap, snap, the cards slapped together, a pause, the deck squared, then, once again, snap, snap, snap.

She wondered who shuffled the cards and why. Was it a frightened passenger, someone aware of just how close is the margin between safety and destruction, who looked at the airplane's curving interior and imagined beyond it the violent sweep of air and wondered at the stress on metal? Or was it merely that the traveler was bored yet not sleepy and too ill-bred to think of others near him?

Snap. Snap. Snap. A pause. The click of the deck. Snap. Snap. Snap.

That kind of irritant drove Greg wild. He would not sit supinely, listening to the endless shuffle of the plastic-backed cards. He would demand quiet and enjoy asking for it. As for her, there was scarcely anything in the world she thought worth a scene.

But she couldn't sleep with the incessant rattle of the cards behind her. She pulled the blanket closer and turned her cheek into the pillow. She did close her eyes but the day flickered in her mind, bright and sharp as the movie on the small screen. There had been so much to do and so little time. She had to get money, no easy task on a Sunday in New Orleans. At first she had thought that would delay her until Monday, but she found, to her surprise and more than a little to her delight, that she functioned under pressure, that she came up with answers. Money—she used her credit card at the automatic outdoor bank teller. Enough money. Of course, it was in cash and she had never traveled with that large a sum, but she would be careful because she had no choice. Then she began to call the airlines and easily got a reservation to New York and another on a flight leaving for London that night.

Time really began to run out then. Only an hour to pack and get to the airport. Calls to make, to Greg, to the University, to her roommate, to Kay and Marjorie's assistant at the shop. And to each she said that her aunt had asked her to join her in London, a matter of business.

She felt a dry ache in her throat when she said it. Please God, that Kay would be in London, that Julie would find her safe and apologetic that she had caused worry and alarm by failing to let them know of a change in her plans. Please God.

In the darkness of the plane, surrounded by nameless, faceless strangers, Julie struggled against late-night fear, a melancholy sense of loss. Don't borrow trouble, that had been her mother's maxim. But when trouble comes, Julie thought coldly, good cheer won't suffice.

She turned restlessly. The cards clicked behind her. What would she do in London? What could she do, really? She turned uneasily again. Was she a fool to be on this plane? The old withering sense of inadequacy swept over her. Then quickly, angrily, the new decisive Julie pushed that feeling away. She knew in her bones that something was wrong, dreadfully wrong. Knew it. She couldn't prove it to a judge. She probably couldn't convince Greg. But she knew Kay, knew her as only kin can ever know one another. And Kay was thoughtful and sensible and utterly dependable.

If Kay missed a flight without canceling her reservation, she must have a compelling reason. And, most frightening of all, was the knowledge that Kay had walked out of her hotel on Thursday—and never returned.

Julie propped the pillow more behind her shoulders and stared somberly up the aisle of the night-shrouded plane. Tomorrow as soon as they landed, she would go to the hotel, find out what she could there. Then, her next move would be to Scotland Yard.

She slept finally, but her dreams were tense and strained and in them she hurried, trying to catch up with a dimly seen figure that was just too far ahead to hear her call.

But nothing ever turns out quite as planned, either asleep or awake.

Julie was so jet-lagged by the time she reached the hotel that it was an effort to walk without shambling, to keep open eyes grainy with fatigue. She had come such a long way to find Kay, to help Kay, but first she must sleep. She followed the porter to the elevator and resisted the impulse to lean against the wall as the cage slowly rose. Once inside the room, she dropped her coat and purse into a chair, handed the porter his tip and didn't even see the quick, curious appraisal he gave her. The door shut behind him, she walked numbly to the bathroom. She took a hot bath, slipped into her nightgown and went directly to bed and plummeted luxuriously into thick, heavy, swirling folds of sleep.

The room was dim, the late-afternoon sunlight pale behind drawn curtains, when the telephone rang. Julie stirred. The phone buzzed again. She rolled over, fumbled with the receiver, held it to her ear.

"Miss Emory? Angus Moray here. I'm just now home again, a day sooner than expected. Thomas gave me your letter. I'm afraid there is some confusion. Thomas didn't understand that you were asking for my father." He paused and Julie had time to think what a nice voice, what a very nice voice he had, and then he continued, slowly, gently, "And obviously you don't know that my father was killed in the war, in 1945. I never actually knew him, you see."

Something in the quality of her silence must have puzzled him. "I say, Miss Emory, I'm very sorry . . ."

"I'm not Miss Emory," Julie began, then quickly, before she lost him, she continued, "I'm her niece, Julie Fremont, and I would like to talk to you, if I may. You see, my aunt . . . Oh, Mr. Moray, she was supposed to come home to New Orleans on Saturday but she wasn't on the plane. Then, when I started calling here I found out that she left the hotel on Thursday and never returned. So I came to London. I arrived early this morning and was so tired I went to bed. But now, I hope to find Kay. And I would like to talk to you, try to find out something of what she did in London."

"I see," he said slowly. "She did not come back to her hotel on Thursday . . . Yes, Miss Fremont, yes, I think I should meet with you. At your hotel? In half an hour?"

She dressed quickly and had time to straighten the room before he knocked. She felt closer to despair as she hung her dresses in the closet, emptied her cosmetic bag, than she had in New Orleans when she had listened to the phone ringing, ringing in an empty room. For here were Kay's things, her face powder, a favorite lipstick, her eye shadow and cleansing cream, her ivory satin negligee. Why would Kay walk away and leave all of her things?

But worst of all, just as a knock sounded at the door, Julie opened a drawer in the bedside table and there was Kay's plane ticket. Julie picked it up, and, still holding it, walked to the door.

When she opened it, he started to speak, then reached out and touched her arm.

"What is it? What's happened?"

"Her ticket! Kay's ticket home. She must have intended to return to the hotel. It is here and all of her things." She spread her hand and he looked around the hotel room, at a book lying open and face down on the bedside table, at the array of cosmetics on the dresser, at the bright-yellow house shoes next to the bed.

He nodded soberly and she liked the solid square of his face. His skin was reddened, by sun or wind, and his light-brown hair flecked with red. He stared down at the plane ticket, then looked up at her, and she was startled at the sharp green of his eyes, as clear and green as a cat's.

"I think you are right to be worried, Miss Fremont. Especially when I show you the letter your aunt left for my father," and he reached into his coat pocket and pulled out an envelope.

He hesitated for a moment, then handed it to her. "Let me explain the circumstances a bit. I was out of England last Thursday. On Thursday evening, not long after dark, my manservant, Thomas, answered the doorbell. There was an American lady standing on the steps." He told Julie about

Kay's visit, her dismay at finding Angus Moray gone, the sense of urgency in her manner. "Thomas said she was very much of a lady, so when she asked to leave a message, he let her into the house." The young man paused, then said, "You'd have to know Thomas to understand what a surprising response that was on his part. It impressed me a good deal. It also makes the message she left that much more . . . disturbing. Here, see what you think."

Julie took the envelope and lifted out the sheet of paper and recognized at once Kay's flowing, graceful handwriting. She read:

"Dear Angus, Do you remember when the jackals were at England's throat? Do you remember Wanborough Manor and Arisaig and Beaulieu? Do you remember Lionel Neal and Kay Emory? You tried, in those short days, you tried with every fiber of your heart, to arm us against the enemy. You helped us in every way you could. Angus, I need your help now, need it every bit as desperately as I did then.

"It's odd, Angus, but I feel closer in time at this moment to the Kay that I was in 1940 than to the woman I am now, should be now. I came to London this week on business, and it was the first time I had been back since the day we left for France in 1941. I was afraid that the memories might be painful but I had no thought at all that the past was not over, not finished for all time. I'm sure you knew, you were always a most perceptive man, that I loved Lionel . . . ."

Julie looked up then, into the young man's vivid green eyes, and shook her head. "We shouldn't be reading this. It isn't . . ."

"I know," he said quickly, "but I had to read it. A friend of my father's had come to him for help—and I thought he would want me to help if I could."

Julie nodded, looked down again at the sheet of paper.

". . . and that we would have married."

The strong, smooth writing faltered here and something was scratched through and Julie couldn't make it out. Then harder, blacker, the sentence picked up. "I don't know if any news of our circuit's collapse reached you. I don't know whether you ever learned what happened. But I am sure you had files on our beginnings, on the plans made for us. I need your help, Angus, to get some confirmation of the fact that I was an agent for F Section of SOE, something that will help prove my story.

"Of course, I know that the war crimes trials were all held long ago. But what would they do now if I could prove that he still lived, the man who betrayed us? Could he be tried for collaboration, for murder? Surely there must be some way of bringing him to justice! I can't believe there is a time limit on prosecution for murder.

"Please, Angus, help me. I ask not for myself but for Lionel and Grand'mère, for the doctor and the priest, for Countess Rakovsky, for all whose blood stains Edmond's hands.

"There must be a way. There must."

And it was signed with the clear bold signature Julie knew so well.

"I knew something was wrong," Julie said faintly, when she had read it through, "but I never dreamed . . ." She looked up at Angus Moray's son. "Do you know what she is writing about? 'SOE' and 'F Section'?"

He nodded. "You didn't know then that your aunt had been a secret agent in the war?"

Julie shook her head. "I wasn't even born during World War II. And later, I did know that Kay had been sick once or that something bad had happened to her. There were some years no one ever mentioned. But I didn't know she'd ever been to England or France, either one."

He thought for a moment. "I'll explain as well as I can. I only know myself what I've been told, years afterward. During the war, my father was a captain and he served in the F Section of the Special Operations Executive. That was the very secret group which trained agents and smuggled them into France where they encouraged all kinds of resistance to the Nazis. Much about SOE's work is still hush-hush. My mother told me that Father helped train agents, and that explains your aunt's reference to Wanborough and Arisaig and Beaulieu. Father was a conducting officer. Mother said that conducting officers usually never did go into the field but that there was a very special mission that he insisted upon accompanying in March 1945. He didn't come back."

It was quiet in the hotel room, both of them for a moment feeling very close to a world they had never known, a world of uniforms and blacked-out cities, of heavy, throbbing bombers and small clandestine craft, of bravery and fear and treachery. A quarter of a century past, and yet words written in haste in a letter brought it as near, made it as real as the muted hum of traffic beneath the hotel window or the muffled slam of a door down the hallway.

Julie pressed one hand hard against her cheek and spoke almost to herself. "So Kay was an agent in France in World War II. And she was betrayed, she and Lionel." She looked up then, at Angus Moray, and saw her next thought in his eyes, "And she came here to London, last week, and somewhere she saw the man who betrayed them." She licked dry lips. "If she saw him then, of course, he could have seen her?"

The young man nodded, slowly, reluctantly.

"It was Thursday evening that she came to your house, so it must have been sometime that day that she saw him."

"More than likely—"

"And she has not been seen since."

CHAPTER 14

Julie took the Northern Line to Leicester Square, then changed to the Piccadilly Line. The third station was Russell Square. She hurried out of the car and wormed past the people ahead of her to walk rapidly up and out of the Underground. She stopped just past the exit and took a deep breath. She was so angry her chest ached. Then, worse than anger, that old withering sense of self-contempt swept over her. Once again, she'd done it wrong, all wrong!

Tears smarted. She reached up, rubbed ferociously at her eyes. She would not cry, she would not! She lifted her face, looked around to get her bearings, then began to cut diagonally across the park.

The sky had darkened while she was at Scotland Yard. Thick, heavy gray-black clouds pressed close to earth and the air was wet with mist. The leaves underfoot lumped into a soft moist carpet. It was damply cold.

Reaching the street, she waited for the light to change. As usual, she looked the wrong way, then realized her error and checked to the right before stepping into the street. At the hotel, she hurried up the broad steps and brushed past the doorman without even looking at him. Nor, once inside, did she glance toward the desk. So she did not see the clerk look up, then move his head, alert, watchful, his cold, predatory eyes following her as she walked toward the elevators.

She stood, waiting for an elevator to reach the lobby, then she knew she did not want to go up to the room, Kay's room, with her things spread in casual disarray as she had left them, expecting to return. Julie jerked around and walked toward the lounge.

The desk clerk still watched her. As she pushed through the swinging door into the lounge, he was lifting a telephone and, checking a slip of paper in his hand, he began to dial.

It was very quiet in the lounge. A very old woman nodded in a rocking chair in the far corner. Two middle-aged ladies sat in an alcove and drank tea and talked inaudibly. Great green fronds of potted plants stretched toward the dark ceiling. A huge fluffy fern flowed like a green wave to break and trail down beside the loveseat where Julie sat. She folded her raincoat and put it on the seat beside her.

She tried to relax. She breathed slowly, slowly, in and out. Gradually, some of the anger and frustration seeped away. Yesterday, when she and Angus had made their plans, it had all seemed simple enough. She would go to Scotland Yard first thing this morning and he would contact friends of his father's and see what access he could manage to the SOE files. They would meet back at Julie's hotel at noon.

She glanced down at her watch. Just on eleven. She had waited almost an hour before the detective inspector was free to see her. Just thinking of that interview made her angry all over again.

But not, she realized miserably, angry at the policeman. Angry at herself. For she had failed. The detective inspector, his name was Reginald Evans, could not have been more courteous, more reasonable. But she had felt, toward the end of their talk, as if she were fighting feathers, flailing at unseen resistance.

She had heard her own voice growing shriller, though there was no overt rejection on his part. He had made notes as he listened, gathered a description of Kay (raven-black hair, white at the temples, violet eyes, high cheekbones, a generous mouth). Yet Julie felt he worked by rote. His gray eyes were empty of feeling, his face expressionless.

She told him of the letter Kay left for Angus. He nodded, again made notes—but said nothing at all. He looked at Julie, listened to her, yet she was sure he wasn't seeing her as another human being. She might as well have been a door or a poster or a blank wall. She tried hard to break through, to make him see the urgency of it.

"You do see how frightening it is! She sees the man who betrayed them and then she disappears!"

She leaned forward, her hands on the dull-gray metal of his desk. Beyond them, past the glass cubicle that was his office, was a room filled with desks where men typed, bent over reports, talked on telephones. There was a restless hum of noise that seeped into the corner. She felt that she was trying to talk over it, trying to catch his attention, though, to be fair, he watched her with attentive brown eyes, listened, even mouthed a response.

"We will, of course, make inquiries, Miss Fremont." He paused, then gave an infinitesimal shrug. "You understand, of course, that Scotland Yard will not make inquiries about . . . supposed Nazi war criminals. That is not in our province. We will, however, try to find your aunt. I quite understand that her disappearance is not in character and is disturbing to you." He glanced at his notepad. "I have your telephone number here. I will be calling you . . . if we have anything to report."

And she had to be content with that, though she knew it was no more substantial than a handful of smoke. He had risen then. Hopelessly, she too had stood. He wasn't going to do anything! He wasn't really going to look for Kay.

And somewhere out in London, Kay needed help.

In the hotel lounge, Julie relived that interview one more time. What should she have done? Why hadn't he listened to her?

Julie pressed her hands against her cheeks. Was it her fault? Had she seemed so silly and unimportant that the detective inspector discounted everything she told him? Would another, stronger personality have impressed him, started a real all-out search for Kay?

No. No. This time it wasn't *her* failure. After all, Angus believed with her that something must have happened to Kay. The thing now was not to despair. If Scotland Yard wouldn't look for Kay, then Julie and Angus would.

It was time to stop stewing about that useless trip to Scotland Yard and start thinking about what to do next. Julie opened her purse, pulled out a pen and small notepad. She frowned at it for a moment, then wrote down Thursday and underlined it twice. It was on Thursday that Kay had turned up on Angus Moray's doorstep, seeking help. So it was very likely that it was earlier in the day that she had, shockingly, come face to face with her past.

Thursday.

Julie's face crinkled in concentration. Kay had expected to return home to America on Saturday, so the auction would have concluded on Friday. Auctions, important ones, often ran several days, so Kay had probably been at the auction on Thursday also.

There was a starting point. The auction. Wasn't it possible that . . .

"Miss Fremont?"

Julie looked up in surprise. The young sandy-haired bellboy who had carried her suitcase to her room was looking down at her and his eyes were friendly and kind.

"I have a message for you."

Angus, of course. He was going to be delayed. Well, that would give her time to look in Kay's room for the name of the gallery.

She reached up for the note, read it and could scarcely believe it. Miss Fremont was requested to meet her aunt at 103 Jeremy Close.

The bellboy had turned away.

"Wait, please." Julie called him back. "Does this mean my aunt called here, to the hotel?"

The boy shrugged. "I don't know, miss, I'm sure. The desk clerk took the message."

Julie jumped up. "When did she call? Just now?"

Again the boy shrugged helplessly.

"Please, show me who took the message," and she was gathering up her purse and raincoat.

"I'm glad everything's all right, miss," the boy said as they started out of the lounge. "I know it's hard for a family when ladies . . . when there is that kind of difficulty. I have an aunt who's sober as a judge most of the time, then, bango, nobody knows where she's off . . ."

Julie stopped in midstride and turned toward the boy.

"What did you say?"

He flushed a bright, sharp red and pulled uneasily at his jacket. "I'm sorry, miss, I didn't mean to speak out of turn. Anyone can tell at first look that your aunt is a very nice lady. But nice ladies can . . . I mean, even the best of . . ."

Julie held up her hand. "No, please, I'm not angry. I just don't understand. Why should you think that my aunt, that Miss Emory would . . . that she would drink too much?"

The boy stared miserably at the floor.

"No, please tell me," Julie said gently. "I'm not angry at all. But so much has happened that I don't understand. Perhaps if I know . . ."

The boy nodded. "I'm sorry, I'm sure, miss, but I thought certainly you would know. You see, it was, well, it was a week ago today, Tuesday evening it was, miss, and your aunt came into the bar, quite proper, and sat down by herself and ordered a drink. That one and a second and, I think, a third, then the first thing you know, she was falling out from the table and onto the floor, and she couldn't walk or talk, miss, she was so . . . well, miss, she was drunk as a lord. That means, of course, that she'd drunk a tidy bit even before she came into the bar. For that's how it takes them, the ones that drink too much. Why, they can down three times as much as a big man and not show it a bit, then, all of a sudden, one drink more, and they're off their feet."

Julie looked at his serious, kind face and knew he believed every word that he said. But Kay drunk! Why, she would as soon imagine her running naked down Bourbon Street. But the boy sounded so certain and he wasn't, she could tell, malicious or ugly.

"You saw her like that?" Julie asked.

He nodded unhappily. "It was me and Alfred that carried her up to her room, miss."

"I see," Julie said. But she didn't see at all. "Thank you for telling me."

"I'm sorry, miss. I wouldn't have said a word if I hadn't thought you would know. And, miss, it happens to the nicest of ladies."

Julie nodded. All the way to the desk, she tried to understand, to fit this tawdry scene to the aunt she knew. Kay never drank too much.

At least, not around Julie. Julie felt a flicker of uncertainty. Was it possible, could Kay possibly . . .

She remembered her aunt so clearly the last time she saw her, remembered Kay's clear violet eyes and smooth fresh face and the faint lemony fragrance of her cologne. Kay was always so self-possessed. To picture her drunk was incredible.

But the bellboy had *seen* it.

Julie reached the desk and waited for the clerk to finish with another guest.

The lobby hadn't changed since she walked into it on Monday morning. But, standing there, waiting for the stocky clerk to turn her way, everything seemed different, tinted by this new, shocking view of her aunt. Julie looked toward the entrance to the bar. She tried to imagine a limp and flaccid Kay being carried through the doorway to the elevator.

"Yes, miss?"

She jerked around to face the clerk and immediately disliked him, disliked his narrow, squinty eyes and thin, tight mouth and his faintly insolent air.

She held out the message to him.

"Did you write this?"

He glanced down, pursed his mouth and said brusquely, "I might have done. I don't keep count of all the messages."

"You should know your own handwriting."

He stared at her and his light-blue eyes were as cold and hard as marbles. "I should." He must have seen the irritation on her face, for he added sourly, "It's mine."

"When did it come?"

"I'm sure I couldn't say, miss. Within the hour, I suppose."

"Exactly what did she say? Please try to remember. It's important."

He stared at her unblinkingly. Five pounds the man had given him to report Miss Emory's return to her room. She hadn't come back, but the niece had come. On the off chance, he called the man, told him of Julie's arrival. Another five pounds promised for delivering the message—and forgetting the number he had dialed.

He dropped his eyes to the message, slowly shook his

head. "I'm sorry, I'm sure, miss, but it came at a busy time and I don't recall anything else. It does seem to me that the speaker was in a hurry, like, but that's all there was to it. If you came quickly to this address, your aunt would meet you." He looked up blandly. "Does that help any, miss?"

The speaker in a hurry. If she came quickly.

Julie snatched back the message and looked again at the address. "Can you tell me, please, where this is?"

"Be glad to, miss," and the clerk pulled out a city map and glanced at the legend, then pointed, "It's about here, miss, in South Kensington."

"Where is the hotel?"

He showed her.

She frowned. "That's a long way."

"A cabby can get you there, oh, in twenty minutes," he estimated.

Twenty minutes. And the message had said to hurry.

She swung around, was almost to the door, when she remembered Angus. She glanced quickly around the lobby and there, near the elevators, was the young bellboy who had been so nice to her. She crossed to him.

"Please," she said breathlessly, "can you help me?"

"Why, miss, I'd be glad to."

"A friend of mine is coming here to the hotel to meet me at noon. He's tall and slender and has reddish hair and looks as though he's been out in the sun."

The bellboy nodded.

"Tell him I've gone to meet my aunt and I'll call him as soon as I can. Will you remember?"

"Of course, miss. Be glad to."

He hoped everything would work out for the young lady. He watched her hurry out of the hotel and jump into a cab and lean forward to speak to the driver. Too bad she had such family troubles. But everything would likely be all right. The cab pulled away and he turned and moved toward the desk to pick up the luggage of some new arrivals.

CHAPTER 15

"Do please hurry," Julie urged.

The driver answered pleasantly but firmly, "I can't go any faster, miss, for the fog. You see, it's coming up fast now."

And it was. The thin gray mist had thickened to swirling dense pockets of fog that wreathed street lamps till they barely glowed and curtained buildings, softening their stone outlines until they seemed as insubstantial as the fog itself. Moisture beaded the taxi windows, blurring still more her view of the fog-shrouded streets. The lights of the taxi couldn't pierce the shifting gauzy fog. Instead, they diffused, shading into ineffectual halos of light.

The taxi slowed to a cautious slither, clinging to the fading red beacons of tail lights moving ahead. The fog always seemed to thin just enough for the car to continue.

Julie pressed her face against the side window, straining to see, but there was nothing but the glisten of wet streets and the fluffy fog and the pale globules of light marking the street lamps high above.

"It's all right, miss, don't be frightened," the driver soothed. "I've driven London's streets for twenty years and I can find my way."

But the driver's hunched shoulders reflected his tension and the cab seemed to feel its way as cautiously as a cat. The minutes stretched to a quarter hour and then a half, and it seemed to Julie that she had been forever in the wide back seat, one hand gripping the leather doorarm tightly, willing the cab to go faster, knowing it could not. The cab had its own particular smell, the sweet scent of soft leather, the lingering aroma of pipe tobacco, the faint overlay of engine fumes.

He stopped the cab twice to get out and check street signs.

"Is it far?" she asked the second time.

"We've gone halfway, miss."

Julie looked down at her watch. How long ago must that message have come? It had been, at the very least, more than an hour ago. Would Kay still be at this address?

Julie looked out at the fog billowing around lampposts and doorsteps, clinging with ghostly fingers to shutters and eaves, and she shivered. A London fog. That was when Jack the Ripper prowled, wasn't it? Slipping along under the cover of heavy mist to reach out and . . .

"Miss?"

Julie jumped, then scolded herself. How idiotic to think about Jack the Ripper when she must in a short while walk out into that eddying, shifting vapor.

"You do say you must hurry?"

"Yes," she answered, "but I understand that we can't go faster."

"Righto. But if you take the Underground, miss, you'll get there much sooner, the way the streets be. We are at Marble Arch station. Do you know your way by tube?"

Julie shook her head.

He parked the cab then, reached into his dash pocket for an Underground map. "Let me show you, miss. You ride the Central Line to Notting Hill Gate, and there you change . . ."

And he also tried to tell her how to find Jeremy Close from the Underground station.

"The streets wind and curve thereabouts, miss. Many of the houses are built around courts with a close leading to them." And he had explained the close to her, a narrow passageway opening onto a bit of parkland with houses on either side. He thought the address she sought was one of these.

Julie scurried down into the Underground and welcomed the brightness after the fog, the cheerful tiles and bright lights, the platform lined with theater posters. Her train came in almost immediately. It was only three stations until she changed to the Circle Line.

The message had urged hurry. Well, she had tried. There was no point now in worrying. She would find Kay or she wouldn't.

Julie relaxed on the hard brown seat and looked curiously around. The car wasn't crowded but, even so, it seemed awfully quiet, only one or two passengers conversing in quiet voices with their companions. And it was very clean. She had been to New York once and ridden the subway to the tip of Manhattan. She remembered it as dirty. This was much nicer.

And it was wonderful, even if only for a moment, to be free of the burden of her search for Kay. There was nothing more at this instant that she could be doing. She was, for this period, a captive to the Underground, powerless to affect its pace or destination. So she was for this brief moment relieved of all necessity to act.

She stared at the ghostly reflection of her face in the train window as it sped through the tunnel. What a revealing thought that was, Julie Fremont. How far had she come to find an honest picture of herself—grateful to be spared decisions.

She had run away from one decision in Louisiana. Now she welcomed any respite from action here.

Her face was almost formless in the window, a pale, insubstantial image. Was the actuality any more real?

Will the real Julie Fremont please stand up?

Yes, she would. She wasn't spineless! She had come to

London, hadn't she? She was, right this minute, on her way to meet Kay, fog or no fog! She lifted her head, battled her fears. She wasn't indecisive. She had even bearded Scotland Yard.

To little avail.

But that was all right. One race didn't make a meet. If you didn't win one, you just tried harder the next. If she couldn't find Kay *with* Scotland Yard, she would find her *without.*

She and Angus.

It was terribly comforting to think of Angus, to picture his plain sunburned face, his steady, bright-green eyes, to remember the kindness in his voice and the touch of his hand on her arm.

Odd. She had known him a part of one day and yet she felt as if she had known him a long time—or waited for him a long time.

This was such a startling thought that she tilted it in her mind, looked it up and down and over again. He was just an ordinary young man, attractive, well-mannered, kindly. Why did she have this sense of companionship, of right-ness?

Because he was trying to help her, a stranger?

She shook her head slowly.

No. It was more than gratitude on her part. Much more. There was an instinctive response—and he had felt it, too, she was sure of it. The two of them had come together and known each other at once.

That was why she hadn't hesitated to leave a message for she knew that he would understand why she had to leave without waiting for him. There was no doubt in her mind that he would understand.

Greg would have been angry.

The prickly little thought darted into her mind like a bright tropical fish, quick and brilliant and impossible to ignore.

Greg. She could always picture him, the long, arrogant length of him, his dark hair and narrow face and sensual mouth. You did not leave messages for Greg. He left them for others. You did not turn to Greg for help. He was too busy.

She saw him from this very long distance, a distance of both time and space, and realized that when he was not beside her, mesmerizing her with his undeniable physical appeal, she could see him clearly, unsentimentally and quite coldly. And she was frightened at how close she had come, and only she knew how near, to meeting his demand. So near.

Yet, once again, as she remembered him, the feel of his mouth on hers, she was not sure of her answer. But she would make a decision. One way or the other. She was sure of that now.

The train was slowing. This was her stop. She gripped her purse, stood, waited for the car to slide up to the platform.

SOUTH KENSINGTON.

She threaded her way past slower travelers, once again hurrying, intent upon her task, wondering what Kay had planned, why she wanted Julie to meet her here.

The important thing, of course, was that Kay was all right. She had been so afraid, Julie admitted to herself, afraid that she and Angus would never find any trace of Kay. And Kay was Julie's only link to a past, to a part of herself that no one else, despite the best of intentions, could ever really share, the past of a family, faces and voices that only lived, now, in Kay's memory and her own.

And she had not, Julie knew, realized until now how fond she was of her graceful, quiet aunt who always smiled so slowly but with such genuine amusement and who was so . . . Julie tried to find the right words to express to herself the aura that surrounded Kay. Refreshing, that was it. In a world that so often seemed tawdry and unkempt and down-at-heel, Kay was always immaculate, like the lemon-fresh house Julie had grown up in. It was funny to compare a person to a house, but Kay was that solid and rock-certain to Julie.

Even before she reached the top of the Underground stairs, Julie felt the cold moistness of the air. She stopped at the top of the steps. She could scarcely see the corner lamp-post and it couldn't be five feet away! This was too much. The fog was worse. No one could find their way in this kind of fog!

An old man stepped around her, pulled his hat down on his head, strode briskly into the fog and promptly disappeared. A young couple, arm in arm, scarcely aware of anything outside themselves, bumped into her, murmured something, and turned away to the right and were swallowed up in the mist.

But they knew where they were going.

"Ay, and it's a sorry lot they are, let me tell you, Abigail! If you ask me, it won't take . . ."

"Pardon me," Julie interrupted.

The old woman paused, looked away from her companion. "Yes?"

"Please, I'm a stranger here. Can you tell me how to find 103 Jeremy Close?"

"Ay. Go to your right, it be one block, then to your left a half a block."

"Thank you."

The woman nodded, turned back to her companion and they moved off into the fog. Julie looked once, longingly, at the steps melting down into the Underground, then she too stepped out into the fog. After only a few steps, she stopped and felt fear flutter in her throat. There was nothing around her but the gray swirling fog. It clung to her hair, touched her face like tendrils of Spanish moss, eddied like smoke, assuming grotesque and frightening shapes.

Julie almost turned back. She wanted to go back. But Kay waited for her, not more than a block and a half away. And Kay must need her.

Slowly, one step after another, she moved on down the street. It was very quiet. It felt eerie to be in the center of a huge city and not hear a single car or bus. There was nothing but the click of her shoes and the soft swish of her raincoat. No sound anywhere. The world as silent as if everyone had gone away and left it empty.

She walked fifty paces, seventy-five, and stopped once again. The fog hung so low, so close and thick to the ground here that she could see nothing else at all. The fog wrapped around her, soft as an eiderdown, gray as a bird's feathers. Gingerly, she put one foot in front of the other and, step by step, she moved ahead.

She was at the end of the block when the fog thinned just a little, enough at least for her to see to make her turn and even to walk a little faster. She could see far enough to make out the iron railings that fenced these houses. It was not quite midway down the block that she came to a stone arch and saw the legend Jeremy Close and knew she had found her destination.

She stood at the arch, one hand on cold wet stone, and tried to see the end of the passageway. Gray stone walls rose on either side. An iron gate barred the arch. She reached out, lifted the handle. The gate moved heavily, its metal hinges creaking.

Julie hesitated. The gate made so much noise! It could not be much used or its hinges wouldn't shriek so. Was this a private way, forbidden to the passerby?

She waited, uncertain. Where was Kay? This was so forbidding. That hideous creaking noise had faded now and there was nothing, nothing but the sound of her breathing and, far away, the thin howl of a dog.

London was a city of millions, yet she stood here, more alone than she had ever been, no human sound to reassure.

"Kay?"

Julie called out.

No answer. No sound at all.

"Kay?"

Then, like diving into cold water, she moved all at once, shoving the gate wider, slipping into the close. She walked slowly forward, one hand out before her, unable to see the end of the passageway.

Now the fog masked before and behind her and she could see only the damp stone walls beside her and the slippery cobblestones at her feet.

The gate squealed on its hinges.

Julie swung around, stared into fog, strained to see something, anything moving in a cloud of fog.

"Kay?" Her voice was high.

The gate slammed shut, a short, quick, final sound. And softly, so softly she wasn't quite sure of them, she heard footsteps coming toward her.

Part III A Settling of Accounts

CHAPTER 16

It all hinged on Angus.

That was the nub of it, Kay knew. If Angus wouldn't help her, if he shrugged away her appeal, then she had no hope of bringing any kind of charge against Edmond.

But Angus wouldn't fail her.

Kay looked once again at her watch. It was almost noon now. It would be best to allow another hour for him to reach home from the airport, time to receive her letter and read it and sweep the years away, time for him to remember her and Lionel and the winter of 1940.

Because he was her only link to that past. He and Edmond.

Edmond.

She remembered the look on his face that night in front of the hotel. He had seen her, oh yes, he had looked up when she stopped so abruptly to catch hold of the railing for support, seen her and turned, and his face was terrible in its fear and uncertainty.

Edmond was afraid. And, in his fear, as dangerous as a water moccasin roused by an unwary footstep. He was waiting to strike and destroy.

She had eluded him that night, turning into an alleyway

and standing, back pressed against rough bricks, as the sound of his following footsteps fell away in the distance.

But she had known better than to return to the hotel. Since that Thursday night, she had remained quietly in the room she had rented, a simple, clean room not too far from the hotel, in a house that catered to students and teachers wishing to be near the Museum. She had gone out only to eat and to cash enough traveler's checks to give her freedom of movement. She had money enough now to go to France, to go wherever necessary in pursuit of Edmond's destruction.

Her thoughts curved around again, full circle. It all depended upon Angus. She had thought it through very carefully, written down, this long weekend, all she could remember. Clearest of all had come the realization that only she could accuse. No one else survived.

Those who had saved her, gambled their own safety to hide her, had been nameless for their sake and her own. What you do not know, you cannot betray. She remembered them well, of course, she could even now picture their faces as clearly as Lionel's. But who they were, where they lived . . . No, she would never be able to find them.

Only Angus could prove the beginning of her story. The end of it? There must be proof if the police would investigate. Even now, surely someone somewhere could support her word. But the police must be willing to search for evidence.

Restlessly, Kay pushed up and out of the easy chair. She crossed to the windows and looked down into the narrow street and instead stared into swirling clouds of fog.

How long had it been like this? Had Angus's plane been able to land? She leaned on the windowsill, her hands gripping the wooden edge. She had waited four days. She was impatient, determined to move after Edmond. Four days—

she would wait four hundred if need be. She would never give up.

New Orleans, her shop, her partner, Julie, John, they were more than half a world away. They were half a lifetime away, as insubstantial as a dream.

She looked down at her watch again. Half-past twelve. She turned away from the window, hurried to the closet for her raincoat. She would walk out now to the call box. It would take longer in the fog. And if she called and he wasn't there yet, why, she would wait a while and ring again. But the man-servant had said his plane was due in at ten on Tuesday morning. That was two and a half hours ago. Surely she had waited long enough.

She closed the door quietly behind her and hurried down the dim hallway to the stairs. The hall carpeting was worn, its muted flower pattern paled into indistinguishable smudges of color. But the hallway glistened with cleanliness and the stair railing was polished until its old brown wood shone. The stairs had been freshly swept and the house itself smelled of camphor and wax and, faintly, of boiled fish. A grandfather clock in the back of the hall began to chime as she reached the foyer. The glass in the front door rattled a little as she shut it behind her.

It was almost like plunging into a cold lake to step out onto the top step. She paused and looked down into the fog and knew she would have to be careful or she could easily lose her way. She was at the bottom step, ready to turn to her left, when the fog eddied and swayed and a little boy popped out and came toward her, one hand outstretched.

"A penny for the guy, mum? A penny for the guy?"

He stared up at Kay and his face was that particular milky-white characteristic of so many English children. He watched her unblinkingly with his dark-blue eyes.

A Settling of Accounts

For an instant, it made no sense to her, this little apparition out of the fog with such a serious face and expectant outstretched hand.

"A penny for the guy," she repeated slowly. Then she smiled. "Oh, of course, for Guy Fawkes Day."

He nodded solemnly.

She opened her handbag then and found her coin purse and fished out several coins and dropped them into that waiting hand. Only then did his face change, breaking up into a huge delighted smile. "Oh thank you, mum, thank you," and he turned and ran off into the fog, and she knew her coins must have been his best sum to date.

She was still smiling to herself as she walked up the street. How did it go? Please to remember the Fifth of November, Gunpowder Treason and Plot.

Hapless Guy Fawkes had conspired to blow up Parliament and King James. Instead, he was discovered and executed very unpleasantly and was remembered by centuries of children as they watched effigies shrivel and burn in a winter bonfire and thrilled to the pop and spangle of firecrackers. She wondered if there would have been a Guy Fawkes Day if he had succeeded and the thirty-six barrels of gunpowder had blown the House of Lords to oblivion? Odd that the exposé of a plot should become folk legend.

A penny for the guy. It would soon be time to build the bonfires. Four more days to November 5.

Where would she be on the fifth of November?

Kay shivered. The damp cold penetrated her raincoat. She began to walk faster and, not far ahead, she saw the call box.

She knew Angus's number now. It took only a moment to drop in the coins and dial.

"May I speak to Mr. Moray, please."

"One moment, please."

211

Welcome words. Words that meant so much more to her than their casual utterance. She blew out a long soft breath and knew how fearful she had been that Angus would not be there. And she was counting on him. Everything depended upon him.

"Hello. Moray here."

No. That wasn't right. She held the receiver hard against her ear, too surprised to respond.

"I say," Angus asked, "is that you, Julie?"

She did not know that voice. And she would know Angus's voice.

"I . . . there must be . . . I have made a mistake. I am calling Angus Moray."

"This is Angus Moray." And then he knew. "Is this Miss Emory?"

So her call was right. And yet it was all wrong.

"I don't . . ." she began.

"Didn't Julie explain to you?" he asked and his voice was gentle.

She understood then. The Angus Moray she had known was *dead,* and she heard with the icy beginnings of shock the name of *her* niece.

"Julie?"

His voice sharpened. "Yes, she left word at the hotel that she had gone to meet you. Didn't you call and ask her to join you?"

They stood by telephones, miles apart in London, and spoke urgently, sharply, interrupted one another. Kay's hand was sweaty on the receiver and her throat ached.

Edmond, of course. He must have continued to watch the hotel, hoping she would return. She had not, but, in his view, Julie would do, would do very well indeed. For once he had Julie, he held the reins.

"We must get on to the police," Angus said angrily.

"No, oh no," Kay cried. "Listen to me, we will never find Julie alive if we call the police. I know him, I tell you. We must not go to the police. It isn't Julie he wants, of course."

She leaned against the cold glass side of the call box, stared hopelessly out into the grayness. Somewhere in this fog-covered city a desperate man held Julie. Kay remembered Julie at her mother's funeral, gray eyes huge in a wan face, frightened and grieved gray eyes, and how they had turned to Kay when the requiem mass ended. Julie growing up, all tanned arms and legs and hair bleached white as bone. Julie in swim meets, driving through the water, harder and faster than seemed possible to her aunt. Julie a college girl, so serious and soft-spoken. Kay wished that she would be more carefree, but perhaps there was a somber strain through their family. And Julie had met death early, and that changed everything. As no one knew better than she.

"Oh damn, damn, damn," Kay said softly.

"Look, Miss Emory, we must call the police. They are equipped to deal with a kidnaper. And the police are circumspect. They are as interested in preventing . . . in rescuing the victim of a crime as anyone could possibly be. They . . ."

She wasn't listening to his well-bred English voice.

Edmond has Julie, that was all she could think, and there was a brackish sick taste in her throat.

"Miss Emory? Miss Emory, are you there? Please, tell me where you are . . ."

She hung up the receiver. She did it gently. She was sorry. She wished that she too could believe in a world of order where the police like plumed knights can rescue damsels. But she knew better. She knew Edmond.

She didn't move from the call box. She huddled in its cold shelter as the fog writhed and curled about it. Soon she must call Edmond, make contact with him, but first she must think. Her only hope, Julie's only hope, lay in how cleverly Kay thought. This was her one moment to plan, this moment alone.

Edmond had Julie, but he would not harm her (surely he would not) as long as she was useful to him. And she was useful as a hostage. Her safety was the carrot he would dangle before Kay.

If she called the police . . .

Kay closed her eyes. Oh God, how she wished she could. But if she didn't call Edmond, didn't rise to the bait, Julie was done.

Perhaps, after she talked to him . . .

She reached up to the receiver, then let her hand fall away. 999. That was the number. She could dial it, be connected immediately with Scotland Yard. She lifted her hand, once again let it fall.

Edmond was merciless. If the police closed in on him, he would kill Julie.

No, somehow she must save Julie herself.

But how?

She had no weapon.

There was a gun in her shop in New Orleans, a .22 pistol. She had even shot it once or twice at cans on top of a country fence. John had given the gun to her because robberies can happen to any shopkeeper.

But that was New Orleans.

She didn't know the laws, but she was sure it wasn't easy to get a gun in London. No cheap available .22s at variety stores.

A knife.

Yes, she could buy a knife. There was a hardware store just up the street.

Did she think Edmond would ever give her a chance to use a knife? But perhaps he was sleek and soft, he had been safe so many years.

And hardware stores carry spools of wire. Thin wire makes an excellent garrote.

Once, years ago, she had slipped through tall grass to drop wire over a sentry's head. She had not drawn the wire taut. That lesson had never been put to practice. Yet.

Julie had gone defenseless to meet her aunt.

"Damn you, Edmond."

Kay looked up the number to the gallery, dropped in her coin, dialed.

"Durand Galleries. May I help you?"

"Is Mr. Durand in?"

"Who is calling, please?"

She drew a quick breath. How hard it is to give your name to the enemy. But her voice was cool and even when she answered, "Kay Emory."

"Just a moment, please."

There was a crackling of papers, thinly heard, the faint tinkle of a bell, the cheerful lilt of a whistle, a scrap of conversation, ". . . got it away from Christie's and that . . ."

Kay held onto the receiver so tightly that her hand ached. Where was Julie now? What had Edmond done to her?

"I'm sorry to have kept you waiting, Miss Emory," the receptionist said impersonally, "but Mr. Durand is out of the office now. Can I connect you with Mr. Henderson?"

Kay didn't answer, couldn't, for a moment, make any answer. There should be a message for her, something telling her where to go, what to do . . . Then she realized that Edmond would not expect her to know so quickly of Julie's disappearance. He had taken Julie hostage, knowing that Kay would move against him, opening up his options, blocking hers. This meant that he was prepared to hold Julie a prisoner for some period unless . . .

"Miss Emory, are you there?"

"Yes," she said thinly. "It is very important that I get in touch with Mr. Durand. Did he leave a number where he can be reached?"

The girl's voice was a little distant now. "No, Mr. Durand did not leave a number."

"Do you expect him to call into the gallery this afternoon?"

"I'm afraid I really don't know."

"Listen to me," and Kay's voice was harsh. "Mr. Durand wants to get in touch with me. He wants it very badly. Tell him that I . . . that I wish to see Julie. Do you have that? Tell him I wish to see Julie." She paused and swallowed. "Tell him I do not have access to a telephone but that I will be at this number," she looked up and told the girl the booth number, "at four o'clock this afternoon, again at five."

"If he should call in, I will give him your message, Miss Emory," the receptionist said coldly.

Kay hung up the receiver, pulled open the door to the booth. Surely Edmond would check with his office. If for no other reason, to demonstrate that he couldn't possibly have been kidnapping anyone on November 1, should the question ever arise. If he didn't, well, she would face that problem when it came. She stepped out into the fog and hurried up the street. She had, at the least, some three hours. She would do what she could.

CHAPTER 17

Some things that policemen learn aren't written in books or listed in a manual or practiced at a school. They aren't even tips shared over a pint of bitter. They are the sum total of being a policeman, of walking the streets and asking questions and listening, mostly listening. A policeman's signposts are words, other people's words, spewed out in anger, whispered in betrayal, whined in self-defense, and, sometimes, just sometimes, offered freely with nothing for the speaker to gain.

Early on, a smart policeman learns how to listen, how to school his face to never show surprise or excitement or too sharp an attention for fear of turning off the spigot of words.

Reggie Evans was a smart policeman and he had been at it for a long time, starting out as a constable on a beat, moving to a station house, making it to the CID, working his way up. Now he was a detective inspector at the Yard with a corner glass cubicle for an office, a squad of men under his supervision, and a face that had been schooled for so long that it no longer expressed anything at all, the muscles at the corners of his mouth slack and soft.

He was listening now. His mild blue eyes watched the young man sitting opposite him and, with no expression on his face at all, Evans was summing up Angus Moray. Good mouth, firm chin. Good color. Clear eyes. No nervous tics, no shifting away of the eyes. Been outdoors recently. Didn't work with his hands. Clothes old but good. One of the better universities, likely. Sensible-sounding chap. And he really had the wind up. But Reggie Evans's face expressed neither approval nor disapproval. He merely listened.

"So it's perfectly clear that Miss Fremont's been kidnapped!"

The detective inspector said nothing for a moment, then offered, "There's been a bad fog. She might be lost, still searching for her aunt."

Angus considered it, gritted his teeth, before he answered quietly, "I don't think that's likely, sir. She is . . . she is a small creature and gentle. I think she would call me if she were lost. Besides, the message asking her to meet her aunt was a fake. It wasn't Miss Emory who called."

Inspector Evans listened and he heard more than the words said. The young man truly believed the girl had been kidnapped and was worried. The inspector checked his notes again. Moray had met Miss Fremont yesterday. A quick attraction there, evidently.

Of course, he had only this fresh-faced youngster's word for any of it, when he had met Miss Fremont, what had happened between them. Could be all a put-up job, Miss Fremont's so-called disappearance, to pull the Yard into hunting for the missing aunt. Or Moray might be fooled himself. Perhaps his small and gentle creature was calculating and crafty.

The inspector remembered Dolly Ammerson. She had been small and gently pretty with huge gentian-blue eyes that had shimmered with tears when the judge sentenced her to life imprisonment for the poisoning of two husbands. In the inspector's judgment, she was as cold and venomous as any murderer he ever tracked.

So, Moray might be in league with his pretty girl, or he might be fooled by her—or they might both be as honest as God.

The inspector thought and nothing showed in his face and

eyes, and Angus Moray exploded.

"Inspector, we've got to hurry!" His voice was rough now, a reasonableness gone, nothing left but urgency and the beginnings of anger.

Inspector Evans rubbed a nicotine-stained finger along his nose. "Don't you find it a little hard to believe in a war criminal, Mr. Moray?"

"No." It was a tough word the way Angus said it.

For the first time there was a flicker of interest in Evans's pale-blue eyes. "Why are you so certain, Mr. Moray?"

Angus reached into his coat pocket then and pulled out the letter Kay had written to his father four days earlier.

"Here is the letter Miss Emory left at my house, and here," he reached into an attaché case that rested on the floor, "are some copies they let me make of some SOE files this morning." He handed all of it to the detective. "You'll see, when you look it over, that everything she says in her letter is true, true in every particular. And the SOE files include some reports my father made, as the conducting officer, on her character." Angus frowned. "He thought very highly of her. Highly indeed. He's not here to vouch for her, but I can tell you what a retired colonel told me this morning. He said it took a very special breed to make it in SOE—and I don't think that kind of woman, even twenty years later, would imagine an enemy. And she is not the least hysterical. I told you that we talked at noon when she called expecting to talk to my father. Instead, of course, she learned that he was dead and that her niece was here in England and had apparently walked into a trap."

The detective was skimming the papers Angus had handed him, but when the pause lengthened, he looked up to meet Angus's steady gaze.

"I want you to understand," Angus said firmly, "that she

was shocked at what she learned and fearful for Julie's safety, but there wasn't a tremor in her voice. She sounded absolutely certain of her course—which didn't include you or me. She felt sure it would be a mistake to call in the police."

"But you came to us anyway."

Angus nodded. "For the very reason she didn't come. This 'Edmond,' whoever he may be, must be very desperate."

The detective looked back down at the papers, read them through, neatly stacked them, then nodded to himself. He looked up at Angus. "The odds that we can discover the identity of this 'Edmond' are not very good, Mr. Moray." He paused, then said crisply, "But we will do the best we can," and he reached for his telephone.

"We must be patient, Miss Fremont. It's very difficult to get about in this kind of fog." He crossed to the kitchen door and pulled the curtain aside. "It does look as though it's beginning to lift." He turned around and smiled at Julie. She schooled her face to smile in return. She did not like him, she did not like this cold, forlorn kitchen, and she wished desperately that Kay would hurry. She huddled in her coat and he said quickly, "Here, I'll just light up this fire and it will be cozy in no time. And I'll make us some tea. I'm sure Kay's friends won't mind," and he busied himself at the old-fashioned small gas range, putting on a teakettle, measuring out tea in a pot, setting out cups. Just two cups. When would Kay come?

She had not been in a kitchen like this one in years. She looked around, at the small stove and the white coil refrigerator and the deep white sink. It reminded her of Great-aunt Emily's old worn house. Of course, that house had not even had running water but a well pump out in the back yard and she used to hang on the pump, up and down, up and down, and watch the water splash out until her great-aunt would hurry out, scolding and shooing her away like a chicken. This kitchen even smelled a little like Great-aunt Emily's the last time she had been in it. The old woman was dead and Julie had come with her mother and Kay to help pack things away and get the house ready for sale. There had been the same dry scent, a room closed, stale, dusty.

He was bringing the tea now. Steam curled from the thick brown mugs and she reached out eagerly, welcoming the heat on her icy hands. At first, it was too hot to drink, and when she did manage a gulp or two, she could scarcely hide her disappointment.

"Have I made it too bitter? Here, take a lump or so of sugar."

That helped. She drank the thick bittersweet tea and, for the first time since she had followed him into the cold little kitchen, she began to feel warm.

Why did they stay in the kitchen? she wondered. And whose friends were these of Kay's that kept such a cold and dusty house? And why had Kay sent this man to meet her?

She looked across the white wooden kitchen table at him, looked into dark, watchful eyes.

"Why did Kay call you?" she asked abruptly.

He lit a cigarette, drew deeply on it, and all the while he watched her and she thought again that she did not like him, did not like him at all.

"We knew each other years ago," and his eyes never left Julie's face. "When she called, asked me to meet you, I was only too glad to stand in."

"What exactly did she say?" Julie asked. She lifted her mug, drank the rest of her tea, felt it rush warm down her throat and once again shuddered a little at its bitterness. She didn't think she would try English tea again though, if she were that cold and, admit it, half scared by the way Kay's friend had loomed up out of the fog, she might welcome it. Then she realized he was saying something. She blinked. Suddenly she was hot. She could feel her face flushing. She shook her head back and forth and saw his eyes staring at her, watching her, black and dark, and they seemed to spread into immense dark pools and she was falling, slipping, hot and sleepy, and she could not keep her head up, could not open her eyes.

She slumped, face down, onto the white wooden table. Her pale-blond hair glistened in the light. He watched her for a moment, then nodded to himself and looked down at his watch.

A bell tinkled as Kay pushed through the shop door. She paused just inside to look around the dim interior. It seemed deserted, then she heard the brisk clump of footsteps on the wooden floor. A dumpy, middle-aged woman with wispy gray hair and a friendly smile greeted her.

"It's a raw day to be about. Can I be helping you?"

"Yes. I would like some wire, the kind of wire used to hang pictures. Strong thin wire."

The woman led her down a narrow aisle, past screwdrivers and chisels, hammers and nails, turned left into an even narrower aisle, and peered nearsightedly into a dark corner. "Right about here, yes, here we are," and she found a spool. She unwound a length of wire, held it up for Kay to see.

"About so much." Kay spread her hands two feet apart.

As the clerk snipped the wire, Kay said, "I also wish to look at your knives."

"What sort of knife would you be needing?"

"I don't know exactly. Something sharp. Do you have a display?"

A Settling of Accounts

The knives were near the front of the store in a wooden display case with a curved glass cover. The clerk unlocked and lifted the lid and Kay bent close to the array of knives. She loosened a long, slender, curved knife from its elastic support and edged out the blade.

"Do be careful now, madam. That is a very sharp blade indeed. Sheffield steel, you know, there is none better."

Kay delicately touched the blade. Yes, it was sharp. It would do very well—if she had a chance to use it.

"This one," Kay said.

At the register, the clerk began to ring up the sale.

Kay was handing her the money when she saw, behind the register, well out of public reach, a temporary display of assorted fireworks and Roman candles. The largest firecrackers were about five inches tall and perhaps an inch in diameter.

Gunpowder Treason and Plot.

She paused, billfold in hand. "How much are those firecrackers, the biggest ones?"

She bought ten of them.

On her way back to the boardinghouse, she stopped at the call box and looked up Edmond's home address and telephone number. If he didn't check with his office, didn't call her at four o'clock, perhaps she would make the first move. Perhaps not. It would take so little to put Julie in greater danger. Julie's safety was all that mattered. Her sister's daughter, the last of her family.

The fog still swirled, curling like smoke from a chimney, but it was thinning, a soft breeze blowing it away, rustling tree branches until they dripped moisture with soft country splats onto the sidewalks. Cars claimed the streets again, people walked briskly along and London was no longer lost and mysterious.

Kay made one last stop, at a small grocery, and bought a tin of crackers. She hurried with her purchases back to the boardinghouse. She locked the door of her room behind her, then emptied out her sacks on the writing table near the window.

A loop of wire, a knife, ten firecrackers, a biscuit tin.

She hung up her coat and sat down across the room from the table. She lit a cigarette, smoked it quietly, thought.

How and how and how?

The wire and the knife, they were easy to conceal.

But how could she use the black powder?

How and how and how?

The cracker tin wouldn't do. Why had she bought it? But, of course, you can't empty gunpowder into any old container, and she had bought the first thing that had occurred to her. But Edmond, no matter how sleek and soft he had become, would not miss anything so obvious as a homemade bomb. And he would search her, she must expect that.

The cigarette burned at her fingers. She stubbed it out, then picked up her purse to fish out her cigarette case—and stopped and looked at her purse.

The alligator hide glistened even in the dim light of the small bedroom. It was rich and warm and lovely, a handbag to last out the years, full size with a broad base so that it could be set down and wouldn't slump or tip. A woman's bag, not a girl's, plenty of room, compartments on each side—but no divider in the middle. She opened it wide, touched the silk-lined interior, then jumped up from the chair and hurried to the bed and dumped everything out.

A big handbag. Odd, a minor thought ran, an obbligato to the clever, concentrated planning, it was the handbag and shoes which had saved her at the department store, catching the pretty young clerk's eye so that she knew Kay had not come to her counter. This very same handbag.

Empty, it seemed even larger. Kay studied it for a moment, ran an exploratory hand along the interior base, then she turned to the table and picked up the knife, the new sharp knife.

CHAPTER 18

It was cold in the call box, cold and damp. Kay waited and worried. She wanted a cigarette, wanted it badly, but this was too enclosed a space to chance it.

The telephone rang promptly at four. She yanked at the receiver.

"Hello."

"So you're there."

"Yes. Where is Julie? Is she all right?"

He hesitated, then asked, his voice so soft as to be almost inaudible, "What makes you think I know where Julie is?"

Clever Edmond. He would take no chances, make no admissions. Yet, he had to know how she had discovered Julie's absence. She had, as she worked and planned that afternoon, known that Edmond would ask, and she knew also that she did not want to tell him about Angus. Angus was her safety line.

"I called the hotel," she said quickly. "To see if there had been any messages for me—and that's when I found out that Julie had left the hotel supposedly to meet me. I knew, of course, what must have happened."

There was a long silence while he considered her answer. She could hear, faintly, the regular, even sound of his breathing. Her hand clung to the receiver. Would he believe her, would he? She must not lose contact with Edmond, must not.

"I don't trust you, Kay."

"You don't have to trust me, Edmond. You have—"

He cut her off sharply. "Save it." He took a deep breath.

"Listen closely, Kay. Follow my directions exactly. If you do not, I am quite sure you will not see—someone you would very much like to see. Do you understand?"

"Yes, Edmond. I understand."

She understood and she didn't doubt him.

"Take the Underground to Trafalgar and wait at Nelson's Column."

And he hung up.

So he wasn't going to take any chances on her calling the police. He was going to be very sure she was alone, that no one was following her, before he approached. If he thought she was observed, he would walk away and she would wait to no avail, and Julie . . . Kay pushed out of the call box and shivered, not only at the sharper cold. He must come to her.

She changed at Piccadilly Circus to the Bakerloo Line and rode the short hop to Trafalgar. It was there that she stopped long enough to buy stamps and mail the bulky letter to Angus. If she did not manage somehow to outwit Edmond, to save Julie and herself, he would not be free of them. This letter would make sure of that, and if he didn't pay for France, he would pay for Julie.

No one fed the pigeons in Trafalgar Square this misty late afternoon. Heads bent, people crossed it on their way to catch buses. The dark cement squares glistened wetly, reflecting headlights and a neon sign that blinked redly across the street. The huge bronze lions on their marble bases reminded her of how London sloughed away the years. She and Lionel had leaned against those bases, fed corn to pigeons. War workers had piled sandbags here. Peace marchers had rallied here. The old had rested on benches, and one day had not returned. Sun and rain and years and Nelson's Column remained. She crossed to it. Her footsteps seemed loud and intrusive in the nearly empty square.

She walked nervously up and down, and the minutes slipped past. Soon it was quite dark and the traffic thickened and the lights swept and curved around the square. She was cold and getting colder and she hunched deep inside her coat and tucked one hand protectively around the end of her purse to try and keep it dry from the all-pervading mist. Five minutes. Ten. Twenty. Where was Edmond? Surely he would come. Please God, have him come.

Every so often she would stop and look searchingly up and down the square and across the streets, toward the National Gallery, then toward the Arch. But nowhere in all the mass of umbrellas and hurrying people did she see Edmond. Her eyes skimmed over the old woman shuffling along, clutching a net shopping bag, and the trio of shop girls and the teen-age boy who slouched toward her, hands deep in his corduroy pants pockets.

So it caught her by surprise when the boy came straight to her, not swerving away at the last minute, and thrust an envelope into her hands.

She looked down at the pale blob of paper, then lifted her head to look for him and he was already gone in the mist and darkness. She took a pointless step or two, then stopped and looked again at the envelope. She tore it open, pulled out the sheet and held it up, but it was too dark where she stood to read what was written. She hurried to the nearest street lamp.

There was a single sentence.

"Walk down the Mall alongside the park."

That was all, no salutation, no signature, nothing more on either side.

Once through the Arch and hurrying along the leaf-strewn sidewalk by the park, she felt every second more vulnerable. She passed no one. Far ahead she saw one solitary walker. Cars streamed past, their lights emphasizing the dark emptiness of the park to her left. The occasional lamp, its light softened and smudged by the mist and darkness, showed only empty paths, heaps of leaves, deserted benches. She could just see, through the bare trees, the dark shape of the bandshell. One summer day, she and Lionel had stretched out in the grass and spent an afternoon, listening to a concert, looking at each other. Their hands had met to hold a book of Keats's poems . . . "Ay, in the very temple of Delight Veil'd Melancholy has her sovereign shrine . . ." She bent against the sharp, cold air, walked faster. Now the bare-branched trees, the whistle of tires over wet pavement, the slap of her shoes over sodden leaves, breathed the essence of melancholy.

Her leg was beginning to tire. She looked back over her shoulder and realized that she had walked a long way. She paused, studied the empty park whose occasional lights only emphasized its gloom, then once again began to walk.

She was almost to the Queen Victoria Memorial when a small Ford slipped up to the curb beside her and the front door swung open.

"Hurry."

It was dim on the sidewalk, the nearest street lamp fifty yards ahead. She came close to the car, bent low to look inside. The interior lights had not come on when the door opened, and it was this that made the car look so forbidding.

The motor raced. "Hurry," he called out brusquely.

There was no turning back now. This was the beginning of the final turn of the wheel, the culmination of those innocent days so long ago in Nice.

She slipped into the seat and the car began to accelerate even before she shut the door. Even so, she twisted to look over into the back seat. The little car was changing lanes, gaining speed, and Edmond checked and rechecked the traffic behind him in his rearview mirror.

"Where is Julie?"

"Waiting for us." He stopped for a traffic light and reached over to take her hands. She shrank back against the door. For an instant his fingers closed painfully about her wrist, then, yanking her hands together, he looped rubber tubing around them, tied it, then tucked the long, loose end of the tubing under his thigh. A horn tooted behind them, he shifted and they were off, veering around the Memorial to the right.

If she moved her hands, tried to grasp anything, he would know it. Clever Edmond. She was as immobilized as if tied hand and foot. But she didn't, at the moment, need her hands. First, she must see Julie.

"Edmond, you will let Julie go?"

"That can be arranged, Kay. It all depends on you."

He was turning again now, into Green Park. He had slowed a little and, though he continued to flick quick glances at the rearview mirror, the air of tension in the car lessened and, when he swerved the car at the last moment to the left as the road forked and no car turned after them, he smiled briefly.

"Everything is going to work out," he said then.

She stared at his profile and wondered at evil in such ordinary guise. He was still handsome, some might even think handsomer than he had been as a young man. Thick black hair that curled slightly, broad curved forehead and slightly hooked nose, but now the face was sharper, harder, more commanding, a tough, elegant face that looked every bit as dangerous as it was. Abruptly, Kay was afraid. She had lost to Edmond in France. How could she think she would do better now?

Because she *had* to. For herself and her sister and for the memory of brave men, she had to succeed. And she would.

He turned then, met her eyes.

"You should have gone back to America." He turned left onto Piccadilly. "Why did you stay in London?"

She didn't answer.

"No one can . . ." He broke off.

She watched him, then she smiled and asked silkily, "Can't they, Edmond? I think a good many things can be proven—if not, you've gone to a good deal of unnecessary bother. Haven't you?"

The car lunged ahead faster.

"If the police look in France, they'll find—"

His left hand slashed out toward her and the back of it caught her full across the cheek. Her head slammed against the seat and she felt blood where she had bitten her tongue, but she almost said it again, wanted to fling accusations at him, watch him worry that she might carry a tiny recorder, luxuriate in the crumbling of his confidence.

She wanted to, the words formed in her mind, but she held them back. Too much too soon and Edmond might strike fatally at her, and then there would be no one to save Julie. That he intended to kill her and to kill Julie was certain. He would delay only until the time seemed safest to him. And there is no question that it is easier to move live hostages than inert bodies. There was a delicate balance. A hostage always hopes and so he will walk one more step, and whether those steps lead ultimately to freedom or to a gas chamber is the gamble both sides take. So Kay clenched her teeth, held her peace.

He hunched over the wheel. He drove faster yet. They sped down Piccadilly, then left it suddenly and began to turn and twist in streets she had never known. She had no idea where they were when he made a final turn into a narrow, dark alley, paved with bricks, that was scarcely large enough for the small car to negotiate. Garage doors lined the way. A wall suddenly loomed up ahead. of them, a gray stone wall slick with moss. He stopped the car and she realized it was a cul-de-sac. He dimmed the lights and turned to look at her.

"I will get out to open the garage door. You understand, Kay, that your cooperation guarantees Julie's continued good health."

It was a light, faint whisper. Nothing that could be picked up by a recorder.

She nodded.

He left nothing to chance. He took the key as he stepped out of the car and he watched her as he pulled up the garage door. He moved quickly, quickly, and she knew he didn't want a neighbor to stray by, to see her in his car. Could she reach her purse, pull it to her . . . But he was back in the car then, shutting the door quietly, turning on the motor, driving the car into the garage, fitting it snugly between the wall and a panel truck with scarcely enough room left on either side to open the doors.

He switched the lights off immediately, then twisted to look out into the dark alley. No lights shone. No one walked by.

"Where is Julie?" she demanded.

"You will be with her in a moment, Kay. But first, I want to be sure that you do not . . . outrage my hospitality," and he was moving across the seat toward her and his hands touched her, searching for a knife, a gun, a transmitter. She sat rigid, hating the feel of his flesh against hers, Judas hands.

He was thorough, but his fingers slipped over the wire that she had twisted about one wrist to simulate a bracelet. If he saw it, of course, he would know, but in the dark, hurrying, did he think it just a piece of primitive jewelry? Then she held her breath, for he was reaching down for her purse.

The clasp clicked open and he was rummaging inside. She breathed out slowly, trying not to attract his attention.

She knew the very instant that he found the knife, knew by the way his face turned toward her, a pale irregular shape in the darkness. It took him a moment to work it free. She had wedged it cleverly, slicing a neat aperture in the lining, pushing it behind the slick silk, but he must have felt its shape. She heard the lining rip as he forced the knife free.

He lifted it out of the purse, turned it this way and that, and once again the pale shape of his face turned toward her and she saw his hand move, and then the tip of the blade pressed against her throat.

CHAPTER 19

"Hush now, Julie, it's all right, it's all right, everything's going to be all right." It was a gentle croon, but still the girl struggled to sit up, and all the while she moaned drowsily.

For this space of time, jostling along in the back of the panel truck, Julie's head on her lap, Kay didn't worry about what was going to happen. She knew that soon, within the next few minutes, the next few hours, she would face Edmond for the final time. She knew, it was so clear when he pressed the tip of the knife against her throat, that he intended to kill her. He had almost done it then, had almost thrust the blade into her flesh, almost. But there would be so much blood, and she thought the little yellow station wagon was his. So much blood, and blood so hard to remove, so difficult to explain.

Edmond would arrange it so that he would have nothing to explain, nothing to link him to the disappearance of an American woman and her niece. She wondered clinically just what he intended. Did he have a country house in thick woods? The ground soft from autumn rains, mounds of leaves humped against fences? Or perhaps a cottage near the sea, the sea which so often does not give up its dead.

Julie struggled again, trying to pull away.

"It's all right, Julie. Everything is all right."

"Kay!" There was thanksgiving and relief and love in Julie's voice, then, abruptly, uncertainty and the beginnings of fear, "Kay, where are we? What's happened? Who . . ."

"At the moment," Kay said calmly, "we are bumping along in the back of Edmond's panel truck. Where we are

234

going more precisely than that, I don't know. But I . . ."

Julie's hand closed tightly on Kay's wrist. "Edmond? Then . . . Oh Kay, he's caught you through me, hasn't he? That's what's happened, isn't it?"

"It's all right, Julie. Edmond and I, well, we would have met, sooner or later. And, since Angus, my Angus, is dead, it would have been sooner."

"Kay, I'm so sorry," and it was an anguished whisper.

"No more of that." Kay's voice was sharp for an instant. "Things happen as they must, Julie. Besides, we aren't helpless, not at all. I don't intend to let Edmond have his way, you know. We will be very alert and there are the two of us. I want you to promise me that you'll do just as I say, exactly as I say. I don't know what will happen, how we can outwit him, but I'm certain that we shall—and I must depend upon you to follow my lead."

Julie was still muzzy from the drug, half sick at her stomach, overwhelmingly aware that she had landed them in the hands of the enemy. "Of course," she said quickly, "I promise, Kay. Don't worry, you can count on me, whatever you say, I'll do."

But she didn't see what they could hope to do and she shivered, remembering those black eyes that had watched her across the white wooden table, bleak, wary black eyes.

"Are you cold?" Kay asked quickly.

"Oh no, no."

Kay slipped her arm around her niece's shoulders, but knew she had no comfort for fear except perhaps the greatest comfort of all, the presence of another human being. "It will be all right," she said once again, and she said it as though it were a fact, irrefutable, certain, destined. And if she were wrong, Julie would still have taken comfort while she could.

"Kay?" Perhaps it was the total blackness, the invisibility

of each to the other, that gave Julie the courage to ask. Perhaps it was the nearness of oblivion and a desperate necessity to know the reason why. "Kay, who is Edmond? What . . . what did he do?"

What did Edmond do?

It was a long moment before Kay said slowly, "It all began that summer in Nice . . ."

The summer of 1938 in Nice. Water so sharply blue it made your eyes ache. Silky, languorous, sun-baked air. The sweet, thick scent of orange blossoms.

Kay celebrated her seventeenth birthday that June, a candlelit dinner and champagne, her grandmother beaming at her from the head of the table. Dear Grand'mère, black-eyed and plump and spritely, loving life, loving Kay, proud of her beautiful granddaughter. Of all the five American grandchildren, it was Kay who chose to visit France most often, who felt most at home, who decided that summer of '38 to stay in France to finish her schooling.

It was late in the summer, when heat lay over Nice in shimmering waves, Kay remembered later especially how hot it was that afternoon, that her grandmother called to her from the shadowy coolness of the drawing room.

Madame Varney laid aside the small leatherbound volume she had been reading and reached up a hand to Kay. "Come sit with me, my dear."

"Oh Grandmama, the others are waiting on the beach. Edmond has found a paddle boat and . . ."

Her grandmother interrupted and her usually soft, kind voice was almost brusque. "Edmond. Edmond Lorillard?"

"Yes." Kay smiled, taking an innocent pride in her conquest, pleased that the handsome young Frenchman followed her with his eyes whenever she was near, moved to be close to her on the beach, was almost openly rude to Lionel, who had come down from Paris to spend a week with his sister, who was Kay's guest. Kay's mouth curved in a satisfied smile. "He's cute, isn't he?"

Her grandmother's plump face creased in a frown. "Are you . . ." She hesitated, then asked, "Do you care for him, Kay?"

"Care for him?"

Kay was seventeen, realizing slowly, delightfully, her own femininity, luxuriating in the caress of sun and water against tanned skin, accepting homage from Edmond as naturally as a flower accepts sunshine, yet, at the same time, aware of Lionel in a different, far more subtle and compelling way.

"Oh Grandmama, you are too serious, *trop serieuse*." She jumped up from the sofa, eager to be down with the others. She paused long enough to drop a kiss on her grandmother's head. "I care for everybody and nobody. Edmond . . ." She shrugged. "Edmond is handsome and he is here this summer and follows me like a spaniel. That doesn't mean anything."

She was turning away when her grandmother caught her wrist. "Kay, it may mean a great deal to Edmond. You see, in France a young lady doesn't encourage a man unless she cares for him. I think Edmond is courting you. It would be a very good match for him."

The dim, shadowy room, shuttered against the heat, seemed suddenly oppressive. "A good match," Kay repeated. "That's scarcely flattering," and her voice was dry.

"I did not mean it to be flattering," her grandmother replied. "Edmond's mother was widowed many years ago. She has worked very hard as a seamstress and she has given him many advantages not usually available to boys of his class. Edmond is a good student and he earned a scholarship to Grenoble, but he has no prospects, Kay. He is studying medieval art when he would do better to work at something practical, engineering or the law. It would be very helpful to Edmond to have a wealthy wife."

Kay was angry now. And she was never angry with her grandmother. "I did not know that . . . that money meant so much to you, Grandmama. Would it be all right for Edmond to court me, as you put it, if he were rich, like Alphonse? Would you . . ."

Her grandmother interrupted sharply, "You mistake me, Kay. I would never object to a young man because he was poor, even if I thought it would always be a struggle for the both of you. But I do not think Edmond will be poor. No, that is not the problem. I think, indeed, that Edmond will do well —at whatever the cost. I have watched him come here, I have seen the way he looks at you—and it is the same way that he looks at my silver, at the Matisse on that wall, at the Aubusson in the study." The old woman pushed back a gray hair that was straggling into her face. "Edmond does not love you, Kay. But he would like to possess you."

Kay felt the hot prick of tears behind her eyes. "That is an awful, a horrible way to talk about Edmond. We are only having fun, Grandmama. It doesn't mean anything, anything at all."

Her grandmother shook her head. "It may mean nothing to you, Kay. I am afraid it means too much to Edmond. In France . . ." Then her voice fell away because Kay was already pushing through the French window, hurrying out into the garden, on her way to the beach.

Lionel's one week stretched into two and then a third. Kay swam and danced and smiled, at Edmond and at Lionel, and, if her eyes held Lionel's longer, if she touched him when she could, if they clung to each other for an instant the afternoon they swam into the depths of a grotto, then only the two of them knew, Kay and Lionel.

And Edmond was always there. Especially he was there after Lionel returned to Paris. Every afternoon, Edmond bicycled out the winding coastal road to Madame Varney's villa to go down to the private shingled beach at the foot of the cliff.

Usually there were four or five bathers, Edmond, Kay, Betty, Jeanne, the daughter of a nearby family, and her brother Alphonse. But this particular August afternoon, the brother and sister had telephoned not to expect them and Betty had picked up too much sun the day before, so only Edmond and Kay were gathering up towels and the hamper with cool fresh orange juice and small thin sandwiches wrapped in linen. They were laughing, balancing the hamper between them, when Madame Varney came into the kitchen.

"Bonjour, madame," Edmond said quickly.

The older woman nodded, looked inquiringly around the kitchen, then turned to Kay. "Where are the others, *cherie?"*

When Kay had explained, her grandmother said slowly, "I don't believe it is a good idea for only two to bathe."

It was abruptly very quiet in the kitchen. Edmond lifted his head, stared at Madame Varney, and a slow flush stained his face. Kay drew in her breath sharply.

"But Grandmama, we bathe every afternoon—and Edmond is our guest."

The old lady raised her chin. "Yes, and I know as our guest that he will wish to please me. The water can be very treacherous—I do not wish two alone to venture into it. Our cliff is so secluded, so private that no one could come to your aid. I only trust bathing when there is a group."

Kay bit her lip, then smiled at her grandmother and said, "You worry so and you needn't. It will be all right. Edmond and I promise not to swim. We will carry down our little lunch and throw rocks into the water. I promise that we won't bathe."

Madame Varney almost spoke, then shook her head and sighed as Kay and Edmond left the kitchen.

As they stepped carefully down the twisting staircase hewn out of the cliff face, Edmond said bitterly, "I should not come again. Your grandmother does not like me. She does not want you to be alone with me."

The steps curved around the cliff now, on the sea side, and the two of them were alone, no one to see them, no one to hear them, only the warm, living rock face next to them and, beneath them, the surging water.

They paused. The wind off the sea blew against them. Sea spume touched them like a magic mist.

Edmond turned to Kay and he was close to her, so close she could feel his warmth.

"You do like me?" he asked.

The sun beat down on her, the spray beaded his skin. "Of course I do, Edmond," and she was suddenly in his arms and the hamper fell at their feet. She was so young and everything was a beginning and his lips were warm and gentle. She kissed him once more and then she broke away and ran on down the steps.

He did not kiss her again, but they lay side by side that warm lovely afternoon and were incredibly aware of each other. She had kissed him that afternoon because her grandmother had embarrassed him, because he was handsome and near, because the sun shone and she was seventeen.

That was the last afternoon that they bathed. A late-summer storm darkened the Provençal sky. Rain plummeted down and the water roiled at the cliff base.

Kay and Betty were packing, ready to return to Paris for school, when the maid knocked at their door to tell Kay that

A Settling of Accounts

Edmond awaited her downstairs.

It was storming again. Rain washed so hard against the windowpanes that the shrubs and bent grass beyond were gray and indistinct. He was staring out the rain-blurred windows, waiting for her.

"Edmond, how nice of you to come."

He jerked around to face her.

She smiled and would have reached out her hand, but he stood so stiff and straight. Then she saw that he wore a black suit and carried a bouquet. The flowers were bent from the force of the rain and still dripped a little. Roses and sprigs of orange blossom. They gave off a heavy, sweet scent that spread through the room like honey oozing from a spilled pot.

He thrust the bouquet toward her.

She took it. "Why, thank you, Edmond. It's so thoughtful of you to come and say good-bye."

He looked suddenly uncertain and she wondered what she could have said that disappointed him, what it was that he expected.

"I would have wished to have spoken to your father," he began. Kay wondered wildly what on earth he was talking about.

"My father?"

Edmond nodded solemnly. "Yes, that would have been more correct. But he is so many miles from here, I cannot do that." He frowned and his face was dark. "I will not speak first to Madame Varney, for she does not like me and would not believe that we love each other."

"Love . . ." Kay said faintly.

Edmond was fumbling at his coat pocket.

Kay watched, hoping that she had misunderstood. Then, triumphantly, he pulled the small square box from his pocket. He held it in his palm and slowly lifted the lid and she could see the silver ring with its tiny diamond stone.

She was shaking her head, back and forth, back and forth.

He looked up, saw that, and his face changed and it was terrible to watch, agonizing to see his shock and humiliation and the beginnings of a great anger.

"I'm so sorry," she began.

He stared at her and the dark flush she had seen once before suffused his face. "You kissed me. On the beach."

She shook her head, back and forth, back and forth. "I didn't mean . . ."

His hand closed on the little box, crushed it, crumpling the cheap pasteboard. Then he stuffed the twisted lump into his pocket. He didn't look at her again. Head down, he stormed past her. He flung back the drawing-room door so hard that a vase teetered on the table beside her, then tipped to roll and fall onto the floor and shatter. It was a Chantilly vase, a pale, delicate cream color, a favorite of her grandmother's. It was shattered beyond repair. Kay knelt. She lay down the damp, drooping bouquet and began to pick up the tiny pieces.

But some things, when broken, can never be restored.

CHAPTER 20

It was cold, riding on the bare metal flooring of the van. They found two moving pads stacked in a near corner and, dusty as they were, spread them out like blankets, and that was better. The van kept a steady pace, tires whishing rhythmically over a wet roadway. Occasionally, it would briefly slow and Kay knew they must be passing through another little town.

Where were they going? What was Edmond going to do with them?

She patted her handbag again. Yes, it was here. She opened it and reached in and her fingers checked for her cigarette lighter. There it was. She wanted a cigarette, but she knew better than to chance it in the darkness. If a spark touched too near . . . Was there anything more volatile than black powder?

Then her fingers strayed to the coil of wire around her wrist. Somehow, one way or the other, she would manage.

Julie moved restlessly and Kay began to talk quietly again. "I didn't see Edmond again, of course, before we left for Paris, Betty and I." How long ago it was, the fall of 1938, and she and Betty traveling northward by train, Lionel meeting them at the station. Odd to think that no one foresaw war. At least, none of them did. They did not know how close death rode to them, had no least inkling that Betty would perish in the ruins of her home, which had stood for two hundred years, and that Lionel . . .

"We never thought of war," Kay said slowly into the darkness. It was the October of Munich, but they scarcely noticed, walking in the Tuileries, sharing roasted chestnuts, watching little boys in gray short pants and ragged sweaters sail homemade boats in the Round Pond. So many little memories, the Reverend Mother leading them in prayer, the news from Czechoslovakia, Betty laughing at a pantomime in the park, and, always, memories of Lionel, for it was that winter when she began to fall in love with him. Some things are difficult to tell.

"We had . . . such a happy winter. Lionel was still at the Sorbonne, you understand. He had at least another year before he would finish. He stayed in Paris the next summer and once again Betty and I went to Nice to visit Grandmama. We did not see Edmond. I heard he had been called up. But, to be honest, I scarcely gave him a thought. Then it was September again, September of 1939, and the Germans crossed into Poland—and the war began."

"Did you leave for England then?"

"No. It's odd, Julie, but that first winter of the war, things were much the same." She tried to explain that winter of the Phony War and everyone's faith in the Maginot Line, their conviction that Hitler couldn't defeat France.

"Hitler started his offensive in the spring," and like so many children's blocks, the countries fell, and, finally, France fell, too, and Kay and Betty were among the thousands of refugees clogging the road to the south. It took them three days to reach Nice.

"I tried, so hard, to persuade Grandmama to come with us to England and then home to America with me."

But the old lady wouldn't budge. Her two widowed sisters, her brother in Bordeaux, she wouldn't leave them even to come to the home of her only daughter in New Orleans.

Kay had begged.

Madame Varney pleated her skirt with nervous fingers. "I know *Les Boches*. I am . . ." and her voice broke, "I am afraid of them. But I cannot leave France." She shook her head slowly, tears in her eyes. "We survived the Great War. We shall survive again."

Kay and Betty stayed long enough to help hide the silver and set by a store of food, then they squeezed aboard a crowded bus to Marseille.

"We caught the last boat out."

A little breathing space in England, the stirrings of pride and hope over Dunkirk, then the Battle of Britain and Lionel in the thick of it.

"I was so glad when his hand was hurt. I'm ashamed now. If he hadn't been wounded, if I hadn't told SOE how well he spoke French . . ."

But she had. And SOE called both of them to serve.

Kay described it as well as she could, that faraway autumn after the bombs destroyed Lionel's home. "We knew what the odds were. We knew we were on our own once we got back to France. We knew what the Gestapo would do." She was silent for a long moment. "But I suppose you never really believe it will happen to you. You can't think that and go into it. We were sure somehow that we would survive, the two of us. Together."

They had worked hard, learned their lessons.

"Je suis Marie Deschamps," Kay said softly.

Everything began beautifully.

A Rumanian countess, Olga Rakovsky, had managed to send word to London that her villa, on a headland south of Nice, would welcome British agents, be willing to provide a base of operations for the setting up of a circuit. The countess had worked for British Intelligence in World War I and had no love for Germans. They had murdered her husband in 1916. She was fifty-four in 1941, an elegant, aloof, somber woman whose rare smile was as striking as a shaft of sunlight in a Velasquez canvas.

The countess was waiting with her manservant, Andre, on the shingle beach when the felucca out of Gibraltar slipped into the deep secluded waters of the cove that balmy spring morning in 1941 and three dim and shadowy shapes debarked, Lionel and Kay and their wireless operator, quiet and steady Lisette.

The countess gave each of them a firm handshake and in less than twenty minutes, before dawn edged the sky with curving, climbing swaths of rose and pearl, the three of them were safe in their new lives, Lisette en route to Grasse, the tiny perfume town in the rolling hills behind Nice, and Lionel and Kay ensconced in the small loft of the stable which the countess had converted to a garage and potting shed and all-purpose storage area. They were now Marie and Paul Deschamps, a couple attending the countess, Marie a maid and Paul a gardener. As an Englishman bred, he was well at home with all growing things, though still awkward with his maimed right hand. The hand was, however, as an actual, evident wound, excellent support for Paul Deschamps' record of service in the French Second Army and his wounding during the fighting near Sedan.

Kay and Lionel's field names were Nicole and Pierre. Their instructions were to set up a network of future sabo-teurs, to explore the countryside and find good dropping areas, to distribute supplies to trusted subagents. They had with them their personal suitcase, a second suitcase with plastic explosive, a third with a supply of pencil-shaped deto-nators, and a shabby velvet valise, stuffed with five hundred thousand francs.

"It began so well," Kay said quietly. "And we had each other for six months." She hesitated. How much should she tell Julie? Then she went ahead, told all of it, for surely Julie would understand. Even with the fear and the horror that would see the end of it, Kay had always been able to look back and know for that space of time she had loved and been loved. And she knew that the reality of love is not measured in hours.

"It was a natural mistake on the countess's part. She assumed that since London had told her to expect Paul and Marie Deschamps, that we were a married couple. And London had warned us never to tell anything about ourselves, that we were Paul and Marie Deschamps, that we should never confide anything about our former selves to the people we met. So we didn't correct the countess that morning we landed.

"That first day was such a busy one. There was so much for us to learn. We had breakfast, rolls and honey and a thick, sweet chocolate, and the countess told us, quickly, quickly, so many things, the name of the couple whose place we had taken, the color of the bus we had ridden from Nantes, the latest announcements from Vichy, the kinds of German officers vacationing on the beaches, the names of collaborators to avoid.

"I was washing up our dishes when there was a brisk knock at the kitchen door. That was the first time I realized how frightening it is to be outside the law. My hands began to shake. I knew I mustn't show fear, but all I could think of was the Gestapo. I plunged my hands into the dishwater to hide them. I know that we were all afraid, even Lionel, for we stood so still and you could not hear a breath in that narrow kitchen, then the knock sounded again and the door opened and this plump face peered around the door, bristly eyebrows and bushy gray hair, smiling eyes. Then I saw his collar and I was able to breathe again."

"Monsieur le cure, bonjour," the countess said in relief.

"Bonjour, mes amis." He bowed to the countess, then looked at Lionel and Kay, his bright, dark eyes noting their damp clothes and closed faces. He listened gravely as the countess introduced them as her servants, explaining that they had been part of the staff at her home in Nantes and she had sent for them to come to Nice for the duration. He nodded gently, then a delighted smile creased his face. He was circumspect, however. "I am so happy to know that madame the countess will have adequate service in her villa now." He paused, then said very clearly, "I wish to welcome you to our village. There are many here who will wish to assist you in doing the very best job that you can."

He stayed for tea with madame and their talk would not have interested any German, about the necessity of some new vestments and how the cloth might be obtained, of the baptism planned on the next Sunday for the new daughter of the *commissaire de police,* of a special collection for orphans. It was only as he was leaving, politely bowing one more time at the door, that he told madame, "If your new man, Paul, has time tomorrow, I would appreciate some help on repairing the roof of the sacristy." He nodded genially to himself. "I'll expect him about nine o'clock."

So the first contact was made, effortlessly. Everything that first day went well. Lionel retrieved the suitcases and, of course, the shabby valise. He carried them out to the converted stable and plumped them into a shadowy corner, not even going upstairs to the loft. Then he hurried out and set to work in the garden under the countess's directions, working and asking quick, soft-voiced questions, learning some of the many things they would need to know, the curfew hour, what control points had been set up, additions to the rationed list, prices on the black market, estimates of the police chief's loyalties, rumors of resistance, patrols on the coastal roads,

Vichy supporters, and more and more.

Kay was busy in the kitchen. She was dismayed at the great age of the stove and the size of the tiny ice box which would hold a jar of milk and a bowl of butter and little else. But the kitchen was spotless, the pans ranged neatly in the cupboards, the shelves recently scrubbed. There was not much food, but she managed a reasonably good dinner.

How clearly she remembered that first dinner, the countess served alone in the dining room, she and Lionel eating together later in the kitchen. An omelet, asparagus with a mild cheese sauce, a green salad, a bottle of chablis. Lionel helped her wash up. They continued to speak in French but, alone together, they could say what they wished.

Lionel was exhilarated.

He stood beside the huge old-fashioned sink in his black wool trousers and heavy black shoes, a white shirt with long sleeves rolled up to the elbow, and dried the dishes awkwardly but swiftly. "Tomorrow I'll try to get us a couple of bicycles. We need to be able to move around better. You can take the ration cards in and do the shopping. Take your time and be on the lookout for good places for drops. I think we'll have some agents on a string as soon as I've talked to the priest tomorrow."

"Lionel, you will be careful?"

"Careful?" He repeated the word as if it were entirely strange to him, then relented at the evident worry in her eyes. "Lady, you can count on me. I've got more reasons than any man I know to hang on to tomorrow."

"Reasons?"

He plopped the dishtowel down on the drainboard and gathered her up in his arms. "You," he kissed her, "and you," he kissed her again, "and you."

Then, abruptly, he pushed her away and said a little indistinctly, "But I have a little trouble sometimes remembering that tomorrow isn't here yet."

They were quiet then as they locked up the kitchen for the night and Kay led the way outside to the stable. She had carried up the suitcases that afternoon, unpacked their personal one, putting away their clothes into the bare wooden drawers of the small chest. The white cotton gown with a bottom row of three ruffles rested atop one pillow, the pink-and-gray pajamas lay on the other.

She walked up the narrow loft stairs, opened the door and waited for Lionel to enter.

He stopped just past the threshold and looked at the small bare room, wooden walls, wooden floor, a small dresser with a cracked mirror, a scarred and peeling chest and scarcely room enough left in the narrow room for the double bed.

He ran a hand through his thick blond hair and half turned toward Kay.

"I say, I hadn't even thought about the couple's room. But this, uh, this won't do. We'll have to see about . . ."

His voice trailed off. The villa wouldn't run to twin beds. There wasn't room for another bed. And what excuse could the cook and gardener give for living in other than their rightful quarters?

Kay smiled a little tremulously. "I'd say, Lionel, that agents in the field have to . . . adjust to the realities."

He stared down at her.

He took a hesitant step toward her and then she moved into his arms and managed to say, "Lionel, I love you," before his mouth covered hers.

CHAPTER 21

So that was love, Julie thought, a gift freely made, not in answer to a demand but in warm and mutual consent. She had come a long way to learn this, to understand that love is giving, not taking.

"I loved him very much," Kay said simply. "We had six months together."

Together. Running the risks they were sent to take, seeking out agents, riding bicycles down country roads to check on drop sites, gathering information on possible sabotage, then night would fall and the sweet scent of orange blossoms drifted into their room and the soft sea-scented breeze rustled palm leaves and they would be together and nothing existed but themselves.

The summer passed. Hillsides glistened with the golden mantles of mimosa. Roses bloomed richly red. The vividly blue water rolled into shore. It was hard to remember danger in the midst of beauty, the shark's hungry mouth, the slither of an electric eel, the sting of bumblebees.

Summer slipped into fall and they moved to the rhythm of Nice. It was in mid-September, as she was walking home from the market, that she heard a car coming up behind, changing into a low, whining growl to manage the steep gradient of the hill. There were few cars in Nice and its outlying villages that summer. For Vichy officials, perhaps. She kept her eyes on the grassy verge, remembered not to walk too fast. Be inconspicuous, unnoticed. Safe. The car came even with her, then it slowed. Her heart thudded but she kept on walking, slowly.

What caught his attention? Was it something about her walk, though she tried to move stolidly? Was it the shape of her back, familiar to him even in the heavy, strange clothing?

The car was stopping now, pulling off the road in front of her. The driver's door opened. She looked up. Her lips moved, whispering over and over, *"Je suis Marie Deschamps,"* and then she stopped, for Edmond was walking toward her, his dark eyes staring into hers.

"Kay!" He stopped a few feet from her and stared, still scarcely believing his eyes. But she saw quick understanding on his face. He knew it was her and he knew there could be but one reason for her to be in France.

Then he nodded very formally and spoke to her in French. "You will forgive me. For a moment, I mistook you for an old friend of mine."

She murmured that it was all right, quite all right.

But he did not move out of her way. "I am Edmond Lorillard."

She hesitated, then said, "I am Marie Deschamps."

"Have you been in Nice long?"

Kay was wary, but what could she do? "We arrived this spring, monsieur."

"We?"

She nodded and looked at him steadily. "Yes. My husband Paul and I." It was better to be clear on it. Edmond must not think, must not hope . . .

Something moved in his dark eyes and she wasn't sure what it was. Disappointment? Anger?

But his face was unchanged, darkly handsome, intense.

"I hope, madame, that you and . . . and your husband are successful in your new situation." He gave a short bow and turned away.

She watched as he climbed into the car, a black Citroën,

and drove away. She watched the car swing around the hill-side and disappear. In a moment, the rattle of the engine could no longer be heard. There was no sound but the soft twitter of the birds and the murmur of the ocean. The quickly dissipating curl of smoke from the exhaust and the rapid, light beating of her heart were the only reminders that she had actually stood face to face with Edmond.

She hurried the rest of the way to the villa. She didn't remember to walk slowly. The heavy shoes wore a blister on her right foot and she was limping and hot by the time she pushed through the wooden gate into the garden.

"Lio . . . Paul, Paul!"

He hurried out of the stable, pruning shears in his left hand, readiness in his dark-blue eyes. He looked past her, listened, then asked, "What's happened? What's frightened you?"

That was the first moment she realized she was afraid. Somehow, his putting it in words made it less frightening, reassured her. How could she, after all, be afraid of Edmond?

She pushed back a tendril of black hair that had fallen loose from its bun and tried to catch her breath. "It's all right," she managed finally, "it's just that I've seen Edmond —and he recognized me."

"Edmond?"

"You remember! The art student. You met him the first summer you came to see Betty and me at Grandmama's."

"Hmm," Lionel grunted, "that one." His thick, fair brows knotted in a frown. "What did he say? Where did he see you?"

He listened closely as she told him and was quiet when she finished. Then he shrugged. "It sounds to me like he's on our side. I mean, why bother with this business of wishing you luck if he's pro-German?" Lionel smiled a little. "And there's no reason for him to have it in for us."

She almost spoke, but Lionel was reaching out to take the heavy basket and turning to carry it to the kitchen. She stood unmoving in the shade of the mimosa and felt a wave of sickness at the thought. To tell Lionel that she had kissed Edmond on the beach and that he had asked her to marry him on the strength of it! What would he think? Would he believe there must be more to it than that, to bring a proposal? And, whether he did or not, he had never hidden his contempt for Edmond.

He stopped at the kitchen door and realized she was not coming and turned to look, then hurried back.

"What's wrong, Kay? You look quite ill. Is there something more that happened? Are you all right?"

She brushed the back of her hand against her mouth and felt the faint sheen of sweat. "It is unseasonably hot today. I think that's it. Nothing more. I hurried . . ."

He took her arm then and helped her gently up the path and insisted she take a quiet lie-down while he put away the groceries. She tried to relax but she moved uneasily on the hard bed. She should tell him, she should, she should.

He brought a glass of orange juice and sat down beside her while she drank it, and she couldn't quite control the trembling of her hand. He took the glass when it was empty and set it on the night table, then turned back to hold her hands in his.

"Kay, tell me what's wrong."

She looked up at him, at his broad, honest face, at the worry in his dark-blue eyes. Dear Lionel. Dear good wonderful Lionel. How could she possibly tell him about Edmond? And what real difference could it make? She shook her head and managed a smile, a smile that grew as she looked at him. "Nothing is wrong, Lionel. Nothing is ever wrong when you're here," and she freed her hands to reach up and draw his face down to hers, caught his mouth with hers.

It was later in the same week, she was once again walking home from the market, when she came around the curve and saw the black Citroën parked on the verge. Edmond sat in it, smoking, watching. Waiting for her.

She saw him check to see if anyone were near, then, assured they were unobserved, he called out softly, "Hurry, Kay. Get in. I need to talk to you."

She hesitated.

"Let's go. Someone pro-Vichy might see us here. I have some important information for you to give to . . . to your husband."

She got in then. He started the car and pulled onto the road.

"I'll make it quick then drop you off. The police are holding an Englishman, a spy. They plan to turn him over to the Gestapo agents tomorrow. That will be the end of him. Even though the Germans haven't occupied the free zone, there are Gestapo everywhere and the police have to hand over captured spies to them."

He let her off just short of the countess's villa, after telling her what time the exchange would take place and how many men Lionel would likely need to rescue the agent.

Lionel and Kay, a son of Dr. Morisant's and two railroad workers made up the rescue party that night. It went off without a hitch.

Twice in the next month, Edmond was helpful, the time of a shipment of petrol through Nice, the name of a collaborationist who had been trying to make contact with Lionel's circuit.

It was in late October that Lionel came home after meeting Edmond on the Promenade and confided to Kay that Edmond wanted ten thousand francs to buy off a

Gestapo captain in exchange for the freedom of a French admiral who would be willing to come to London and broadcast over BBC to France.

"I told him I'd have to check with Baker Street, but he's adamant that there isn't time, that it's a now-or-never situation. I told him I'd have to think about it for a day or two."

Kay was kneading dough. She stopped, her hands floury and warm, and asked slowly, "How can Edmond know this kind of thing, Lionel? How can he possibly?"

Lionel leaned against the drainboard. "Edmond was hired to inventory the Fleury estate. It was confiscated by the Germans. Edmond is evaluating the artwork. He makes his reports to Miller, the Gestapo captain. So it all falls in place. And Edmond's been right on everything else he's told us."

"Yes," Kay agreed. "But still . . ."

It was the next afternoon and Kay was scrubbing the stone floor of the kitchen when the door opened behind her. "Arretez," she called. She stopped and half turned and saw unfamiliar gray trousers and looked up, her heart beginning an irregular, uneven thump.

"Edmond," she whispered.

He held a finger to his mouth, then gestured for her to come.

"What are you doing here?" she asked sharply.

"Who is here?"

She hesitated and his hand reached out for her wrist. "Quickly, quickly, who is here?"

"Only the countess and I."

"Where is . . . Paul?"

Lionel had been gone an hour or so to talk to Father Lombard about the ten thousand francs that Edmond wanted. He should be back at any time.

"I'm not sure," she said warily.

Edmond frowned, "Look, Kay—"

She interrupted. "Marie. My name is Marie."

He nodded impatiently. "All right, all right. You will do as well. I need the ten thousand francs. Now. Lionel told you, didn't he?" Edmond's dark eyes fastened on her, bright and hard.

"Yes."

His eyes never left her face. "You have the money here, don't you?"

She started to shake her head, but he held her wrist and he yanked her toward him.

"Don't lie, Kay. I'm sure. Lionel said he needed a day or two to think it over. That means he has money, has it here, for he couldn't get it from London in a day or two."

"But I can't give it . . ." She cut off her words, but it was too late. Now there was no doubt at all. The money was at the villa and Edmond knew it.

He smiled, and his smile frightened her more than anything. "I knew it. I thought you'd have money, that first day I saw you. And I made up my mind to get it."

"There isn't any admiral," she cried.

He laughed.

"But why, Edmond? Why do you want money?"

"I've got to get out of here."

"Why?"

"Müller presses me. All the time. He wants to know a little more. But you can't trust Germans. He'll use me but he won't give me any protection. And if I don't cooperate, I'll end up on one of those damned labor trains going to Germany."

"Cooperate? You mean collaborate, don't you?"

He saw the contempt in her eyes. But he only smiled, then said very clearly, "You are the fools. But useful fools. You have money. I need money. And I'm going to take it." He smiled again, a thin, dry smile. "And there's not a thing in the world you can do about it, is there? You can't call the police, can you?"

A dry smile and dry rot in his soul. Edmond would do for Edmond and let his country lie under the Germans' heel. Kay stared at him and wondered how she had ever thought him handsome.

"We won't give you a penny. We didn't bring money to France for collaborators."

"You're wrong, Kay. You will give it—and gladly." His hand cut upward so quickly that she only saw a blur of movement. His knuckles slashed across her mouth and the pain was sharp and violent. She heard a moan and realized she had made that cry, and then there was the slam of the door against a wall and Lionel was suddenly there and she heard him swear and there was a sickening thump as he struck Edmond, flinging him across the kitchen and into the wooden table, which tipped to crash in a noisy heap. The bowl of fruit clattered to the floor. Apples and oranges and pears thumped and bounced and rolled across the stone floor and over the smell and taste of her own blood, Kay could smell the faint sweetness of the bruised pear near her foot.

Lionel was halfway across the kitchen, lunging toward Edmond, when he staggered. Kay saw him begin to fall even as she heard the sound of the shot.

Edmond still lay on the stone floor, but there was a pistol in his hand.

"Lionel! Lionel!"

She thought she screamed it but it was only a ragged, anguished whisper. She ran to him and knelt and lifted his head and tried to pull him up. He looked at her and his dark-blue eyes were clear and aware.

A Settling of Accounts

The front of his dark shirt was wet now, wet and sticky, and the blood spread and began to drip onto the clean flagstones that she had just mopped, and the dark-red pool widened with such frightening speed.

She had to stop that flow of blood before his life drained into an ugly dark splotch on the stone floor! She gently laid down his head and jumped up to run and grab up clean dishtowels and hurry back to press them against his chest.

His eyes were closed now and his ruddy face as pale as candle wax.

There was blood everywhere, on her hands, her dress, spreading on the floor, seeping into the sharp white of the dishtowels, staining them like spilled claret.

Dimly she heard the countess's cry and Edmond's sharp order.

"Lionel, oh Lionel, please." She was calling to him, but he lay heavy and still and his eyes didn't open. But he was still breathing, wasn't he? There was the ever so slight rise and fall of those sticky, reddish-white cloths on his chest.

"Madame," she called out, screamed it out, "get the doctor, call, hurry, hurry!"

"No."

She had almost forgotten Edmond, forgotten the hated cause. She looked up now. He stood by the door and the gun pointed at them.

"We must call the doctor." She said it so reasonably. He could see that, couldn't he? Could see the awful spread of the blood. They had to call the doctor. She looked at the countess. "Hurry, madame, call Dr. Morisant."

"The money," Edmond said harshly. "First, the money."

She stared at him. The words were meaningless. What did money matter now? Money couldn't help Lionel.

The countess tried to move past Edmond but he raised the

gun to her head. "The money. Tell Kay to get the money, then you can call the doctor."

"The stables. In the loft," Kay said tonelessly. "The blue velvet valise in the bottom of the wardrobe." Then she nodded at Countess Rakovsky. "Call now."

Edmond hesitated for a moment, then let the countess pass. "If you try to trick me, I will shoot all of you, Kay."

She didn't even bother to answer. She was holding Lionel's head now, her face close to his, her cheek against his hair. Was he breathing? His face was faintly blue now. Oh God, why didn't the bleeding stop!

It took Dr. Morisant fifteen minutes to come, his old car laboring up the steep curving road to the villa. He was kneeling beside Lionel when Father Lombard arrived, red-faced from riding his bicycle so hard.

The four of them were settling Lionel, a scarcely breathing Lionel, into the back seat of the doctor's shabby sedan when a heavy saloon car roared into the narrow drive, squealed to a stop and its occupants spilled out, guns in hand.

The Gestapo.

CHAPTER 22

Odd-shaped pieces in a puzzle mystify until they are turned rightside up. A crescent moon, a silver bridge, a shallow bowl, it all depends upon the angle. Once seen, it seems impossible that the correct shape wasn't obvious.

Angus pushed up from his desk and began to pace back and forth on the faded brown rug in his study. Two women couldn't disappear utterly from view without leaving any trace at all!

(Certainly they could, Moray, if they . . .)

Somewhere there had to be a trail, the beginning, the track of Edmond. He wasn't a magician! He must have revealed himself a dozen times in the abduction of two women. He must have been seen, talked to people.

Angus turned again, began to pace the other way. Of course, he had spoken on the phone to the desk clerk, told him the message to give to Julie . . .

Angus stopped, stared at the bookcases in front of him without seeing them.

The message to Julie—but how had he known that Julie was at the hotel? How could he possibly have known?

It was raining, a steady, cold November drizzle when Angus slammed out of his house. He rarely drove in London but he did keep a car, an Austin coupe. He went first to the hotel, but the clerk was off duty.

The manager shook his head. "It isn't our policy to give out our employees' home addresses."

"It's important. It could be a matter of life or death." That was a mistake. The hint of danger, the possibility that the clerk might be involved only succeeded in frightening the manager, making him even more determined not to talk to Angus at all.

The door was closing. Angus said loudly, "Look, I'll keep the police out of it if you'll just give me the address. I only want to talk to him."

But he was shouting at the unresponsive white panels of a closed door. He began to pound on it, bruising his knuckles but making a satisfyingly thunderous noise. He heard a high squeak of outrage from beyond the panel, stayed his hand for a moment and heard the manager threatening shrilly to call the police.

"Do," Angus shouted. "Call. Call now. They'll get the address for me." And he began to pound louder than before.

"Sir! Sir!"

It was more of a hiss than a whisper. Angus turned and saw a narrow, clever face peering around a corner at him. Bright-blue eyes looked Angus up and down, a hand gestured for him to come, then the face disappeared. It was the bellboy who had given him Julie's message when he came to the hotel at noon.

Angus hesitated, then turned and hurried around the corner. The bellboy was waiting near the stairwell.

"Do you want Mick's address on account of the young lady on seven?"

Julie's room, her aunt's room, was 706.

"Is Mick the desk clerk who told Miss Fremont that her aunt had called?"

The young man nodded vigorously. "I heard you asking Mr. Graves. He's a poor fish."

And Angus knew he was going to get the address. When he had it, tucked into his hand by the grinning bellboy, he hesitated for a moment by the rank of phones. Should he call

Inspector Evans? Then Angus swung around and hurried out of the hotel. Not yet. He had ideas, lots of them, but nothing tangible. If he could find this Mick, lean on him a little bit . . . If the desk clerk weren't home, then it was time for the inspector and time to hope he saw the glimmer Angus saw so clearly.

In his car, he pulled a map and flashlight from the car pocket. He checked the street index. Yes, there it was, off Clerkenwell Road, not a long distance at all.

It was a respectable street, narrow gray-stone houses with glistening front steps and curtained bow windows. Number 26 was along on the right, next to the end. Angus found a parking spot in the next block and hurried back to the house.

The old house, converted to small flats, smelled damp when he stepped into the vestibule. Too little warmth for too many years. Ryan was scrawled in pencil on a scrap of paper tucked in a third-floor letter box.

The stairs were a little shabbier at each floor, and those leading to the third were narrow and uncarpeted.

Angus knocked at Ryan's flat. Faintly he heard movement beyond the door. Impatiently, he knocked again.

"A minute, can't you?" The door opened, and the face on a level with Angus's was as surly as the voice.

Angus looked at the small, mean eyes, the thin, tight mouth, the bright, cheap striped shirt.

"Mick Ryan?"

"Right, mate."

"You have some information that I'm willing to pay for." Angus pulled out his billfold and slowly drew out three ten-pound notes and balanced them in his hand. The mean little eyes flickered from Angus's hand to his face and back again to the money.

"What can I do for you, mate?"

"I want the name of the man who called and asked you to give a message to Miss Fremont and say it was from her aunt."

The cold little blue eyes were wary. "It's no crime to pass on a message."

So the clerk had known full well it was a trick, had pretended to Julie that it was her aunt who called. Angus would have liked to stove in that wary, mean face, but instead he said mildly, "Nobody's talking about a crime. This is between us. A little information. A lot of money."

"You'll keep me out of it?"

"Sure."

Ryan rubbed at his sallow cheek. "Look, mister, I'll tell you straight, I don't know the bloke's name."

Angus's hand started to close around the three bills, and the raspy, whiny voice hurried on, "But I'll give you the phone number I used to call and tell him the niece had come." He paused and added silkily, "And for another ten quid, I'll tell you the address the American girl went to."

Angus didn't change expression but he felt a quick surge of triumph. Edmond had revealed himself. He had indeed.

"But he had the money!" Julie cried, outrage in her voice. "Wasn't that enough? Why did he turn you in to the Gestapo?"

"It wasn't even for revenge," Kay said emptily. She could perhaps have understood the ugly workings of outraged pride or the blind malice of a rejected love. But it wasn't that at all.

"Looking back, it is all easy to understand. Edmond didn't, of course, care for me at all. He saw me as a passport to comfort, to money. He was sure I was that mythical creature, the American heiress, and, even if I weren't all that rich, he knew that Grandmama was . . . very comfortable. He had hoped to marry me. When I turned him down, I think he was furious, not at losing me, but at coming so near to wealth and then having it slip through his grasp. When he saw me trudging up that hill, he knew I must be back in France as a British agent and he must have, from that very first instant, begun to figure how that knowledge could help him the most. He was careful, he gained our confidence first. But, as soon as he was sure we had a secret store of funds, he made his move."

It was easy, terribly easy in the cold darkness of the moving van, to remember, to see again scenes she had so long tried to forget.

"The valise was a pale gray-blue. Its leather handles were shabby. I was surprised, the first time I saw it, that it could hold so much money." Five hundred thousand francs. Worth, at that time, ten thousand dollars. A nice sum.

Julie reached out and took Kay's hands, held them tightly, but nothing could warm the cold, dark emptiness in her heart.

"I met Edmond's mother once," Kay said in that dry, dead voice. "She was a pale, drawn little woman and she scurried around that afternoon bringing an extra lump of sugar to Edmond, patting his shoulder, fetching him matches. Everyone always praised her, how hard she had worked to educate him, how selfless she was, how devoted." Kay shuddered. "Praised her," she repeated, and her voice was hard now, hard and angry. "How to create a monster! An overweening ego that will seek its own comforts, its safety, and destroy everything and everyone as thoughtlessly as a machine threshes wheat."

He had fed them, the countess and Lionel, the priest, the doctor and Kay, to the Gestapo not because he hated them but to ensure his own safety.

"If he left us there, just ran with the money," Kay explained, "the word would have gone out to Resistance groups and the search would have begun to find Edmond, recover the money—kill him. So he alerted the Gestapo, said two British agents, a man, wounded, and a woman were at the Countess Rakovsky's villa. When the Gestapo came, we couldn't say Edmond had shot Lionel for the money—where would a poor maid and her husband have obtained that kind of money? We told them that Edmond had tried to attack me, and my husband came and Edmond shot him. We said it was all a lie, Edmond's lie, that we were British agents, we were Paul and Marie Deschamps."

"What . . ." Julie stopped, tried again, "how . . ." But she couldn't ask. There was an echo of horror in Kay's level voice.

"I don't think," Kay said carefully, parceling out the words like so many stones, "that Lionel would have lived anyway. I don't think so."

But how many dreams had she endured, her mind twisting away from reality, dreaming of a hospital and Dr. Morisant smiling beside the bed and a wan but living Lionel looking up at her? How many?

There was to be no hospital for Lionel Neal.

"The drive was made of crushed oyster shells. There were four Gestapo men. Two of them held Schmeisser machine pistols. The fat one told everyone what to do."

Fat, a huge protruding stomach, pendulous jaws, pudgy fingers, he planted his shiny black boots on the oyster shells, pointed at Dr. Morisant's old car, "Pull the man out!"

Two of them yanked Lionel out of the back seat, dumped him onto the drive and blood spread on the white oyster shells, was darkly red on the gray-white of the shells.

"Dr. Morisant tried to stop them. They clubbed him

down. He said Lionel would die if he weren't taken to the hospital. They said no one could leave until the English spies confessed."

She tried to run to Lionel, to kneel beside him, but one of the men caught her in unexpectedly strong hands, held her as she struggled.

She watched Lionel die, saw his life's blood spread sluggishly on the white crushed shells.

"Herr Doctor, do you not wish to save your patient?" the fat one asked.

Dr. Morisant, the side of his face swelling from the blows of the gun, stared down at Lionel's twisted, humped body. "My patient is dead."

Indescribable pain creates its own defense. Kay was with them, of them, jammed in the back of the Citroën, the butt of a gun hard against her hip, but she was withdrawn, unhearing, uncaring.

The Gestapo had taken over a small hotel not far from the beachfront. Gay striped awnings flapped in the gentle sea breeze. Plump pigeons ambled along window ledges. The only difference from before the war was the flag that hung over the entrance, the black of the swastika sharp against the red background.

They marched the four of them into the lobby, herded them into a corner, left them guarded by a young hard-faced private.

They sat on the brocaded chairs, the countess, the doctor, the priest and Kay. Kay stared dry-eyed at nothing while Father Lombard gripped her hands in his. But she could take no comfort there. Over and over again in her mind she saw the slow red welling of blood, Lionel's blood, and she wanted to cry, to scream, to strike out, but she only sat on the dusty couch, sat and looked at nothing.

And she never even wondered why they were kept in the lobby, what was going to happen. There was no room for anything in her mind but the slow red welling of blood.

She had no defense when the voice cried out:

"Kay!"

Her head swung around, before she thought, and she looked up into the frightened, worried eyes of her grandmother.

She turned her head—and wrote death warrants for all of them.

She felt the blood drain from her face and the sick thumping of her heart, Oh God what had she done!, and she shook her head back and forth and whispered, *"Non, non, je suis Marie Deschamps."*

Edmond had brought Madame Varney into the hotel through a side door, not beneath the ugly arrogance of the Nazi flag. And now, Madame Varney looked around the lobby, saw the sentry and the other men, and then she turned and looked up at Edmond and her old face crumpled. "You said that Kay needed help—and you have brought me here to betray her."

Kay swallowed once, twice. Deny everything, deny it all, London had said. No matter how much the Gestapo seemed to know. She shook her head, once again. *"Je suis Marie Deschamps."*

And her grandmother, knowing it was too late, forever too late, began to cry, tears running down her soft and wrinkled cheeks.

The fat man, the one who had directed the others at the countess's villa, moved to Kay, took her arm, pulled her along with him. He said something briefly in German to another, younger man who turned on his heel and gestured to Madame Varney to come along.

A Settling of Accounts

They led Kay and her grandmother across the lobby. Kay thought with despair of how she had battled the temptation to go and see her grandmother all the months they had been in Nice. The countess's villa was far from her grandmother's, there had been no danger their paths would accidentally cross. And Kay had been firm with herself. She would do nothing to endanger Grandmama.

At the archway opening into the foyer, Kay twisted her head to look back and saw the countess and the doctor and the priest watching and their faces were gray and slack and she knew with a sickening sense of shock that they saw Death walking beside her. The fat man yanked on Kay's arm and they walked on.

She never saw any of them, the countess or the priest or the doctor, again.

The heavy man stopped at the hotel desk, spoke to a brown-suited orderly, who nodded and reached around for a room key and handed it over.

A room for . . . for what?

Part of Kay was still withdrawn, untouched, but another part of her was swept with fear. She felt and knew that she was absolutely vulnerable, absolutely defenseless. All the rules and laws which had, in her lifetime, protected her, no longer applied. These men could do anything they wished to her, anything at all. She could twist and scream and cry and plead and there was no succor. Anywhere.

The plump-jowled man led the way into the open-grilled elevator. There was room just for the four of them, Kay, her grandmother, the plump-jowled leader and his underling, still carrying the Schmeisser pistol. The cage was rattling slowly up when somewhere above them a high-pitched, hideous scream began, rose, shrieked, then choked off in an awful guttural growl. Kay's breath caught in her chest, her heart thudded and she began, uncontrollably, to shake. Her grandmother slipped an arm around her shoulder.

When the cage stopped at the fourth floor, they were roughly pushed out into the hall, the pistol jabbing at them. It was intended to frighten them more, to reinforce their sense of helplessness.

The ugly black snout of the gun poked her grandmother in the side and the old woman gave a gasp of pain.

Something exploded inside Kay, the culmination of the day's horrors. She whirled toward the man who held the Schmeisser. She had not, until now, actually looked at him. In the instant before her hands swept up, she saw him clearly, arrogant blue eyes, dark narrow face, thin bristly mustache. He was her age, her generation, but they were separated by more than nationality or language. They were separated by experience of evil. She knew it even as she moved, knew, but she was beyond all hope now and she would, at least this one time, trade pain for pain.

Her nails, sharp as an animal's claws, tore at his eyes, gouged deep bloody marks down his cheeks, her knee came up fast and hard into the softness of his groin.

He whooped in pain and pulled away, doubling up. Her right foot in its hard black shoe came down to grind into his instep.

Pain exploded across the back of her head. She crashed into the wall, slid down it to the floor. She lay in a dazed heap and the pain ran in hot scarlet waves down her back and arm. It had receded a little, was just bearable, when she heard her grandmother scream, "Non, non."

Kay was pulling up on her hands and knees, turning to look, when he began to kick her. Blood ran down from her scratches in his face. As he bent over her, the blood dripped down. He kicked and kicked and kicked, the blunt toe of his heavy boot smashing into her arm, her ribs, her hip. She bunched up, an animal turning in on itself seeking ease, and he kicked her leg again and again and again.

She retched into her own screams and was so ravaged by pain that she did not even know when the kicking stopped.

He shouted at her to get up. She didn't move at all.

A sharp short scream.

She lifted her head and saw her grandmother's hands tight against her chest, her face crumpled in agony. The snout of the Schmeisser hurtled toward the old woman again and Kay made a strangled cry.

Kay tried to get up, tried with all her heart, but her right leg gave way beneath her and she fell back down, her face thudding into the dusty frayed carpet.

Her grandmother screamed again.

Kay crawled the rest of the way down the hall. Whenever she paused too long, the Schmeisser lunged.

She thought that once she pulled her throbbing, agonized body into the room, that he would leave her grandmother alone, once again turn on her.

He waited until Kay had crawled into the far corner where he had pointed, and then he stood her grandmother in the middle of the room. The fat man nodded gently as he watched the young man, with the dark-blue eyes and the bristly mustache, methodically jam the snub of the pistol into Kay's grandmother until the old woman fell to the floor and didn't move again.

CHAPTER 23

"She never regained consciousness," Kay said finally. "God's mercy."

It was quiet in the van, only the whistle of the tires, the muted hum of the motor to remind them that they traveled through darkness to a destination unknown.

"I knew what I had to do when she died," Kay said simply. "I knew that somehow I had to escape. It wasn't then that I was fighting to live. It wasn't that at all. But I could not bear to be hurt any more—and I knew too much, too many names, too many places. Estelle, who passed letters for us, she was sixteen and had the brightest, clearest brown eyes. Old Marc, the baker, carved wooden animals for his grandchildren and rubbed his eyes when he told us of his son Noel who died in the fighting at Montreuil. Madame Latour, Henri, Jacques, Helene . . . The safety, the lives of all of them, depended on me. I was very desperate, very determined."

Her leg still would not support her. She did manage to pull herself upright, to cling to the wall. She had to walk. She had to!

She took a step. She would walk, she had no choice and the men might return at any time . . . The leg crumpled beneath her and it took another agonizing effort to pull up again, to lean and support herself on one leg.

She stared around the room, refusing to see the dark lump of black that had been her grandmother. It was an ordinary hotel room, had been an ordinary room until it was given over to evil.

One narrow bed, a chest, a chair, one window with heavy gold drapes.

A Settling of Accounts

She worked her way around the room to the drapes. She had no particular hope, no plan, but the window was a place to start. She pulled the drapes open. The window was nailed shut. Just past it was an ornamental ledge, perhaps sixteen inches wide. She looked up. The drapes hung from a brass curtain rod. She stared at the rod for a long moment, then reached up and yanked at the drapes, pulled as hard as she could. They did not tear. The material was old but strong. Viciously, she pulled again. The rod jumped out of its supports and rod, rings and drapes clattered down on her head. She held the bunch of it and tried to listen over the erratic thump of her heart.

What a horrendous noise it had made! But no one came.

She worked feverishly then, pulling the rod apart and, yes, one segment was long enough. She took the thick cord that banded the drapes and used it to truss the rod the length of her injured leg to serve as a splint. The knob of the rod was level with her hipbone and she could grab it to steady and direct the rod as she tried to move.

She could now, painfully, walk.

She looked again at the window.

It was nailed shut, yes, but if she broke out the glass . . . The heavy thickness of the drapes muffled the crash as she jabbed the other half of the rod again and again against the glass. The glass tinkled and clinked as it broke, but nearby windows were shut and the alleyway was five stories below.

It was getting dark now, the sun slipping behind a thick bank of clouds in the west, staining the sky with deep red fingers of sunset. The air that swept into the room felt cold and Kay realized she was sweating heavily.

Shards of glass still clung to the edges of the window frame. She wrenched loose one sharp wedge and held it in her hand. If she sliced across her wrist, quickly, roughly . . . She

273

tucked that piece into her waistband. If she did not escape, and, she looked down the dizzying distance to the alley, if she did not plummet onto the ground, then she would have that piece of glass.

She felt the hot sweet sickness in her stomach as she lifted her injured leg and maneuvered it through the window. She struggled out to sit on the ledge, her legs parallel to the window, and then, slowly, inches at a time, she struggled to stand.

It was dark before she managed. That made it easier, for now she could not see the ground below. She didn't look down. She thought only of moving, a foot at a time, along that ledge, clinging with hot wet fingers to the bulges and clumps of the decorative masonry. She did not look to see if a window was draped when she came to it. She had no more choices to make. Her whole being centered on the awkward stiff jerk of her injured leg, then the cautious step of her other leg along the ledge. On and on and on, and then her reaching hand groped into nothingness.

How long she stood there, her face pressed against the cold stone, she never knew, and then, finally, she looked and it was very simple to understand. She had reached the back of the hotel.

Was there a ledge along the back?

It was another long while before she could force her foot to reach out, testing, seeking. The ledge was there. If it hadn't been . . . She managed the corner and then, once again, her being centered on moving along that narrow strip, foot by foot by foot.

When the hard iron bars blocked her way, she didn't recognize the barrier at first. It was just another obstacle. She held onto the bars and knew she could not go much farther. And what was the point of going at all, round and round the hotel like a wind-up toy? Now the way was blocked and the only answer was to turn and retrace that impossibly long distance. Why bother at all? If she let go, if her tiring hands relaxed, she would topple off the ledge. Then it would all be over, the pain and the fear and the pointless, endless struggle along the ledge.

She looked down then, looked down into darkness and saw, dimly, outlined by patches of light that marked shaded windows, the dark hulking shape of iron, projecting out from the hotel. The very mass of iron that she clung to. It slanted one way and then the other down the side of . . .

A fire escape.

Her hands tightened convulsively on the cold iron bars.

A fire escape.

"So you managed to escape!"

Kay nodded in the darkness of the van. "Yes. It was the fire escape that saved me. I'll never know how I got onto it, made my way down. It seemed to take hours. Then, at the last, I thought it was going to be useless after all. The escape stopped at the first floor, didn't reach to the ground."

"What did you do?"

"I dropped."

Julie winced. Two simple words but how hideous it must have been for Kay, injured as she was.

"I undid the curtain rod, dropped it first. I guess I was hoping to find it if I made it down. Then I hung by my hands. But it was still so far . . . The last thing I remember was the jolt as I landed and then nothing. They told me later that I slept for almost two days and nights. When I woke, it was to find my leg in a cast and myself cleaned and bathed and in a fresh white nightgown.

"I never knew their names, it was better so. I called them Michel and Dede. He collected the garbage from behind the

275

hotel. He was late that night in finishing his rounds. He found me just as the Klaxon sounded. They had discovered my escape. He said it was only a matter of minutes for both of us. He knew, when he saw me, that I had been beaten by the Gestapo. He pulled me to his cart and pushed me up into it and dumped three cans of garbage over me, only making sure there was a little space for me to breathe. They flashed lights into the cart, asked him if he had seen anyone. If I had wakened, cried out . . .”

It had taken a long time for her leg to mend. She had lain quietly in the only bedroom they had, on a trundle bed that would hide beneath their own when anyone came.

“They saved me, nursed me back to health, and, finally, bought papers for me out of their own tiny income and, in the spring, sent me off to find a way into Spain. They had so little but it was everything to them, and they risked it all for a stranger.”

She paused and then said so softly that Julie could scarcely hear, “Whenever I remember the ugliness, Edmond’s greed and the viciousness of the Gestapo, and it threatens to make me bitter and hateful, then I remember Michel and Dede, too, who were good and brave and kind. It is another triumph of evil if we do not believe in the good.”

The van slowed. Both of them listened intently. It stopped, paused, started up again. Another town obviously. Again it slowed, stopped.

“Should we try to pound, make some noise?” Julie asked.

But before the question could do more than move in their minds, the van lurched ahead. They moved clumsily in the darkness, searching the van, hunting for something to pound with. But there was nothing, and their hands made only useless slapping sounds.

Then the van began to pick up speed.

A Settling of Accounts

They were both near the back of the van now.

"He intends to kill us, doesn't he?" Julie asked.

"Yes. But we won't let it happen, Julie."

The certainty in Kay's voice was reassuring beyond all reason.

"We can't guess what he has in mind. But remember, it is easier by far for him to manage us as prisoners than to try and move our bodies. So our time won't run out until he has us right at the spot where he hopes to hide our bodies. Between now and then we will find a chance to escape. Or make one."

"All right, Kay. Tell me what to do when the time comes and, whatever it is, I promise I'll do it."

Kay patted her niece's shoulder. Julie had been abducted, drugged, jolted about in the darkness of a van, knowing that its driver planned her death, and, with all of it, she was still defiant, ready to struggle.

It was then that she told Julie of the coil of wire on her wrist and the dangerous black powder packed in the bottom of her purse.

CHAPTER 24

"I know it's after hours. Ring people at home. Track them down. I want to know everything you can find out about Henri Durand." The inspector watched as his assistant hurried from the office. As the door closed, he turned to look at Angus Moray.

"You may be wrong."

"I may," Angus agreed. "But it would be a bit of a coincidence, don't you think?"

Slowly, Detective Inspector Evans nodded. It had been a frantic hour since Angus arrived with the telephone number provided by the hotel desk clerk. Traced, it proved to be a private line on the desk of the owner of Durand Galleries. And it was to Durand Galleries that Kay Emory had gone that last Thursday before she disappeared. And the address in South Kensington led to a house whose contents were being appraised by Durand Galleries for auction. Henri Durand had keys to that house.

Bit by bit the information came in. It was so much more than they had hoped for, yet it was still only a signpost. They had a man's name, and every fact they found made it more likely. He was French. He was the right age.

And he could not be found anywhere.

The rear door to the van opened slowly. In comparison to the utter darkness of the last hours, it seemed sharply bright, though night had long since fallen. The thin glow of a November moon shone bone-white on Edmond's face. Behind him, slender spiky fronds of silvery marsh grass undu-

lated in the cold rush of the wind off the darkly surging water.
The rustle of the grasses, the soft sucking sound of the restless water, the smell of fish and salt water and decaying vege-
tation—Kay's heart began to pound. Of course, of course, all
England is an island, and if you wish to be rid of anything,
what better place than the depths of dark cold water?

Edmond spoke not a word. The moonlight glittered on the
pistol he held in his right hand. He beckoned to them and the
metal glistened, a beacon to destruction.

They hesitated at the edge of the van, staring down at him.
If they stepped down to the road, was it then that he would
raise the pistol, point it? Would they see the flash of gunpowder, hear the sharp crack as the hammer struck?

He flicked on the flashlight that he held in his other hand.
He stepped a little closer and the bright narrow beam probed
the farthest corners of the van, then jumped back to them and
moved until the thin string of light touched Kay's purse, and
there it held.

Kay stood rigid. How could he possibly suspect? He had
looked in her purse, found the knife, poked past all the mis-
cellany, keys, lipstick, handkerchief, eye shadow, powder, to
touch the bottom, the lining she had so carefully replaced and
tightly tucked. He had been satisfied with the knife, not
thought beyond it. How could he possibly suspect?

Her hand tightened on the handle. If she flung it as hard as
possible, would it throw him off balance enough for her to . . .

But he was moving now, stepping back a little, and the
beam of light dropped to the rutted roadway, a narrow half-
track scarcely visible beneath mounds of leaves and matted
winter-bleached weeds.

Kay began to breathe again. He did not suspect her
handbag, he was only checking to make sure that she carried
it, that it was not left behind in the van, and that must mean

they had farther yet to go, that the pistol would not make its final explosion yet.

He gestured once again with the pistol. Kay took Julie's arm and they jumped awkwardly out of the van, stiff from the long, uncomfortable ride. Now the flashlight beam pointed past the van to a faint path. Kay and Julie began to walk, stumbling a little on the uneven ground. The path curved rightward. Small twisted trees pressed close on the left and, abruptly, perhaps a matter of yards to the right, the ground sank into a marshy expanse, and beyond the waving, moving grasses was the darkness of the sea. The wind was sharp and cold, rustling the grasses, tugging at their raincoats, skittering leaves in a restless, erratic dance.

A night for witches and warlocks to call Satan up, to link bloodstained hands and chant incantations, bringing evil abroad.

Kay stopped suddenly. Julie walked a half step more, then she paused. The light moved, pulled back, swung toward Kay. Edmond stopped, too, and his awful impatience to be done with them, his brittle, scarcely concealed excitement sickened Kay.

"Hurry!" he ordered. "Hurry!"

Kay reached an arm around Julie. All her fine plans and brave hopes made on that long dark ride to the coast, they were all going to come to nothing. It was too late, already too late! They should have beaten on the back of the van, screamed, jumped Edmond when the door first opened! Now they were miles from anywhere, alone on a dark, wind-ridden, marshy coast, alone with a killer. Tears of despair burned at the back of Kay's dry, aching eyes. And Julie was depending on her! Perhaps, if they ran now, one in one direction, one the other way, perhaps . . .

Edmond reached out, gripped Kay's arm with hard, angry

fingers. "Hurry, damn you."

"Where?"

Yes, Edmond, where do you lead us, to what unimaginable final horror? Will we die face down in cold moving water, the marsh grass moving gently above us?

"There," and he pointed ahead.

The weathered boards glimmered as soft as cobwebs in the thin moonlight, and the water foamed in soft white swirls as it moved gently alongside the boathouse.

A boat.

Something moved in Kay's mind and she wasn't sure whether it was false hope, the fool's gold of the mind, or whether it was the sharp, quick instinct for survival.

She began to move and Julie kept step, and the wild, dangerous force that was Edmond came behind them.

She might be wrong, fatally wrong. This might be the very place they would die, in the muffled hollowness of a boathouse.

But it must be *his* boathouse, *his* boat, and bloodstains are so hard to remove.

If he brought them all this way, he must have a plan in mind. And what better place to dispose of two bodies in the dark heaving sea. They needn't even be dead when plunged overboard. Not a drop of blood to mark his boat.

One more gamble, one more walk.

It was warmer in the shelter of the boathouse, out of the sharp wind. Edmond moved quickly, once inside, hurrying them onto the boat, herding them down the companionway from the deck into the saloon and on to a forward cabin. He closed them in it and once again they were in darkness. Neither of them spoke as they listened to his footsteps padding above them and heard rattles and clangs and soft thumping sounds.

From the broad, sleek profile of the boat seen in the beam of Edmond's flashlight, Kay judged it to be a good-sized cabin cruiser. Diesel engines, no doubt. Perhaps with a hundred-gallon fuel capacity. And it was built much like John's boat. How many times had she and John cruised into the Gulf of Mexico, heavy swells lifting the boat's white hull up and down, up and down? How many times had they fished, watched through the clear blue waters for the silver flash of bonito or the bright blue-green of kingfish? And how many times had they smiled lazily and their bodies, warm from the sun, damp from salt spray, moved together? All her memories were sunlit, and never in those warm easy days had the faintest black hint flickered from the future.

Abruptly, shockingly, the motors roared, their thick hum magnified by the walls of the boathouse. The overhead light came on in their cabin prison. It was the forward cabin, odd-shaped to accommodate the locker. Kay turned and looked at it. John kept his extra life preservers there and . . .

Julie, too, a child of the sea, understood at once and was the first to reach and open the locker door. Not much storage space, but all space is used by a careful skipper.

Kay tugged at the pile of wet-weather gear, caps, slickers. Was that all the cupboard held? Surely there would be something useful, something! Three pairs of rubber boots, two extra life preservers, a coil of sturdy rope, a plastic air pump, and the rest of the space taken up by the bright orange of the collapsed life raft.

Everything for an emergency. Everything except something they could use in their defense. What good would any of this do against Edmond and his pistol?

Kay looked briefly at Julie, who was very carefully not looking at her aunt. Julie's face in the soft cabin light was sunken and strained, and Kay knew how her niece would look as a very old woman. Except, at this moment, there seemed little likelihood Julie would attain any great age.

They were, wordlessly, wearily, replacing the air pump, the rope, the life preservers when Kay whispered, "Wait! Wait!," and once again began to empty the locker. She pulled out everything until once again they could see the bright orange of the extra raft, and now she leaned inside the little space and began to tussle with the awkward, heavy, uninflated mass of rubber and, yes, there, beneath the life raft were two small paddles.

Perspiration was sticky on her face, her hands were damp, when she had them both free and lying on the bright-blue leatherette cushions between them.

Julie stared down at the small yellow-white paddles, and there was an odd mixture of despair and determination on her face as Kay spoke in soft urgent whispers. Julie listened and, finally, she nodded.

Kay said insistently, "You do see, don't you? It is the only chance we have. And all of it, Julie, depends on you. You mustn't stop, not for a second, no matter what happens, what you hear, whether you think I'm hurt, nothing matters but for you to get away, to swim for help. And, don't you see, he won't dare kill me if you get away. He won't dare."

Then, paddles in hand, they began to wait.

Norfolk P. C. Samuel Monks had lost his way twice, well as he knew the twisting country roads, but it is hard to find a particular boathouse in The Broads, the network of rivers and marshes between Norwich and the cold waters of the North Sea. He would have given up on this narrow lane except for the bright flash of light reflected from the parked van when the headlights of the police car touched it. And he knew, once he saw the van, that he had found the right spot.

He was, however, a careful middle-aged police constable. Due care had brought him to middle age. He intended to enjoy old age, so he called on his two-way radio, reported the van, the apparently deserted van, before he ever slipped out of his seat and warily began his approach. Word had already reached London of the van's discovery by the time P. C. Monks stood at the door of the boathouse and flashed his flashlight into an empty slip. He checked out the boathouse methodically, bending down on one knee to flash his light beneath the pier at the foaming water.

Nothing. Nothing anywhere.

He rose a little stiffly, stepped out the door and paused to swing the light slowly back and forth along the pier to the shore and there, just off the path, was a footprint. A woman's footprint. For the first time since the radio call from Scotland Yard, P. C. Monks felt an electric prickle of excitement down his back.

Dear God, how far out into the ocean was he going? Kay rubbed at her cheek. Julie could swim, Lord yes, she could swim, but the water would be so cold. Kay bit at her lip, than looked up in surprise when Julie patted her hand.

"Don't worry. If I can get away, I can swim it."

"The waves," Kay began, but Julie shook her head.

"I can do it. I will do it."

Kay forced a smile. Yes, Julie was confident and, wonderfully, she had accepted Kay's judgment that this was the only possible way to save both of them.

Kay had no illusions there. Her goal was, at this point, a simple one. Get Julie into the water. That was the only possible hope of saving her niece. As for what would happen when Julie went overboard, well, the mind could only plan so far ahead, bear to imagine just so much.

Likely, the engines would fall away and the anchor chain

rattle before he ever came to their cabin. Likely, but she had come too far to be easy here. She watched the door and listened, listened over the heavy wash of the sea and the creaking of the hull and the thrum of the diesels, listened and watched the door and held the paddle hard in firm hands, and tried to imagine that first quick instant, the only instant they would have, and the thrust of the paddle against flesh.

And there was in that tight concentration no room for memory or farewell, for a husbanding of sensation, the sticky feel of the blue leatherette cushion, the musty smell of the cabin, the plunging rhythm of the boat, bulling its way to sea.

The roll and pitch of the boat increased sharply when the engines quit.

There was that instant of warning, of preparation. Kay held the paddle like a battering ram. She would shove it, hard as possible, the instant the door opened. There was no room in the small cabin to wield it overhead, to smash down. One shove, that's all, when you pared it down. One shove.

Julie was just behind her, paddle in hand. But Julie knew her job, and, please God, don't let her think of anything else, don't let her question whether this would save both of them, don't let her think beyond running and reaching the water.

As the door opened, Kay was pushing it with her shoulder and lunging out into the main saloon.

The sharp edge of the paddle caught him squarely in the chest and Kay felt for one brief second an absolute certainty of success. He grunted, stumbled backward and Julie was, oh thank God, she was past them and running up the companionway, and Edmond was falling. Kay was raising the paddle, free now to strike down, and then she lurched and began to fall and scarcely understood why, even when she heard the horrendous roar of the pistol, and it was only as she slid heavily to the floor and felt the warmth of her own blood that she realized she had been shot.

The cruiser heaved up and down, up and down, and there was no sound but the creaking of the hull and the slap of the water. No sound.

Julie must have reached the deck, must now be in the icy water, swimming, swimming faster and harder than she ever had before.

Time passed then, but how much Kay had no inkling. She was sliding up and down, up and down, and hazily realized it was the tilting of the floor, but nothing mattered now because Julie was safe. Julie was swimming, swimming . . . Kay almost closed her eyes then, for good, let it all go, for now everything would be all right.

And she heard Edmond move.

She lay heavily on one side. She opened her eyes and could see him moving unsteadily toward the companionway. It took him a long time to cross the saloon, longer still to reach the top deck.

But it wouldn't take any time at all for the cruiser to follow Julie, and in that bright, sharp moonlight he would find her and run her down.

The anchor chain rattled.

Slowly, Kay raised her face. She wanted so desperately to rest, for now there was a burning ache that spread over her chest, and every time she breathed it hurt a little more and soon there would be nothing but pain, billowing, burning pain. She blinked. The clanking of the winched chain stopped. The anchor was up now. He would be underway in only a moment.

How far had Julie swum now? How far?

With infinite slowness, Kay began to pull her knees up to her body, the first struggling effort of a grievously wounded animal to move.

CHAPTER 25

Cold, cold, colder than blue ice or a blizzard's wind, colder than the iceberg's tip or a Himalayan peak, cold as death, the numbing, frigid water pulled at Julie, and the faint splash as she swam seemed to mock her effort.

She changed to breaststroke. Pull, Julie, pull. You can always do breaststroke. Keep on going, Julie.

She could feel her strength going, could feel the shock of the icy waters pulling her down.

She must swim, swim and swim, until she could swim no more, she could do it, she would, for Kay, for herself, for Angus. Freestyle again now. Finish, Julie, finish. She lifted aching arms, kicked muscle-tightened legs, dragged breath into burning lungs.

Then, faintly over the water, she heard diesel motors rumble to life. She lifted her head, trying desperately to see back over the waters, but the heavy swell reared behind her, then, slowly, slowly, she rose in the water and she saw the cabin cruiser. A spotlight burned on, cutting a sharp white swath through the night. She had swum as fast as she could, but it wouldn't take five minutes for the cruiser to overtake her. Could Kay possibly have taken over the boat? Julie hoped and waited a moment yet, the cold pressing into her, and watched the empty deck. But no familiar figure came to the side, waved, called. No, it wasn't Kay coming after her.

Desperately, her already straining heart fluttering now with fear, Julie began to beat through the cold waters. There, ahead of her, she could see a moving light across the waters, a car on the coastal road. She couldn't be more than a half mile from shore now.

How far could she go, how fast? Could she swim underwater when the cruiser came near? Oh yes. But only for a while. And now, added to the cold and the fatigue, there was a hot rush of anger. Damn Edmond! Damn him!

And now she raced for her life, hers and Kay's, elbows high, legs thrumming, hard and straight. She would swim, she would swim to the very last instant even though she knew the race was lost.

Kay inched over the moving deck. She must hurry, knew she must hurry. Every second that passed, the heavy cruiser slammed through the water nearer to Julie. Oh God, she had to hurry!

Kay had trouble seeing now. Nothing was quite as it should be, blurring and merging and moving, but she had pulled herself, a laborious half foot at a time, across the beautiful teak floor, leaving a thick red smear of her blood along the way. At the cabin doorway, she managed to lift her head. Please God, let her be able to see just a while longer, just a while.

How far was Julie now?

Kay's glazing eyes swept the floor and there was her handbag, the alligator handbag she had always carried with such pleasure.

She reached out, ignoring the quick, fiery spread of pain. No time now for pain. No time now for anything.

She grabbed at the handle, pulled it close and, before the pain swept her with faintness, managed to open the clasps.

Now she didn't need to see. A small smile touched her face. Her handbag. How many times had she reached into it for her lighter and pulled it out to briskly click, then use its flame to light a cigarette. Her fingers closed on the lighter. And now, if weak and fumbling fingers could manage one last task, one final task, then all would be done.

Slowly, carefully, she pulled out the coil of wick from the bottom of the purse where she had so cunningly worked it, then took the lighter and held it close. Black powder and, only feet away, the fuel tanks, a hundred gallons of diesel fuel.

One quick flick of her thumb and Julie would be safe.

Her thumb lifted.

For Julie. And, too, for the doctor and the priest, for the countess, for Grandmama, and for Lionel.

Lionel. In that last tiny fragment of time, she saw his face, those vivid blue eyes, that square honest stubborn jaw, that broad smiling generous mouth.

And her thumb flicked down.

The employees of Five Star hope you have enjoyed this book. All our books are made to last. Other Five Star books are available at your library, through selected bookstores, or directly from us.

For more information about titles, please call:

(800) 223-1244

or visit our Web site at:

www.gale.com/fivestar

To share your comments, please write:

Publisher
Five Star
295 Kennedy Memorial Drive
Waterville, ME 04901